Romantic Recon

Blake Allwood

Blake Allwood Publishing

Content Warnings

Violence

Death or Dying

Murder

Join Blake's email list to get advance notice of new books and receive his occasional newsletter:

www.blakeallwood.com

MM Romance
By Blake Allwood

<u>Transitions Series</u>
Aiden Inspired
Suzie Empowered (MF Romance)
Bobby Transformed

<u>Chance Series</u>
Love By Chance
Another Chance <u>With</u> Love
Taking A Chance <u>For</u> Love

<u>Romantic Series</u>
Romantic Renovations (1)
Romantic Rescue (2)
Romantic Recon (3)

<u>Melody Series</u>
Melody of the Heart
Melody of the Snow

<u>Road to Rocktoberfest Anthology</u>
Changing His Tune - 2022

<u>Coming Home Series (2023)</u>
A Long Way Home
Family Home
Discovering Home
Finding Home
Bound For Home
…and many more

<u>Novellas</u>
Tenacious
Moon's Place

Romantic Fantasy
By Adam J. Ridley

<u>Big Bend Series</u>
Love's Legacy (1)
Love's Heirloom (2)
Love's Bequest (3)

<u>The Witch Brothers Series</u>
Emerald Earth (1)
Diamond Air (2)
Ruby Fire (3)
Sapphire Water (4)

Content Warnings

Violence

Death or Dying

Murder

Join Blake's email list to get advance notice of new books and receive his occasional newsletter:

www.blakeallwood.com

MM Romance
By Blake Allwood

<u>Transitions Series</u>
Aiden Inspired
Suzie Empowered (MF Romance)
Bobby Transformed

<u>Chance Series</u>
Love By Chance
Another Chance <u>With</u> Love
Taking A Chance <u>For</u> Love

<u>Romantic Series</u>
Romantic Renovations (1)
Romantic Rescue (2)
Romantic Recon (3)

<u>Melody Series</u>
Melody of the Heart
Melody of the Snow

<u>Road to Rocktoberfest Anthology</u>
Changing His Tune - 2022

<u>Coming Home Series (2023)</u>
A Long Way Home
Family Home
Discovering Home
Finding Home
Bound For Home
…and many more

<u>Novellas</u>
Tenacious
Moon's Place

Romantic Fantasy
By Adam J. Ridley

<u>Big Bend Series</u>
Love's Legacy (1)
Love's Heirloom (2)
Love's Bequest (3)

<u>The Witch Brothers Series</u>
Emerald Earth (1)
Diamond Air (2)
Ruby Fire (3)
Sapphire Water (4)

Acknowledgments

A special thank you to

John Gilchrist – Beta Reader
Ryan Eagan – Developmental Editor
Jo Bird - Copy Editor
Ann Attwood – Line Editor
Renee Mizar - Proofreader

And of course, a big thank you to my husband who encourages me to keep going down these rabbit holes never knowing where I might end up.

One

Prologue: Bentley Cummings

I DROVE MY DAD's brand-new Cadillac to the abbey. He'd said I should give Sister Clarissa, my mom's cousin, a ride in style, since she'd denied herself any comfort after becoming a nun with the Poor Clares.

Before getting out of the car, I put my head on the steering wheel and sighed. Life was about to change, and I had no idea if it would be for the better, or lead to my death.

I closed my eyes, remembering the day, months ago now, that I'd slipped away from my parents while at church and sought out Sister Clarissa for help.

She'd hugged me, but when I told her that I needed to talk to her about something Dad was doing, she'd pulled away and acted like she hadn't heard me. Of course, that made my heart drop. Sister Clarissa had always been like a mom to me. She'd been watching out for me all my life, but now, in my most desperate time of need, was she going to desert me? Leave me and innocent young women to be destroyed by the monsters in my family?

Before leaving church that day, Father Thomas approached my father to ask him if I could assist the sisters set up for the church's annual New Year's fundraiser, commenting on how I was easily twice as strong as the younger kids who'd normally help out.

My dad, who was still a devout Catholic despite what he did for a living, smiled at the compliment. He'd always thought of my size and strength as a reflection of his own virility.

"We can spare him," Mom finally said. "It does him good to do the Lord's work anyway."

My father nodded his approval.

I smiled, hope filling me once again. I knew deep down, Sister Clarissa had something to do with this.

The morning I arrived at the abbey, nothing seemed out of the ordinary as I helped Mother Olive with the usual set-up for the New Year's Bazaar the church held every year. I was about to leave when Sister Clarissa came out of the backroom rubbing her hands together.

Oh, Bentley, you're still here, good. I wondered if you'd come help me put some stuff away before you go home."

I shrugged. "Sure, I guess." I followed her down the winding hallways of the abbey and the school, until we were alone in one of the classrooms.

"We only have a few moments before someone will notice I'm missing. What did you need to speak with me about?"

I sighed in relief. She wasn't abandoning me.

A week later, I sat in Sister Clarissa's room overwhelmed by what I needed to tell her. "We're trafficking young girls," I blurted out, my face blooming in a bright-red blush of embarrassment. Besides telling her I was gay, I'd never even come close to discussing sex with her. "Not to mention prostitution."

"You are going to calm down," she said, her voice stern.

"I'm going to help you handle this, but Bentley, I'm afraid you will end up in the middle of some nasty crosshairs. Are you willing to go against your father and his organization?"

I nodded. "I won't be a part of it. Maybe I should just tell him that. Maybe he'll just let me go to college, and we'll be done with it all."

Sister Clarissa shook her head. "I'm so sorry, dear boy, but no, he'll kill you before he lets you out of the organization. I've spoken to your mother about this. You'll take your seat at the table, or you'll be taken out permanently."

"What do you mean? Why would my father have such a black-and-white way of thinking about this?" I asked.

She shook her head again before pushing me toward the door. "There's more going on than you realize. Keep your head down and I'll help you survive. Bentley..." she said, making me look at her, "...I love you... stay safe."

I went home that night feeling confident we'd save those girls... that was all I could ask for.

———

I raised my head up off the steering wheel. It'd been months since my confession to Sister Clarissa. Now, we were ready to move to the next phase of our plan. The one where the girls would be saved... the one where I might die as a result of what we'd done.

I took a long, deep breath, opened the door of the Cadillac, and slipped out. No one greeted me when I entered the abbey, and when I arrived at Sister Clarissa's room, I was met by her and two men I'd never seen before. She quickly motioned for me to come inside and sit at the small table.

"This is Agent Fred Sepia and Agent Luke Wilson. They're both with the FBI," she said when I sat down.

I could tell she was tired, so I leaned toward her, and said quietly, "Mom told me about the cancer."

Sister Clarissa nodded. "It's not really that big of an issue. I've been doing chemo for months now, it's just the stress of all this." She waved her hand dismissively, before adding, "It's all just getting to be a bit much."

"Should we stop then?" I asked, then looked over at the men.

"It's a little late for that," she said. "This is the night they're going to raid the family. You're here, so we can keep you safe.

"Okay, son, tell us what you know," Agent Sepia said, cutting off our conversation.

I looked over at Sister Clarissa, who nodded for me to go ahead.

"Well, um, I know what we are. I mean, it's not like I've ever participated in the family business, b-but I knew."

Sister Clarissa broke in. "Bentley's mother is my first cousin, and she stood her ground when he was born that he wouldn't be involved with the business until he got through school," she clarified, then nodded at me to continue.

The two agents watched me like a hawk, writing down my every word, even though they told me the conversation was being recorded. "I knew when people were gonna be killed. Uncle Joey and Uncle Christopher, they, um, they aren't really my uncles, but..." I stammered, feeling nervous talking about things I'd been taught from birth never to mention. "Um, so I think they're Dad's enforcers, and Dad would tell them about people who needed to be 'dealt with.'"

"When were you supposed to take over the business?" Agent Wilson, the man in the brown suit, asked.

I shrugged. "I hadn't been told. It was never that clear."

"Why don't you start from the beginning, Bentley," Sister Clarissa said. "I'll fill in the gaps."

I nodded at her before I did as she recommended. "Sister Clarissa, here, she... she has always taught me to be, um, better than my dad," I said, getting nods of affirmation from the men.

"In high school, I was in football, and Dad's influence there was strong. Teachers would let me get away with stuff, and I didn't have to compete... you know?" I paused and waited as the thoughts of my life spun through my head. Finally, I looked up, and continued, "If it wasn't for Sister Clarissa, I'm sure I'd have been more like them..."

Clarissa chuckled next to me, and rubbed my arm trying to comfort me, not unlike she used to do when I was small. "I was pretty hard on him, and it's good that I was," she said, a look of pride and love showing on her face. "He graduated at the top of his class."

"Let's stay on topic," Agent Wilson interrupted. "Tell us more about why things were different in high school."

I paused, wanting to find a good example, but all I could think of was football. "Well, like I said, I played football and I was good, and because of Sister Clarissa, I did good in school, too, but I-I never really felt like I had any competition. I never had to deal with it, at least, not until the night of my eighteenth birthday That's when my dad really began to teach me about what we did."

I blushed, because I knew it was confession time, and I hated to admit this stuff in front of Sister Clarissa more than the agents. One thing I'd had pushed into my head early on was that confession was good for the soul, even if it left your bottom sore.

"So, um, to be honest, at first, I didn't worry so much about the stuff my father did, or the crimes he told me about—a little money laundering here and there, some illegal drug activity—of course, all of it smaller scale, small enough not to attract too much attention."

"Did he tell you everything?" Agent Sepia asked.

"No, definitely not at first. I knew I was being tested. He was showing me just enough to see if I'd squeal. I knew what he'd shown me wasn't enough to make all the money my family had, and I also knew it wasn't enough to put my dad on top of the organization in the city. Since I was little, he'd brag about that all the time."

"Did they tell you more later?" the same agent asked.

I nodded and swallowed hard. "Yeah. After I graduated from high school, that's when things changed. My dad took me to a gentlemen's club, and told me to pick the woman I wanted."

I looked over and saw Sister Clarissa's eyes fixed on me, drilling into me. She was sending the message that I still needed to keep a certain detail to myself. I'd told her when I turned fifteen that I was gay, but she admonished me to keep it a secret. "Your life depends on you keeping that secret," she'd warned me. I could tell this was *still* a time to keep it secret.

"So," I continued, "I looked at the women who were all dancing on the stage and just pointed. I ended up with a young woman, not a whole lot older than me."

"So, your dad bought you a-a date?" Agent Sepia asked, his face registering his distaste. My dad had been insistent, and I knew if I hadn't gone all the way with her, he'd have guessed the truth about my sexuality. That memory stood out as one of the worst nights I could remember and also something that changed my life for the good.

I nodded. "Yeah, and she's pregnant. I should ask now that you all make sure my kid will be safe, no matter how this turns out for me. Okay?" I asked.

"So, when did you decide to go against your dad?" Agent Wilson asked, ignoring my question. I looked at both men, searching their faces for any indication they thought what I was doing was wrong. I was already worried these guys were in my dad's pocket. A lot of the local police were. Sister Clarissa had convinced me the FBI wasn't. Luckily, what I saw in their faces was more akin to greed. They were about to take down a huge crime syndicate, and I was the tool that made that possible.

Greed was something I understood from living with and being around my dad's men. They cared for nothing and no one, other than themselves. Seeing that same motivation in these men reassured me enough to continue. "It wasn't until the week before Christmas that the shit hit the fan," I said, and cringed when I realized I'd said shit in front of Sister Clarissa. Usually, she'd say something, but her face didn't even register it. She, like the agents, was listening to my story.

"That night he took me to the western side of the state, to a small town close to the borders of New York and New Hampshire. I followed my dad and his men into a rundown hotel that looked like it had been built a long time ago. We walked down the smelly, poorly lit hallway and into a room with two full beds."

My stomach turned as I thought about it. I would never forget what I saw.

"There were two young girls, younger than me, maybe fourteen, maybe fifteen, both tied down. They were bloody and both were only semi-conscious. Clearly, several men had, um, used them."

I felt the bile rise in my throat as I remembered how they looked.

"I knew I needed to hide my disgust from my dad, at least until I could figure out how to help the two girls. That night I met over fifty girls and women just like them, ranging from twelve to twenty. All were being sold for sex, and it was my own father doing it," I said, and crossed myself, warding off the evil I knew surrounded that kind of stuff.

I didn't tell the agents, but that night, I prayed to Saint Jude, the patron saint of lost causes, to help me through and get those women help.

"We spent a full three days in that nasty hotel," I continued. "I had a room to myself, but I didn't dare call Sister Clarissa, not until I knew it was safe to talk to her. My father half-heartedly offered me time with 'the girls,' as he called them, and I acted like it disgusted me to fuck someone who was a common whore. My dad laughed, and said I was 'too damned picky,' but he didn't push me any further. We got back home the day before

Christmas Eve, and I bided my time until Christmas Mass, the next night. After the service, I sought out Sister Clarissa."

"That's when we set the ball in motion that has led us to tonight," Sister Clarissa said.

I forced myself not to get emotional as I glanced over at her just as she told the agents, "Over the next few months, Bentley became my informant."

Agent Sepia took a deep breath then and said, "I guess I don't have to tell you exactly how much danger you are in, son."

He then looked over at Sister Clarissa, saying, "We'd suggest you go into witness protection, but because we have so much information on your family, I doubt we'll need you as a witness."

"So, I'm just going to be left to die?" I asked as real anger rose up inside of me.

"No," Sister Clarissa said, pinning the agents with her most authoritative look. "They are going to protect you, but for now, you're going to hide out until all this is over."

"Where?" I asked. "I don't know anyone outside Boston."

"Well, I think hiding you in plain sight is the best and most secure thing," she said. "That's why you're going to stay with your aunt."

"My aunt?" I all but yelled. "She hates us!"

Sister Clarissa chuckled. "No, she doesn't hate you. She hates what your father has been up to, but, Bentley, she doesn't hate you and never has. She's already agreed to keep you safe while all this blows over."

"Blows over? This isn't something that can blow over," I said, feeling my time on earth was coming to an end.

"It'll be okay, sweet boy," she said. "These agents are going to take you to your aunt's place. No one will think to look for you there."

"But, they will come here," I said.

Sister Clarissa nodded. "Probably, but that's why these men are going to take you out in handcuffs. The other sisters will witness you being taken against your will. When word gets around, they will just assume you were arrested, like the rest of the folks involved."

It is pretty ingenious, I thought to myself. It would look like I was being arrested. I'd be taken to an estranged family member's house, where I'd sit out the massive storm that was bound to hit. It was also unlikely anyone would suspect Sister Clarissa was a part of setting all this up.

I let the FBI agents handcuff me and lead me out the side entrance of the abbey. Sister Clarissa got into their car with me, but she wasn't handcuffed. Several of the sisters were in the yard and witnessed what was happening. When the car door closed behind her, she explained she was coming with us in order to have an excuse for not calling my parents to let them know I'd been arrested. The story would go that the FBI had followed me as I drove my dad's car to the abbey, then arrested me after I went into the church.

I was taken first to the FBI headquarters, but instead of going in, I was immediately stuck in a nondescript car and told to lie down. They drove me to my aunt's house, and after doing surveillance, I was allowed to go inside.

My aunt met me along with my cousin Melissa, who introduced me to her new husband, Vince Cooper.

After I was pulled into a hug, my aunt said, "We're so sorry, Bentley. I can't imagine how difficult this is."

"What's gonna be difficult is staying alive."

"We agree," Vince said. "That's why you're going to hide out in our apartment with us. We just moved into one of my dad's apartment buildings he's fixing up to resell. It's got three bedrooms, and nobody's going to think to look for you there."

The night I went with Vince and Melissa, I had no idea how big a role they would play in keeping me alive.

The arrests started that night, and by Monday afternoon, everyone was out on bail. That's when the bullets started flying. The evening news showed body after body turning up in various places around the city. I kept watching the news to see if maybe my father was one of the victims, but he never was. I did, however, recognize several of the men my father had brought to the house with him through the years.

One afternoon, two weeks into the storm, my aunt called my cousin crying. Thugs had broken into her house and roughed her up. They were looking for me.

She said she could tell they weren't too convinced I wasn't with her, and I should probably hide someplace else for a while, since they were seemingly checking all the family for me.

I knew then, I had to do something, or else I was going to put a lot of innocent people in jeopardy.

I took public transport back to my parents' house. I'd decided if I had to die, I might as well get it over with.

Before I got three blocks, though, the bus was pulled over and I was taken off. Three men tossed me into the back of a Lincoln Town Car. I figured my time was up.

The guy in the back with me reached into his coat pocket and pulled out a badge. "Where were you going, Junior?" he asked with a smirk.

I shrugged. "Home to face the music."

The man's smirk changed to shock. "You can't go home, they'll kill you."

"I couldn't stay where I was, and let them kill innocent people either." Despite the badge, I didn't trust these guys yet, and just in case they weren't actually FBI agents, I decided to keep my mouth shut about where I was coming from. My cousins really were in danger for helping me.

Luckily, I was taken back to FBI headquarters, and left in a room for a long time. When the door eventually opened, I wasn't surprised to see the two agents who'd I'd met in Sister Clarissa's room.

They sat down and looked at me for a long time, before passing me a manila envelope. Inside was a passport, driver's license, and birth certificate, all under the name of "Alex Truman."

"What's this?" I asked.

"That's your ticket to survival," Agent Wilson said.

"Witness protection?" I asked.

"Sort of, except you'll never be a witness. It's more of a thank you between the FBI and the Sister for working with us for so long to bring down your father and grandfather's organization."

"So, where am I going?" I asked.

The two men looked at each other, and Agent Wilson reached into his shirt pocket and pulled out a photo ID. It took a moment for me to realize what it was.

I looked at it funny, then back at the men. "You're putting me in the Army?"

He shook his head. "No, son, you're going into the Marines."

That was the last time I saw my beloved Sister Clarissa. She died a few months later while I was still in basic training. The FBI, who were technically in charge of me, notified me, but also said I couldn't come home. After that, I was resolved to do whatever was necessary to finish off the crap my family had been involved in, once and for all.

One summer, after I separated from the military, I stood in front of my parents' house, having done surveillance for weeks. I'd had a buddy who'd been in the Marines with me, and now worked in the Department of Homeland Security, look up my family. After the arrests and basic dismantling of the assets, the business hadn't been able to come back. Despite that, I knew I was taking a chance coming back here.

I still had my key from when I was a kid. I'd given it to my cousin Melissa for safekeeping before I'd left for boot camp. My parents were sitting in the living room, watching TV, when I let myself in and sat across from them.

My dad hesitated a moment before he jumped up to grab his gun. Mine was out faster. "There's two ways this could go down. You can try to shoot me, and I'll finish this right here and right now, or you can put that gun down and we can talk and come to an agreement." I hesitated for effect, then said, "But, know this, after what I've been through, I promise I'm good either way."

My dad looked at me for several long moments before he put his gun down. I didn't wait for a response. Instead, I launched into my prepared speech. "Here's what I'm thinking. You've pretty much lost everything since the raids. I've been keeping tabs, and even the street gangs have more power than you do now, but I'm guessing you know more than a little bit about what's going on in this town."

"What, you think I'm gonna be a rat like you?" he asked, then spat at my feet.

"Yeah, I do, 'cause I've got something going on that's worth a shit ton more than the crimes you've been trying to build back up."

I could tell my dad was interested. The man might be a no-good crook, but he never turned away from a possible good deal.

"What's in it for me?" he finally asked.

"You've gotten sloppy in your old age, Dad. They have you on tape talking to a cop about your business dealings. They're finally going to take you down, unless you agree to work with us to take out some of the worst of the worst, the ones who want to blow up our city. You may not know, at least I hope you don't, but you've been feeding Al Qaeda. Loosely of course, but they can link you to them. That means Guantanamo, or maybe they'll just kill you and be done with it."

My dad stared at me with disgust. Up until then my mom hadn't moved or said anything, but she looked at my father, and said, "You'd better do what he says."

I personally escorted both my parents to a nondescript building I'd prearranged with my Homeland Security buddy. I knew there were more than a few people who'd like to take my father out, and I'd lied about there being a tape, but my dad didn't know that.

As his son, I had a way in, and I took advantage of it.

In the end, because of the information my father had given them, they were able to take down a terrorist ring. That had made me popular.

After that, I was recruited by various organizations, but I knew exactly what I wanted to do. I wanted to be the one the government turned to when they needed something delicate done—the things they couldn't do themselves—and I sure as hell didn't want bureaucrats breathing down my neck while I was handling their delicate business.

So, my career as a governmental consultant started then and there. A life filled with the dark and ugly underbelly of our government. I had reclaimed my identity as Bentley Cummings, and also became wealthier and more powerful than my father or his cronies ever were.

The only question was, if Sister Clarissa were still alive, would she think I'd sold my soul to the devil after all she'd done to save me?

Two

Bentley – Present Day

Sandra came home unannounced, sat in a chair across from where I sat, and stared at me for fifteen minutes before she finally broke down and cried.

I didn't know what to do. Sandra had never broken down in front of me before. She'd gotten angry, hurt by a boy occasionally, but she'd never broken down where I could see her.

I came over tentatively, knowing my daughter now knew just as many ways to kill a person as I did. "Sandra, are you okay?" I asked.

She didn't respond. Instead, she continued crying, so I knelt in front of her, until she was finally ready to respond, "You're one of the good guys," she said, the shock and surprise flowing out of her. "You're one of the good guys."

I took her hand in mine, admiring how small hers looked inside my own. Despite that, I knew she was powerful inside and out.

"What makes you say that?" I asked, even though I knew the reason.

"You saved those girls when you were just a kid yourself. That's why you had to be hidden away. You were so brave, Dad."

To hear Sandra call me "Dad" almost undid me. She never called me that, and only used "Father" occasionally, but usually she avoided referring to me at all.

"Then you fought in all those wars, and saved more people, innocent people, then you came home, exposed your dad, and saved even more."

I just sat watching her. I wasn't sure how to respond. Sandra had never really trusted me, hadn't really ever needed me. Still, I'd always wanted to be her father, to have her in my life in a real parent-daughter way. I just never thought the day would come.

The next thing I knew, Sandra threw herself into my arms, and that's when I was no longer able to keep my own water-works from flowing. We held each other and cried for what felt like hours, long and amazing hours.

When she pulled back, she said, "I'm so sorry, Dad, I never…"

"You've never had reason to, honey. I couldn't tell you what I'd been through, and during your most formidable years, I wasn't here. You didn't even know me."

I felt the hot tears fall down my face as I acknowledged what I had always considered was my biggest failure in this life, not being able to be there for my daughter when she'd needed me.

Sandra had joined the CIA as soon as she was out of college. I was sure her personal mission had been to bring me down, not unlike I had done with my father. Of course, she hadn't known any of that, and knew relatively few things about the real me. All she knew was that one day, when she'd just turned seven years old, I showed back up in her life, and barely saved her from being thrust into foster care. Her wariness toward me, not to mention my family's criminal ties, also explained why she'd kept her mother's maiden name all these years later, rather than claiming the Cummings name as her own.

She smiled at me then. "So, you're gay."

I almost swallowed my tongue. "Damn, they didn't leave anything out, did they?" I asked, shocked.

Sandra chuckled. "Well, no one really gave me your information. I got a boosted clearance level yesterday and looked you up. Your file is pretty thorough."

I blushed. "I only dated a few people seriously, but more than one were important government officials, including a cousin to one of the presidents."

"Why didn't you tell me, Dad?" she asked.

I chuckled. "Well, you've never really seemed interested in my love life, or my life in general. It just never came up, and since I've never had a relationship that lasted more than a few weeks, it wasn't like I was going to bring anyone home that you'd have to deal with."

Sandra sighed. "I love you, Dad, I always have, but I was so afraid of you, so afraid of what you were, or who I thought you might've been. I sort of thought there'd be a day when I'd take you down."

I chuckled. "I figured that's what you thought, and, sweet girl, I love you, too. You've been one of the most important people in my life since before you were even born."

She cleared her throat then, and said, "I want to work on us. I want to build the parts of our relationship that I refused to allow to develop. Can we do that, Dad, or is it too late?" Another tear slipped down her face, and I wiped it away.

"It'll never be too late. I'm here for you, baby, all you had to do was let me in."

She started crying again, but this time she just melted in my arms. At twenty-four years old, my baby girl had finally *become* my baby girl.

Three

Cliff Sparks

"**G**RANDMA, DO YOU WANT me to turn off the oven?" I yelled into the living room.

"Yes, dear. I'll be out in a minute," she hollered back.

"Take your time. I don't have to go in until late today."

She came out of the back room dressed to the max.

"Dang, Grandma, are you going on a date?"

"Well, with my grandson, yes I am!"

"Where are we going?" I asked, concerned maybe I'd missed a planned event.

"We're going right here. I just felt like dressing up. Since I moved into this place, all I ever see are these old women who walk around in those hideous house dresses."

I chuckled. That was the one thing she complained about the most since moving into the independent living home in Edmonds. My grandmother used to be a fashion designer in the nineteen seventies. I'd heard enough stories about her life with

Brenda David and other famous Seattle designers that I could probably write a book.

"So, what? You're now dressing to the nines every day just to show off?"

She gave me her look, which always put me firmly in my place, and shook her head. "You are still such a brat," she said, and kissed my cheek. "As a matter of pride, yes. I figured if someone showed up looking decent, maybe some of the other ladies in this establishment might take a hint, and show a little more pride in their appearance as well."

She walked into her kitchen, donned her apron and pulled out the tray of cooked store-bought biscuits. "Just because I'm old, and living in this old people's hellhole, doesn't mean I have to lose all that's left of my pride."

She threw the frozen sausages into the pan to fry and turned to look at me. When she caught my expression, she exhaled. "Oh, honey, I didn't mean to make you feel bad. I'm just frustrated. I'm eighty-three. My mom lived into her nineties and never once set foot in one of... these places."

I sighed. "We can try it again. You know hiring a nurse was an option, and I can try to reduce my hours."

She shook her head. "No, honey, don't listen to me. I'm just being silly. Now, how do you want your eggs?" she asked, changing the subject.

Grandma had suffered a mild stroke, but still got around well. Her face had only had that characteristic droop for a couple months, and she was now able to function better, but not well enough to be on her own. When she started forgetting to take her medication, she also began to forget other things, like turning off the stove, and leaving her keys in the door. When she almost burned the house down, it scared her enough that she shopped around, and finally put herself in here.

I didn't even know she was considering it until she'd already made the arrangements and started packing.

She plopped the plate of food in front of me as unceremoniously as she always had. Mom had been our cook. Grandma was a career woman and always had been. Mom, on the other hand, had married my dad when she was eighteen before he headed off to war and had fully embraced her role as the woman of the house.

I didn't have many memories of my early years, but Mom had told many stories of moving around from city to city as my dad advanced through his military career.

When he was killed, I was only six years old. Grandma insisted we live with her, until we got back on our feet. We never left.

There were so many blessings wrapped up in that. Grandma and I were peas in a pod. We were more alike than Mom and I were, and unfortunately for my mom, it was often us against her.

But, she'd taken care of us. When Mom got leukemia my junior year of high school, then died just three months later, it left both Grandma and me rudderless.

Somehow the two of us had managed.

We ate in silence like we usually did. Even though Mom's passing had been nearly fifteen years ago, we'd never gotten back to the idle chatter that used to fill our table before she died.

After we finished eating, I took the plates to the sink and washed them off, before loading the dishwasher. When I came back to the table, Grandma plopped a large white envelope in front of me, and sat down.

I couldn't read her expression, but she usually only schooled her face when things were important. I opened the envelope, pulled the papers out, and gasped audibly when I saw what they were.

"Grandma, you can't..."

"I can and I already have. That house was built by your grandpa, and even though you never knew him, he was a good man, and he'd have wanted his grandson to have it."

I stared speechless at the paperwork. "What about... his son?" I asked, thinking of my half-uncle, Ralph. The man wanted nothing to do with us, so I'd only met him once.

"Ralph inherited what he inherited when Elvin died. That house was built for me and your mom. Now that I'm not living there, it belongs to you."

Grandma and my grandfather Elvin weren't married. In fact, he'd been married to Ralph's mother when Grandma got pregnant with my mom. It'd been quite the ordeal. Grandma swore she didn't know he was married. Mom never talked about it. All that drama had happened long before I was born.

"Grandma, you might get better and want to go home."

"Psht," she said. "Son, we both know I'm not ever gonna leave here."

She got up and came over to sit next to me. Putting her hand over mine, she spoke quietly, something she never did unless she was trying to get my attention. "Cliff, my time here is limited. I want to finish my days knowing I've left you with as few problems as possible. You're the only thing left of me on this earth."

"Grandma, your designs are..."

"My designs are stuck in some musty old museum. Clothes are supposed to be worn, not hang in the back of some old smelly building."

"I may be wrong, but I'm pretty sure the Smithsonian isn't that musty."

"Regardless, you're what's left of me that matters," she said sternly, returning to her normal professional demeanor.

The shift almost made me smile. The truth was, I preferred my no-nonsense grandma. I thought in more ways than one, she was who taught me how to keep my shit together well enough to be a cop on the streets of Seattle.

I leaned over and kissed her cheek. "Thank you, I promise not to hock it until you kick the bucket."

I jumped up and dashed out of her reach before she could get to me. We were both laughing when we finally plopped down onto her living room furniture.

She looked over at me, serious once again. "You'll need to have all that stuff notarized at my attorney's office. He'll file all the official documents that need to be filed."

I nodded, the smile falling from my face. "When I go, son, my instructions are clearly written in the envelope you've got there. The arrangements are already made, and all you'll have to do is show up."

I looked over at the envelope that still sat on the kitchen table. "You don't plan to go soon, do you?" I asked, more to make the atmosphere lighter, but it didn't come out that way. Even I could hear the sadness in my voice.

She shrugged. "I'm eighty-three and have had a stroke. We both know it's gonna happen sooner rather than later."

"I'd prefer later, if you don't mind."

She chuckled. "You never could just accept what was," she said.

"Nope, I took after you."

She smiled. "That you did, son... that you did."

Four

Bentley

"**I**F HE'S NOT CORRUPT, then how does a street cop afford a three-million-dollar mansion right on the water?" Sandra asked.

"It's his family home, Sandra," Agent Ford, our colleague in the FBI, replied. "His grandmother owns it."

Sandra looked at Ford and sighed, clearly frustrated her relatively new partner hadn't disclosed this to her before the meeting. "That doesn't mean he isn't corrupt. Dad, I'm sorry, but we need to keep the investigation open. At least for another cursory look."

"The client—" Both of us knew I meant my CIA contact, KOPATICAL, "—has already said to shut it down," I explained, but Sandra just looked at me and shook her head. We'd been cleaning up a high-profile international scandal in Seattle for the past few months, which was why Sandra was even involved in the case. Unfortunately, my entire family—at least the ones I acknowledged—were involved. My cousin Melissa's son, Les, had inadvertently ended up deep in the middle of it, and I'd even had to take his boyfriend, now fiancé, Bennett, to Boston to keep him safe. Ultimately, we took down the Seattle criminal gang that included Bennett's father, dirty cops, and corrupt, high-ranking officials.

Sandra continued to argue. "Dad, if you tell *your contact* that you're chasing a lead, especially one that involves a Picasso *and* a Van Gogh, not to mention the—"

I put my hand up. "Sandra, you don't have any evidence that you're chasing *that* particular lead."

She stared at me for a moment before sitting back down. "When will we have another chance to pursue this?" Ford asked.

"Have either of you spoken to your bosses?" I asked, and both of them shook their heads.

"Sandra, what about Interpol? Are they interested?" She continued to shake her head.

"So, in other words, this is going to end up being a pro bono case." Neither of them would make eye contact with me.

I took a deep breath. "Sandra, I know your love of art. But, we're paying out the ass to continue being set up here in Seattle." She looked up at me and I laughed. "I know what you're going to say, and yes, we made out well with the Seattle crime ring that we busted open, but Seattle's proving to be expensive. We... no, I—" I corrected, remembering my daughter didn't actually work for me, "—need to move on to our next job."

"Where do they want to send you?" Ford asked, which made me laugh.

"You know I can't tell you any of that. They'd fire all three of us if I started divulging sensitive information."

Sandra sighed deeply. "So, let me put a little pressure on this guy," she said, pointing at the pictures of the local cop. "If I can't find anything tying him to the art, I'll back off."

Both Ford and I chuckled. Sandra didn't back off from anything, not even when she was told to, which, incidentally, was why she was now assigned to me, her dad, the Mafia lawman.

"Okay, but…" I pointed my finger at her and gave her my most intimidating look. "…you don't start investigating anything until I clear it with FBI headquarters. They are still technically in charge here, and have told me to begin breaking things down."

"Deal. Come on, Kevin, we can investigate without… investigating," she said, and bounced up from her chair and out the door before I could respond.

Ford deferred to her, shrugging and stifling a smile, before following my daughter out the door.

All I could do was shake my head, and hope she didn't blow this. She was a good agent. Smart, level-headed, but sometimes she'd charge into a situation prematurely. My daughter passionately hated crime.

Five

Cliff

"OFFICER SPARKS, PLEASE HAVE a seat," the Chief said as I walked into my sergeant's office. I'd been called to see him before I could even turn my computer on. That was never a good sign.

I sat down and looked expectantly at the two men in front of me. "We are beginning an investigation against you, Officer Sparks. Until the investigation is concluded, you're being placed on administrative leave," the Chief said.

I looked confused. "What am I being investigated for?"

When neither man responded, I shook my head. "So, you're just randomly investigating us now? I know there was a lot of crap that's hit the fan recently, but not all of us are guilty!"

I'd been on edge for months, watching one cop after another be taken down in an FBI sweep of the Seattle area that put many of our most prominent politicians, business owners, and several judges in prison. Luckily, I'd never even been approached by the bad guys, but apparently, I was going to get drawn into the criminal conspiracy now, even though I was never involved. Guilt by association.

My sergeant looked at me. "You know if we investigate and find anything, anything at all, Cliff, your career will end once and for all."

"There's nothing to find. Hell, you won't even tell me why this has even started."

The Chief shook his head. "You should listen to your sergeant. Resigning now won't hurt your chances of getting another job on a different force."

My heart had been beating wildly until then, but now that I was catching on to what they were saying, it dropped into my stomach.

"You want me to quit?"

"Cliff..." my sergeant said, looking over at the Chief before continuing, "...we've had an FBI agent and his CIA counterpart show up asking questions about you. You know our investigators are looking at everything now. The mayor's office is all up in arms, Cliff. Just by having an investigation, you'll be considered guilty, and they will do everything to bring you down."

I slumped in my chair. My first thought was to ask why they were asking questions about me, but the moment I looked into their faces, I knew they'd never tell me. I was considered a criminal now, just like the real scumbags that'd caused all this to happen. I took a deep breath and let it out slowly before asking, "What do I need to do?"

I gave my official two weeks notice, they put me on administrative leave until my resignation took effect, and I grabbed all my belongings, few as they were, and left the building. I turned back to look at the precinct for the last time. I'd been so proud to work there. That was before all hell broke loose. I guessed it was smart to leave now, even if an investigation hadn't begun.

Despite still being in my uniform, I decided against going home. Instead, I headed over to Jeff's gallery for some best-buddy comfort. Jeff met me at the door, concern on his face. "What's going on?" he asked.

"Why does something have to be going on?" I asked, before walking into the gallery's back office.

"'Cause you never come here during the day. You're either chasing bad guys or sleeping."

"Well, my days of chasing bad guys appear to be over, or at least on hiatus."

"Wait, what?" he asked, alarmed. "Did you get fired?"

"I quit before they could fire me."

Jeff just stood looking at me, slack-jawed.

I sat down on the comfy couch that sat against the side wall of his large office. "Some government agents were asking my Chief questions about me. Just that... just some questions, and now they're doing a full investigation."

I shook my head as I thought how insane it was. "If it hadn't been now, after all the corruption, well, no one would've batted an eye. Now, however, it's turned into a witch hunt." I looked up at my best friend and sighed. "Guilty despite being innocent." I got up and paced the room, while Jeff sat down behind his desk. "Both my chief and sergeant said I should resign before I got stuck with something that'd end my career."

Jeff shook his head and sighed with sympathy. "I'm sorry, Cliff, but you can still get a job elsewhere, right?"

"No," I said with frustration. "I can't move away, not with Grandma just going into the senior home. And if I'm being investigated in Seattle, I'll be investigated in any of the surrounding towns. So, I'm all but fucked."

"You still have your parents' trust-fund money, right?" he asked.

I nodded. I hadn't used a penny of it since Mom had died. It represented all that was left of both my dad and my mom. Grandma had put me through college. She and I had both all but decided it was best not to touch it.

"I'd prefer not to use it," I admitted.

Jeff knew me better than most people. I'd talked to him about losing my parents many times, and he'd talked to me equally as much about how smothering his family was. The empathy I saw in his expression was exactly the balm I needed.

"Well, you can move in with us if you need to."

I laughed. "Well, believe it or not, my grandma just signed the house over to me."

Jeff's eyes widened. "Forget what I just said, we're moving in with you."

I couldn't help but laugh. Jeff had been obsessed with my grandma's mid-century Elvin Jennings design home since he'd first come to visit us.

Several architectural magazines had featured the home since my grandfather built it for my grandmother. The fact that it still sat on over an acre of land and overlooked the Puget Sound in Edmonds, one of Seattle's more trendy suburbs, made it that much more appealing.

"I'm not sure Paul would approve."

"Screw Paul, if he doesn't want to move in with you, I'll keep him as my side piece," Jeff said of his husband.

I burst out laughing. Paul and Jeff were almost literally attached at the hip. In the eight years since they'd gotten together, they seemed to only fall more in love with each other as time went on.

"So, you're willing to leave Paul for my house?"

He thought for a moment. "I have a better idea. You move into our home, and Paul and I will move into your house. You know that place is too big for you. You'll be so uncomfortable there."

"Thanks for making this about you," I said, standing, and when Jeff looked like he was about to apologize, I grabbed him into a bear hug. "For real, thanks for making me laugh. I needed that."

When I pulled back, he looked me in the eyes. "Why don't you come to dinner tonight? Paul's finishing a new piece, which he's obsessing about, so I doubt I'll even see him. I can order pizza and we'll pretend to be two cool college kids again. Like easy, footloose and fancy-free."

I laughed. "You've never been footloose and fancy-free, dweeb."

"God, you're so stuck in the eighties. Tell me again how you missed your generation?"

I couldn't help but chuckle. I had been addicted to nineteen-eighties movies in college and had caught onto all the lingo when Jeff and I were roommates. I'd started calling him a dweeb then, and eighties or not, it still fit.

"Tonight sounds good," I said, and walked with him following me, out of his office and right into two suits.

The hair on the back of my neck rose, and I was immediately suspicious. The moment we locked eyes, I saw the recognition in their faces, and knew these were the two who'd approached my superiors.

They didn't address me, however. Instead, the woman looked past me and, seeing Jeff, asked if he was Jeffrey Langston.

Jeff moved around me and shook her hand. "Yes, I'm he."

I rolled my eyes at the formality he put on. These are government agents, Jeff, I thought, not potential customers.

"I'm Special Agent Sandra Inman and this is Agent Kevin Ford. We'd like to ask you a few questions," she said as the man with her showed his FBI badge. I naturally assumed these were the two who'd questioned my sergeant and chief about me.

Jeff agreed and walked back toward his office with the agents in tow. When I followed, they both looked confused, and Jeff looked embarrassed.

I wanted them to say this was private, that I needed to let them conduct this interview without me present, but to my surprise, they didn't. When we all got to Jeff's office, he pointed at his couch and turned the two client chairs around for himself and me.

"Do you know a Colin Churchill?" the woman named Sandra asked.

Jeff nodded. "Yes, I've been liquidating his estate. Why?"

"When was the last time you were in contact with him?"

Jeff shook his head. "Mr. Churchill is deceased. I'm working with his nephew and heir, Anderson Churchill."

"Did you see the papers that gave Anderson the rights to sell his uncle's belongings?" the man, Ford, asked this time.

Jeff nodded. "Of course, we have to have a documented provenance for all art sold through our gallery."

"Can we see the paperwork?" she asked.

Jeff hesitated and looked over at me. When I nodded, he turned to his computer and after a few moments, printed something which he collected and brought back to the desk.

When he handed the paperwork to them, they both looked at it.

"I'm afraid these papers are fraudulent, Mr. Langston. Mr. Colin Churchill is still very much alive."

Jeff looked alarmed. "I don't understand. I checked the state records and pulled his death certificate from there."

Sandra nodded. "Hacked."

"Oh, heavens," Jeff said, and I noticed his face pale. "Am I being arrested?" Jeff asked.

Both agents shook their heads. "No, but we need your help tracking these people down. Can you tell us what you know?"

I listened as Jeff filled the two in on what little he knew. Anderson Churchill had come in and presented Jeff with a list of moderately priced art pieces that he needed to liquidate. Colin Churchill had reportedly resided on one of the regional islands accessible by ferry, so the nephew had decided to sell from here, instead of taking the art back to Vancouver, BC, where he lived.

Now, I understood why the CIA was involved. The Churchills had allegedly crossed international lines.

When Jeff finished, had I not known him, even I would've been suspicious. I did a quick internet search of obituaries using my phone, but found nothing for a Colin Churchill in Washington. Not that it was any major indication. Not everyone had obituaries written about them, but it was a red flag.

The two stood up, and Agent Ford handed Jeff his card. "If you think of anything else, let us know."

When they turned, I asked, "And me? Why are you investigating me?"

They both froze and didn't respond for a beat.

Then Agent Ford replied, "We aren't investigating you, Mr. Sparks."

"No, well, you might want to inform my superiors at the Seattle Police Department of that, because I was asked to resign today, and I'm guessing that's because you two paid them a visit."

I noticed shock register on their faces before they schooled their features. "We're very sorry, sir, but we aren't allowed to discuss an open investigation."

"Of course, you aren't," I responded angrily.

Jeff quickly escorted the two from his office and out the front door. I didn't bother to follow them. Instead, I waited in Jeff's office until he returned.

When he did, he ignored me, much to my surprise. Jeff was hard to upset, but he clearly was now.

"Hi, Todd Riley, please." Jeff didn't look at me while he waited for Todd, an attorney he'd recently met through his brother, to answer the phone. "Hi, Todd... Hey, do you have some time to meet with me?" I could tell Todd said he did. "Good, how about now?" he asked, nodding at Todd's apparent response. "That works. I'll head your way. No, I'd rather not discuss it until we're face to face. Okay, perfect, see you in a few."

He hung up and asked if I wanted to come with him to visit with his attorney.

"Do you want me to?" I asked.

Jeff thought for a moment, then nodded. "Yeah, I think I do."

"Okay, I'll ride with you."

Six

Bentley

"**S**ANDRA, WHAT THE FUCK were you thinking? Didn't I tell you not to do anything until I've had a chance to talk to the head of this investigation? Now you've gotten the one linchpin in all of this fired?"

She had the decency to look chagrined. If it had been anyone but my daughter, whom I'd just made amends with, I'd have fired them. That was the tactic I decided to take.

I stood up and stared out the window. "I'm not going to act like this isn't a major problem, Sandra, and if you'd have been anyone else, I'd have sent you back to the CIA with your tail between your legs. This stunt you and Mr. Follow You Where You Go pulled, may have set us back months. If I'm going to be doing this without pay, I can't afford months, Sandra!"

She nodded. "I-I honestly didn't think they'd fire him."

"Technically, they didn't. They asked for his resignation. But the outcome is the same. Had you waited, done what I asked you to do, the FBI agent in charge of this case could've and would've simply called over to the police department, and said, 'We've got some questions for one of your officers, but don't freak out…'"

I was getting angrier the more I talked. She and Ford really had set us back.

I plopped down in my chair, looking at them both. "Before I send you out, what else have you done?"

I felt my stomach tie in knots as I watched their expressions. "Well, we sort of went to speak to the gallery owner."

I closed my eyes and prayed to the Virgin Mary that I would find the patience not to throttle my daughter. When I opened them, several long moments later, Sandra was chewing on her bottom lip. A sign that she knew how much she'd fucked up.

"Spit it out. What did you learn?"

"Well, he admitted he knew Colin Churchill, the owner. He also admitted to knowing the nephew, Anderson. He's been selling their art for several months."

"Okay, that's not horrible. We can save this, I think, by putting someone on the cop, someone to befriend him maybe."

I was just beginning to let my mind go with it. I could still fix this.

"Um, well, he was there."

I looked over at Sandra, my thoughts still zooming through my mind. "Who was there?"

She paled a bit, and I realized this had just gotten a lot worse. "The officer, he was there."

"Fuck! You interrogated your suspect while your other suspect was there?"

"We didn't have much choice," Ford interrupted, causing me to look in his direction.

My anger must've shown, because he visibly swallowed. He continued, though, "If we'd made a stink about him being there, both of them would've shut down."

"If you hadn't gone behind my back and questioned suspects, when I specifically told you not to, then they wouldn't have even known you were looking."

"Dad, we screwed up. I realized it when we walked in and saw the officer, but don't you think it's suspicious that he went directly to the gallery owner's place immediately after being fired or resigning?"

"Of course, it's fucking suspicious, Sandra, that's why we're even discussing this, but you know, or at least should know at this point, you don't go barging in. You make strategic decisions and work as a fucking team. Okay, I need time to think. Have you done anything else I need to know about?" I asked, and when both of them shook their heads, I ordered them out.

"Oh, and you're both grounded, like don't come out of your fucking holes until I've figured out what to do, and Sandra, I don't fucking care whether you're my daughter or not, if you disobey my command again, you'll not work with me again! Got it?" She swallowed and nodded. "Good, now get out of here!"

I watched the two of them go. Damn, I knew working with my daughter was a bad idea. I'd told my contacts at the CIA it was a bad idea. I'd told my contact at the FBI it was a bad idea. But fuck if I wasn't here dealing with the entire fucked-up mess. The reality was, after all this time, I'd just got my daughter back, and now this fucking case was going to be the reason I would lose her again.

I wanted to put my head down and weep. Instead, I leaned back in the office chair, propped my feet on the desk, and letting my hands rest behind my head, I let my mind ponder what I could do to fix the fucked-up mess now, before it got worse.

If I hadn't already alerted KOPATICAL, my contact at the CIA, that we possibly had our hands on the Verde Thieves, I could've just pretended none of this had happened, but fuck, I'd let Sandra convince me to put my name on the line. Now, I was stuck. I could chase down the leads, and if there was a God, then these two would be innocent, and I'd tell her there was, in fact, nothing here and we could head out.

I ignored the ball of frustration that swirled around in the pit of my stomach, warning me this was never going to be cut and dried.

Might as well move forward and figure it out, like I'd been figuring things out since I was eighteen fucking years old.

Seven

Cliff

THE MEETING WITH JEFF'S attorney, Todd, was matter of fact. I really wasn't able to add much more to what Jeff told him, other than that the two agents had shown up at my place of employment, and ended up causing my superiors to request my resignation.

The next day, I spent the morning visiting my grandma, before she sent me off to her attorney's office to finish up the paperwork on the house.

Two days with attorneys was enough to make anyone feel a bit itchy, so the following morning, I decided to go kidnap my grandma, and take her for a nice long drive. Somewhere both of us could get our minds off our troubles.

I knocked on the door, and not hearing an answer, went straight in. "Grandma, I'm here."

"Cliff, what are you doing back already?" my grandma asked as I walked into her apartment.

I looked around. "What, you don't want me to come visit?"

"I want you to have a life. You were just here a few days ago."

"Um, we lived together before that. Come on, can't a grandson visit his only living relative?"

She shook her head. "You need a man."

I stopped in my tracks and turned to glare at her. "Did my feminist, not-had-a-man-living-with-her-in-my-entire-lifetime grandma, just tell me I need a man?"

She chuckled. "Well, it was different for me. Women were completely suppressed when I was your age. I had to keep my men on a leash. You're a big, strapping, handsome, young man. No one is going to try to control you."

She winked at me, and I knew I was about to be embarrassed by what she said next. "Besides, I might have kept the men in my life on a leash, but I always kept one."

"If that's the case, I never met them."

"Well, of course, you didn't. I wasn't going to parade my toys in front of my grandson."

"Ugh, okay, subject change," I said, and she laughed. That was what I was going for. I wanted her to laugh, but I also didn't want to talk about her love life.

"So, what's your plan for today?" I asked.

She pointed at the kitchen. "I'm going to sit over there this morning, then this afternoon, I'm going to sit over there. Then tonight..."

"Okay, enough, I'm taking you out."

She stopped and turned toward me. "Taking me out where? How do you have time?"

"I took some time off. Why do you care how? You're always nagging me to take you places after you, um, well, after…" Shit, I forgot not to mention her losing her license.

"You mean after your friends shanghaied me and took my liberties away?"

"Yep, that's what I meant."

She gave me her typical *I could squash you with my high heels* look, then turned to go back into her bedroom. "Where are you taking me, so I can change into something appropriate?"

"I thought we'd go to The Mandrel Reserve."

"Oh, Frank and Ida's place? I spent some wonderful days there in my youth."

She disappeared into her bedroom, and I sat on her living-room chair, waiting for her to return. I knew I was in for a day of listening to the shenanigans of her teenage years.

When she came out, she was dressed like she was headed to church. Hat and all.

No way was I going to squash her imaginings of what people wore to those gardens now. Seriously, she'd be the only person there not in shorts.

As we drove, we talked about everything from the beautiful views from the ferry to the history of the area when she was growing up. The conversation switched to her friends who'd once occupied the Mandrel's estate, before it had been turned to a public reserve, and the many people she'd met while partying here.

I let her take the lead, and although the doctor had specifically said she was to always use her walker, she flat-out refused. So, when we went to tour the house, I requested the wheelchair I knew they kept in the back for emergencies.

Of course, the curator knew my grandma well. "Oh, how nice to see you, Mrs. Montgomery," she said, the moment she saw her. My grandma beamed with pride.

As soon as I had the chair in place, she slipped into it without any argument, which was unusual. She usually put on airs about not needing such contraptions. Her lack of argument made me sad. I shook it off though, not wanting her to feel anything but happiness during our outing.

We toured the reserve looking at the different sections, her pointing out where we should go and then telling me stories of the parties, and the people she'd met and played with.

When we came to the Zen water feature, she asked me to leave her there for a few moments to pay her respects.

I knew from previous trips this had at one time been a pool, and that a famous artist had died there. She never told me much about her experience with him, but I figured she must've had a serious connection to the man. My instincts told me they were more than friends, but she never told me, and I never asked.

On one of her visits long ago, I hadn't gone far enough away. I'd heard her quoting some poem. The pain I heard in her voice was so sad and deep, I decided from then on to go further away, so as not to eavesdrop on such a meaningful and private conversation again.

On the way, she'd insisted we stop at the little deli in Kingston before driving the rest of the way down, then once we were sitting on the beach looking out over the Sound, she handed me a sandwich and unwrapped her own.

The two of us sat in silence, listening to the waves gently lapping against the rocky shore. A couple of seals popped their heads up as we sat watching, and we both laughed at their antics.

Finally, I pushed her back to the car, returned the wheelchair, and we drove back toward the city.

She put her hand on my knee as we neared the home. "Thank you, sweetheart. I needed those memories."

I winked at her before taking her hand and squeezing it. "You're welcome. I needed the memories we made today, too."

She nodded at that and fell silent, until I helped her get back into her room.

She sent me on my way after that, telling me she was too tired to entertain me any longer.

I'd seen acceptance on her face as we'd driven back. I thought we both knew that could be her last time visiting there. Part of me wanted to scream and rant about it, to pick her up tomorrow and take her again, and maybe the next day, too, but you couldn't outrun time.

I smiled sadly as I pulled up to the old mid-century home I'd grown up in and still lived in. That was something she'd told me after Mom had died. *Time will have its due, and none of us know when our number will be called.* Strangely, those words had comforted me all those years ago. They weren't very comforting now though, not when losing her meant I would be without family and alone.

I walked into the house and tossed my keys into the box in the middle of the old wooden hall tree my grandfather had designed and built himself.

I walked through the old home and maybe for the first time, I took in the beauty of it all. My grandma hadn't done much to remodel since she'd moved in. She'd allowed my mom to update the kitchen in the nineties, but that was the extent of it.

By signing all of the necessary paperwork at the attorney's office yesterday, this home and all its contents were now officially mine. I also knew, based on the notes she'd given her attorney, which items she designated be sent to the schools, museums, and other notable places that would preserve and honor her place in fashion-design history.

I sat down on the old sofa, still covered in plastic, and resisted the urge to scream and throw things like I had done when I was little.

Instead, I closed my eyes and sighed with acceptance. "You can't outrun time," I said out loud, and knowing I'd never be able to part with anything once she was gone, I went to her bedroom and began the process of boxing up her life's work.

I knew she wouldn't want me back at her place for at least a week, so since I didn't have a job, and still had no idea how I was going to get one, I threw my efforts into fulfilling what were, in some respects, my grandma's final wishes.

Eight

Bentley

I SAT SANDRA AND her lackey, Ford, down, and had a serious talk. "I'm not going to pretend like the two of you didn't make a huge mess of things, because you did, and I want you to learn from that. Sandra, I know for a fact my contacts at the CIA have every intention of keeping you on my team, and Ford, I'm guessing the success you had with our team during the Seattle takedown is going to keep you on my team as well.

"So, I expect you'll learn from this. From now on, when I say leave it be, you'll *leave it be*. However, we have a lot to clean up now. We're already on the line for this case, so we'll be working it."

Sandra smiled and I couldn't help but glare at her. She quickly stifled the smile and I kept talking. "You and Ford are going to completely disappear. I mean completely. I don't want you in Seattle again, until I call on you to come. If I see you, you're fired from my team. Got it?"

They both nodded, even though I could see Sandra wanted to argue. "We know the Churchills also have homes in Portland, Oregon, so that's where you're going to be. Hopefully, you'll find something there, and we won't have to deal with Canadian officials in Vancouver. Do your job as you've been trained. Watch them, follow them, talk to the people who know them. Find out everything you can from the FBI, CIA, and Interpol about the robberies, and where they think the stolen art has been stashed.

"By the time we meet back up here, you two need to be experts on this robbery. Can you do that?" I asked.

They both nodded. "How are you going to investigate the cop?" Sandra asked.

"You mean ex-cop? Now that he's not on the force, it's going to be more difficult." I let the recrimination sink in, before continuing, "That's why you can't be anywhere near here. I'm going to hire the cop to work for our security team. I need to get close, so he doesn't see through our scheme."

The light brightened in Sandra's and Ford's eyes at the same time, and they both smiled. "That's perfect, Dad."

"No, working him through the police department was perfect, this is next to perfect."

She nodded, but I knew she didn't agree. I almost chuckled as I remembered the years of conflict between the two of us. When she'd been a teenager, she'd contradict me, I'd come down hard on her, and she'd get this look—the same look she had right now—and I knew nothing I said or did would change her mind.

God help me, this woman is going to be my death, I thought. I forced myself to keep a straight face. She was right, hiring the cop was the best way to keep tabs. Had he still been a cop, we'd have had to dance through a lot of hoops, and there was no guarantee we had fished out all the corruption within their ranks. In fact, the very reason we were here was because, I was fairly certain we hadn't.

As soon as Sandra and Ford left, I climbed into my BMW and drove down to the police station, and after being escorted into the Chief's office, I began to weave the plan.

"I'm needing to hire a security detail. I was told by my FBI friends you might be able to help me find a few retired cops who could fill the role."

Nine

Cliff

"HI, CHIEF," I ANSWERED the phone, surprised the man was calling me directly. For just a moment, when he asked about my career prospects, I thought maybe he was calling to give me my job back.

"No," I answered excitedly. "I've not taken another job yet... Of course, I'm looking."

When he mentioned a private security firm, my heart fell. "I called my contacts at the FBI, and this firm has an incredibly good reputation. Cliff, it could bolster your career."

"Thank you," I responded, trying not to sound disappointed, then before losing my nerve, I asked, "Sir, why are you helping me?"

"Son, you got caught up in this mess. I felt bad about how it went down, but they would've crucified you. This is a great opportunity and maybe once things cool down..."

"Yes, sir," I said, but he and I both knew I'd never be hired back on the Seattle PD. That life was behind me.

I hung up and stared at my scrawl of the name and number he'd given me over the phone. *Cummings Security.* "Well, why the hell not?" I asked the room, and quickly typed the number into my phone.

"Cummings Security," a chipper woman's voice answered.

"Um, yeah. I'm, um, I'm Clifford Sparks. I was given this number to call about an inquiry into employment."

I was already blowing this. If they were recording all the ums, they would be sure to kick me to the curb.

"Oh, yes, sir, let me transfer you over to Human Resources," the chipper voice said.

I shook my head to get it on straight before I talked to anyone else.

"You've reached the Cummings Security Human Resources Department. Please leave your name and number after the beep. If you are applying for a job, you can apply online, or you can send your resumé to our office directly..."

I quickly jotted down the website and address before hanging up. I guess I should've thought this through a bit more. Maybe this was all bullshit. I wasn't designed for private security. Staring at some famous person's house all hours of the night? No, that wouldn't work for me.

I'd just decided I wasn't going to pursue it when my phone rang.

"Hi, is this Cliff Sparks?" the voice asked.

"Yes, who is this?" I asked, concerned something had happened to my grandma.

"This is Bentley Cummings. My secretary was supposed to send you directly to my number if you called. Your Chief gave you a high recommendation. I'm sorry you were given the run-around."

"That's, um, that's okay."

"Very good, so it's my understanding you have over six years' experience on the force, and the Chief said you'd left due to personal reasons. Are you available for employment, or are you still needing time off?"

The question took me aback. I didn't know what to say other than, "No, I'm actively seeking employment."

"Good, then why don't we meet. What's your day look like today?"

"It's good."

"Then let's meet for lunch. There's a terrific pub near my office in Edmonds."

He gave me the pub's address, and disconnected before I could tell him my resumé was six years out of date.

If I was quick, I could at least present a half-decent resumé and still have time to shower and dress for the interview. I sighed, turned my laptop on, and quickly went to work updating it.

I arrived a full thirty minutes early, which I thought was too early, so I stayed in my car sweating bullets, until I thought the time was more appropriate.

If I played my cards right and got this job, even if it paid less, I could avoid using any of my trust-fund money. Life was throwing me way too many punches, and dealing with the stress of using that money was more than I could handle.

I looked around and didn't see anyone who appeared to be waiting for someone. I was just about to find a table when I turned around and came face to face with one of the tallest, most well-built men I'd ever seen in my life.

My libido immediately kicked in, and had I not been about to go for an interview, I'd have begun flirting with him.

"Are you Clifford Sparks?" the giant hunk of solid testosterone asked me.

For a moment the saliva pooled so heavily in the bottom of my mouth that all I could do was nod stupidly. How did this hunky man know me? Was I in a dream or something? I rarely ran into guys that turned me on, since mostly I was attracted to men bigger and stockier than me, and I was six three and weighed one ninety. I worked out almost daily, building and toning my muscles, so the options for me to be this gaga over a man were slim to none.

"I'm Bentley Cummings. Nice to meet you."

That was enough to knock me out of my lustful haze. "You're Bentley Cummings?" I asked. I was sure anyone with the name Bentley would be a small man with glasses and a wisp of hair on an otherwise bald head, but no, this wasn't that kind of Bentley, this was a...

"Shall we find a seat?"

I cleared my throat, hoping it would clear my mind as well. "Um, sure," I squeaked.

Bentley chuckled, and I'd swear I almost choked on my saliva. Even his chuckle was sexy.

Once we were seated, Bentley began looking over the menu, which spurred me to do the same. Jeff and I ate at this pub occasionally when his artistic husband Paul was in a painting frenzy. The food was pretty good, so I knew already what I was going to get. A burger with steamed veggies instead of fries. Now that I was unemployed, I was afraid I was going to start gaining weight, and I was still too depressed to up my training, so fries were off the table.

I was in my head about what I wasn't going to eat, when the server came over to get our orders.

"I'll have the steak medium rare, with a side salad and garlic cauliflower," Bentley replied. I watched him order, the muscles in his neck tightening so deliciously as he spoke, and almost forgot where I was.

"Um..." I said, when the server turned to me, "I'll um..." My mind was blank. I had my order in mind. "I'll... I'll just have the same," I said.

I blushed when she nodded and turned away.

I was getting embarrassed. It was just so unusual to find someone I was this attracted to. I was about to get up to leave, convinced I'd already spoiled this, when Bentley asked, "So, tell me about your experience."

More for something to do with my hands than anything else, I reached over and pulled the folder I'd brought with me that contained my newly typed and printed resumé. I handed him a copy and began reading off the resumé, hoping that if I didn't look at him, I wouldn't lose my train of thought.

Finally, I reached the end. "So, mostly, I was just on the police force," I admitted.

"That actually sounds good. For the job I'm looking to hire for, we need a former police officer who has experience doing investigation," he said.

My interest piqued then. One of my goals had been to make detective. I hadn't even applied yet, wanting to get more experience as a cop under my belt before I pursued it, but if I could get some experience in the private sector, maybe that could help me in the future if I ever found another police force around here to hire me.

"I'd like more information. What would I be investigating?" I asked, focusing on something other than the man's overwhelmingly handsome physique for the first time since we sat down.

"We've had a stream of robberies involving several wealthier clients throughout the Pacific Northwest. Our goal is to see if we can recover some of the stolen merchandise."

"What was stolen?" I asked, wondering what would be worth hiring a private security company to investigate.

"Well, lots of different things, jewelry, some personal heirlooms, but the main reason we've been brought in is to recover stolen art."

I immediately became suspicious. First, the CIA and FBI sent agents in that ended up costing me my job. Then those two showed up at Jeff's place of business. Now my Chief, who had asked for my resignation, calls me out of the blue, recommends this guy, and he's been hired to hunt down stolen art?

I looked the man in the eye for several long moments, before I said, "I'm sorry, I'm not sure this job is for me."

"I thought you might say that," he said, sighing. "I know you and your friend are being targeted by the FBI and probably even the CIA in relation to these robberies. I also know that your Chief thinks you're innocent. So, if you are, this is a chance for you to help me clear your name."

I was about to leave, but my curiosity got the better of me. "Why me? Why am I being considered complicit?"

The man shrugged. "You're a cop, on a force that's proven to be deeply corrupt, and you're friends with one of the primary suspects in the crime."

"And you're wanting me to spy on and help take down said friend."

"If he's guilty... Is he guilty?" he asked.

"No!" I said and stood up. "He's not. That's not who he is. I'm sorry, Mr. Cummings, I'm not your man."

"You know…" he said as I walked away, "…this makes you look guilty."

I momentarily looked back. "It doesn't matter what I look like, Mr. Cummings. It only matters what's true."

I left without my resumé and without eating. I was so fucking angry, I could beat someone to a pulp. I thought about heading to the gym to do that with a punching bag, but decided I'd better warn Jeff. If this guy's presence was any indication, the heat was about to come down, and I should alert Jeff of that first.

I picked my phone up and called over to the gallery. Paul answered. "Hi, Paul. Is Jeff there?"

"No, sorry, Cliff. He's trying to handle this whole mess with the Churchills. He's meeting with our attorney, and won't be back until late afternoon."

"Okay, well, tell him I called, and Paul, I'm going to go work out, then come over to the gallery. We need to talk about the Churchill thing. I just had a private security company approach me about it. This is bigger than I think Jeff realizes, and I'm in the middle of it with him."

Paul said he'd tell him, so I turned my car toward the gym, and a very unlucky punching bag.

Ten

Bentley

T HE GUY'S REACTION HAD been confusing. I hadn't felt that much lust coming off someone since I had to deal with Gergana Ivanov with the Bulgarian National Intelligence Service. I'd told her a dozen times I was gay and not interested, before she finally slapped me and disappeared out the back of the building. For months I expected to be shot in the back.

I admit, this guy's attraction felt very different than Gergana's had. I had to force myself to focus on the task at hand. Cliff Sparks was shorter than me, but no surprise there. Most people were shorter than me. He was solid, but sculpted, with strong arms and a nice build, and you could tell he focused attention on his entire body, not like the men who built their arm muscles so big they were mismatched to the rest of their physique.

If I weren't trying to figure out if he was someone I was about to take down, I probably would've asked him out.

Now, that realization shocked me more than anything else. I hadn't been out with a man in... well, besides an occasional hookup, it'd been years.

The thought of being attracted to this... asset? That was really confusing.

I had managed to keep my personal lust under control as the conversation moved toward the inevitable. I knew his Chief would reach out to him. I'd managed to get him to tell me about Cliff Sparks, and had gotten him to say positive things before he said he'd reach out to Sparks himself.

I'd decided I wasn't going to be able to hide what I was up to for long, so my goal was to see how quickly he caught on to the conspiracy against him and his friend. Why was he so quick to catch on? That was another question altogether. Was it because he was guilty? Probably. But, I had two things on my side now. First, innocent or not, he was afraid. And second, if he was innocent, I had a legitimate way for him to prove it. Or, if he was guilty, he could keep his eye on me, all the while unaware Sandra and Ford were working this from the back end.

I left the restaurant after eating, knowing that would give him time to do whatever he needed to do to blow off steam. Then, if my prediction was right, he'd head over to his friend's to talk it over with him.

I had his meal put in a to-go container, and headed over to my office to collect what I needed for part two of my plan.

When my surveillance team alerted me that he'd arrived at the gallery, I drove the few blocks from my office to the gallery in downtown Edmonds, and went inside.

Eleven

Cliff

I F SEEING BENTLEY CUMMINGS caused me to lust after him the first time I met him, seeing him at my friend Jeff's place made me equally angry.

"Mr. Cummings, why are you here?" I asked. "I've already told you, I'm not your man."

"You did, but I'm not here to see you. I'm here to speak with your friend, Mr. Langston."

Jeff stepped in front of Paul and me, and shook the man's hand. "I'm Jeff Langston, and this is my husband, Paul Porter. How can we help you?" he asked.

Bentley smiled, and even though the smile stretched across his face, I could feel there was no humor in it. "I'm Bentley Cummings. My company, Cummings Security, has been hired to investigate a string of art thefts. I'm hoping you and your friends will be able to help me."

"He's not a cop, Jeff," I warned. "Be careful what you say to him."

"That's true, I'm not a cop, but I can tell you all now, it's just a matter of time before they come knocking, along with the FBI and other law enforcement agencies. Unless they've already shown up."

I schooled my face, but Jeff audibly gasped. Shit, I needed to work with Jeff on his poker face.

"We aren't involved with any thefts," Jeff said.

"No, but you are most certainly involved with the sale of illicitly traded cultural property."

"There is no proof of that," I interjected.

"No, maybe not yet." He walked over to a painting on the wall and stared at it for several long moments. "Do you know all the ways an art smuggler can offload stolen merchandise onto the market?" he asked. Jeff, Paul, and I just stared at him. "No, I guess you don't. One of the most popular ways is to place a canvas under a different canvas and sell at a legitimate auction. The art sells, it's all legal, above board, and no one is any the wiser."

He walked over and looked at another painting.

"Of course, that all works out fine, until law enforcement crack open the frame and find the stolen piece."

Jeff sucked in a breath and shook his head. "We didn't—"

I put my hand on Jeff's shoulder to stop him from speaking.

"Mr. Cummings, what proof do you have that this is what's happened in this gallery?" I asked, determined to trip him up.

"None," the man remarked without hesitation, but his smile had become even more sly. "That's what I'm hoping you can show me."

"I think it's time for you to go," I said, and moved to open the door.

"I can and will, but, Mr. Langston," he said, looking away from me and at Jeff. "If you're innocent... if you have nothing to hide... even if you've accidentally been pulled into this, you're better off working with a private company. If we find something, we simply return the items to the owners and discreetly alert the FBI to what we know. Your cooperation becomes part of the problem-solving process, instead of you being part of the theft."

"Bullshit, you're better off working with the police or FBI," I countered. "If you somehow got involved, Jeff, you need the prosecution to work with you. This... this guy, he'll use you and then set you up for the fall."

The giant man shook his head. "I'm sorry you see it that way, Mr. Sparks. I'll tell you what, I'll have one of the FBI agents visit you, and I promise, if you or your friends are able to help us solve this case, we will be able to do more for you than anything they can."

He pulled his business cards out, and handed one to Jeff and another to Paul, who'd stood silently biting his nails as the conversation unfolded. "As for you, Mr. Sparks, your employment with my company could go a long way to protecting your friends, especially if we bring down the bad guys."

"How do we know *you* aren't the bad guy?" I spat out.

Bentley chuckled, before responding, "You don't, Mr. Sparks. But, if I can prove to you that I'm one of the good guys, does that mean you'll consider my offer?"

I stared at him before I opened the door and pointed outside. He left without my answer. If I wasn't so fucking pissed, I'd have noticed his beautiful backside as he walked arrogantly out the door. I mentally shook my head, and told myself I needed to end this dry spell soon, for even now, I was looking at this possible rattlesnake, and thinking about how hot he was.

Twelve

Bentley

T HAT WENT BETTER THAN planned. I'd expected the cop to throw me to the curb. The fact that he hadn't, that he'd stood up for his friend, and suggested he work with law enforcement, went a long way toward making me feel there was a small chance he might be innocent after all.

I got into my car and called Sandra. "Hi, it's Dad," I said.

"Yeah, Dad, I have caller ID."

"Don't get smart with me. I need you and Ford to come back up and pay a visit to the gallery owner and the cop. Can you come up tomorrow?" I asked.

Sandra sighed. "Why the change?"

"I need them to know we're working together. Right now, cop man thinks I'm one of the bad guys, but he's not sure. That's got him off-kilter. I'd like to keep it that way. I'm guessing he's nervous enough that if you and Ford verify my identity and say we're working together, he might agree to come work for me."

"Sure, what time tomorrow?"

"Langston in the morning, then the cop. I want you to hand them my card, too."

"Dad, that'll be weird."

"Yep, and it might be just weird enough to push Sparks into our court."

She ended up agreeing, as I figured she would. Sandra was a pill ninety percent of the time, but when she'd gone too far, she tended to play it cool for a while before she went back to her old ways. That worked for me, and it worked for the case. A CIA officer and an FBI agent handing my card to these guys was the best way to make me look trustworthy.

Sandra and Ford showed up at my office in the afternoon. Both of them looked pleased. "It worked, we handed them the card, and Cliff Sparks sat us down in his dining room, and asked a bunch of questions."

"Like what?" I asked.

"He seemed to be wanting to know if you were for real. Where you came from, what part of the government you worked for, could you be trusted...?"

"What did you tell him?" I asked, concerned.

"Not much. Just that you were a private citizen but had the support of the government."

I sighed. "I guess that couldn't be helped, but from now on, you should try not to divulge that last part unless it's absolutely necessary."

Sandra nodded. "So, what next?"

"I'll give him until tomorrow to call. If he doesn't, I'll show back up tomorrow morning"

We talked strategy for the rest of the evening, planning out what we'd do when we had him on board. Sandra and Ford were finding some interesting leads down in Oregon, which they'd been pursuing. I guessed things would start getting hot for Jeffrey Langston sooner than later, once Sandra and Ford began ruffling feathers. I wanted to have him and Sparks as assets before that happened, so time was of the essence.

That night, as I climbed into bed, I closed my eyes and thought of the handsome man, and what a shame it was that he was probably a dirty cop. Despite that, I hadn't felt this kind of attraction in a long time, and it caused my heart to beat a bit faster just thinking about him.

I turned over, deliberately forcing my mind off of him. It would do no good for me to think of Cliff Sparks as anything other than an asset and someone to get the job done. My libido would just have to calm itself down... even if it required me to shove it into the recesses of my mind, and lock it up with a metaphorical key.

Thirteen

Cliff

"Cliff, if you're comfortable working with this guy, it might be best," Todd, Jeff's attorney, said. "I mean, you know as well as I do that working with a private agency is a gamble, but I think Jeff is more at risk with the cops at this moment, especially with the crooked mess that just went down in Seattle."

I sighed as I considered it. Todd was a good guy. He'd helped Daniel, Jeff's brother-in-law, out of some hot water not long ago. In the end, that probably saved the kid's life. Now he was trying to help Jeff.

"But, Todd, this guy has no good written all over him."

"Yeah, Jeff said the same thing. The reality is, if Jeff is innocent and a private agency working for the owners of the stolen art finds it and sets the arrests in motion, that will go in Jeff's favor. You and I both know they want the big fish here, not Jeff."

"So, I should work for the big muscle man?"

Todd's left eyebrow lifted but he quickly looked down, probably so I wouldn't notice. *Yeah, Todd,* I thought. *The guy isn't just dangerous, he's hotter than fucking hell!*

"Okay, fuck," I said. "But if this goes south, you've got my back, right?"

"As long as you keep me in the loop and don't do anything illegal, I'll do what I can to protect you legally."

I shook my head. I couldn't believe I was going to back myself into this freaking corner. Visions of any number of movies where an asset was lured into the game only to be murdered in a horrific way filled my imagination, and there was no doubt I was the asset here, Jeff, too, but the muscle-god of a man wasn't chasing Jeff, he was chasing me.

I left Todd's office and headed over to the gallery. I figured I'd let Jeff know before I committed, and hopefully, he'd talk me out of it.

Unfortunately, Jeff wasn't at the gallery. The lady that worked for him occasionally said he had gone home early. No doubt it was because of those government agents paying him a morning visit. I called Jeff's number as I left the gallery.

"Hey, Cliff. It's Paul," the voice on the other end greeted me.

"Hi, Paul. I'm guessing Jeff isn't doing too well, huh?"

"No, he's lying down. I made him leave his phone with me."

"Yeah, that was a good idea. Paul?" I asked.

"Yeah?"

"I'm going to go work for that private security guy. Todd thinks it's a good idea. I just wanted Jeff to know."

"Are you sure?" he asked.

"No, I'm almost certain it's a bad idea, but it's a better idea than the alternative."

Paul was silent for several moments before he responded. "Cliff, how did all this happen?"

"Criminals don't give a shit about who they hurt, Paul. Usually, the good guys come out on top, but with all that organized crime that has been uprooted in Seattle this past year, everyone is looking for the next head to chop off," I said. Once again, I felt the sting of my city being caught up in a major crime bust of drug dealers and human traffickers. The national scandal involved corrupt cops and crooked politicians and had screwed up more than just my life... "Paul, It's just bad timing."

"Yeah, okay, I'll let Jeff know you called. He'll probably have questions."

"He can call when he gets up. I'm going to phone the security company now."

"Good luck," Paul said before we hung up.

I drove over to my favorite bar, Angela's Place, a small watering hole on the outskirts of Seattle. It'd been built after World War Two and hadn't changed much since then. The beer was cold, and the patrons usually minded their own business. It was exactly what I would need after making my next phone call.

Still sitting in my car, I picked up my phone and dialed.

"Hello," the sexy jerk answered on the first ring.

"Yeah, it's Cliff Sparks. I'm in."

"Good," the man purred. The sound sent lustful sensations through me, and a knot formed in the pit of my stomach. My physical reaction to simply hearing Bentley Cumming's voice frustrated me as much as the situation in which I now found myself.

"Where are you right now?" he asked.

I looked at the little bar I considered my safe space, and decided this wasn't where I would meet him. "Let's meet back at the pub where we first met," I said.

"No, I have a better idea. We need to talk in private. My office is just around the corner from the pub, meet me there."

And so, the games begin, I thought. "Fine, text me the address and I'll put it in my GPS."

I didn't bother to wait for his reply. Instead, I hung up and drove in that general direction. I was already on high alert, and hearing his sultry voice didn't ease my agitation. I hated this situation with everything I had in me. My dad had died in the name of our country, and my mom and grandma were both fiercely loyal to right versus wrong.

I'd become a cop because I wanted to help keep the world safe from monsters that preyed on the innocent. My instincts told me where Bentley Cummings was concerned, there were very fine lines between protecting the innocent and breaking the law. I already knew this would be a test of my resolve.

When I pulled into the parking lot behind the large non-descript building, I immediately knew two things. One, this security company wasn't open for business in the traditional sense. And two, they, like most things that were kept hidden, were probably up to no good.

I got out of my car and did a quick visual scan of the perimeter. There was no one in the vicinity that I could see, so I walked up to the single grey door that displayed the address, but no other identifying information. I expected the door to be locked, but when I twisted the knob it opened, and I walked through.

I was immediately confronted by a well-laid-out office. A woman, who I figured was a sort of secretary, sat at a desk directly in front of me. There were meeting rooms on either side of me leading to the secretary's desk. The décor was nice, if not minimalist. Everything about this space said reserved and intensely controlled.

"Mr. Sparks, please come with me," the woman said when she spotted me. "Mr. Cummings is expecting you."

I just bet he is, I thought bitterly.

I followed her down a long corridor and was shown to an office in the back corner of the building. She waited for me to go in and shut the door behind me.

I expected to see Bentley, but instead, I was met by yet another woman. This one was much more severe-looking, like a cross between an angry nun and an elementary-school librarian.

"Mr. Sparks, nice to meet you. I'm Margarette Jeffers and I run Human Resources for Cummings Security. I have some employment paperwork for you to fill out. Do you have your Social Security card and driver's license with you?" she asked.

I walked in and sat across from her, pulling my wallet out and handing her my identification. I then began to fill out the documents she placed in front of me. I wasn't sure what I expected. Everything with Bentley Cummings had felt so cloak-and-dagger-like, I guess I didn't think I'd be filling out employment paperwork.

Margarette made copies of my identification, and took what I'd filled out, then began asking questions about retirement savings plans. "Our employees have a match plan..."

This is so surreal, I thought to myself, as the HR woman droned on and on about company benefits and OSHA policies. I was really becoming an employee. Was I disappointed this wasn't more... more what?

I had to admit the reality versus what I thought I was getting into had thrown me. I shook it off, got serious, and acted like the professional I knew myself to be. If this was a real, bona fide job, then I'd be a real, bona fide employee.

By the time Margarette was finishing up, I was feeling significantly better about my situation. Legitimate companies had HR people. However, when she handed me the final document, the one that listed my salary, I about choked. My income was twice what I'd made as a cop.

"W-why so much?" I asked like an idiot.

This was the first time I'd seen the woman smile. At that moment, I realized that when she wasn't busy being the HR person at Cummings Security, she was probably a fun person.

"I see you've not worked in the private sector before."

I shook my head and she smiled again. "You'll notice a lot of nice perks. I was a policewoman for twelve years before going private."

"Really?" I asked, shocked. "And you volunteered for a desk job?"

Margarette laughed out loud. "I have six children, Mr. Sparks. My oldest starts college this year. Yes, when you have those sort of costs coming at you, you volunteer for a good-paying desk job."

I shook my head. "May the Lord bless you then," I said, quoting my mom's go-to when someone did something she didn't want. I at least gave myself credit for not making the sign of the cross when I said it.

She just chuckled. "Okay, Mr. Cummings wants to meet with you. I'll take you to his office if you're ready."

I wasn't sure I would ever be ready for that. This was when the feet hit the pavement, so to speak, not to mention I'd just signed a whole ream of documents saying I understood the sexual harassment policy. Even though I'd just scanned them, I didn't see stated anywhere that I could jump my boss's bones and not get fired for it.

As we walked into Cummings's giant office, I knew for a fact my resolve was going to be challenged here more than ever. The huge man was leaned back in an equally sizeable office chair. His back was slightly turned from the door, and he was talking on the phone. Margarette cleared her throat as we came in and

Bentley turned immediately. When he saw us, he quickly ended his phone call.

He was smiling brightly at Margarette, not the same smile I'd seen on him before, but one of affection. One that indicated he liked and appreciated his employee. Was it strange I was jealous that his look of affection wasn't being directed at me? Hell yes, it was strange and weird, and...

"Is all the paperwork done then?" he asked Margarette, and she smiled and nodded.

"All done. Mr. Sparks is now an official member of Cummings Security."

"Excellent. I'll take it from here then," he said.

Margarette patted my arm as she walked out. "Good luck."

Good luck? What the hell does good luck mean?

"Okay, now that you're official, let's get started."

Bentley opened his desk, pulled out a folder, and began taking items out, showing me pictures of myself and Jeff at gallery openings.

He also showed me suspect paintings, with Jeff and me standing in front of them.

We spent almost an hour doing this, him showing me one incriminating piece of evidence after another that involved both Jeff and me.

I truly didn't know what to think. If I had been the one gathering the evidence, instead of the one being investigated, I'd think I was as guilty as a man could be. Bentley pulled the photos of the paintings back out, pointed to them again and, while looking me in the eye, said, "These were taken at the gallery the night of the Churchill opening."

I looked at him and shrugged. "I have no fucking clue about any stolen art, but I understand now why you think I do."

"And your friend?" he asked.

"Jeff?" I hesitated as I thought. I remembered the time in college when our fraternity brothers wanted to go tag various statues on campus. He'd absolutely thrown a fit. That night he almost got us both booted from the fraternity, because, of course, I'd had his back.

I also thought of the time when Paul and he had just met. Paul had been in trouble with the law, and Jeff had helped pull him up and out of the fray. Jeff was one-hundred-percent law-abiding.

I smiled confidently. "He's innocent. I'd bet my life on it."

Bentley regarded me for a long moment. "You may have to before this is said and done."

I felt the impact of the statement and knew it was true. To shake off my shudder, I nodded. "I'm happy to, if it's ever necessary."

That seemed to satisfy him. "So—" he said almost cheerfully, "—let's start to break this down. There are only two valid scenarios in this situation. Either you're guilty and lying to my face, or you're innocent and someone has been working on setting you and your friend up for the fall."

"Which do you believe is the case?" I asked.

The big man shrugged and smiled. "It makes no difference on my end. My job is to find and recover stolen art and..." He hesitated a moment before looking me in the eye. "...to bring the bad guys to justice."

I wanted to push further. Did he believe Jeff and I were the bad guys? Instead, I shook off my ego and focused on the task ahead. Now that I knew the incriminating evidence against us, I needed to prove it wrong, and find out who the real criminals were. My ego was of no consequence here.

"Now that I've seen all this, I'm glad you approached us. Like you said, it makes no difference what you believe. I'm innocent, and if you are what you said you are, and you can offer what you said you can offer, we will prove Jeff's and my innocence before this is all said and done."

Bentley smiled and nodded. "Okay, then let's get started."

By the time the day ended, I had a list of art pieces sold at Jeff's gallery that needed to be checked out. I called Jeff and asked if Bentley and I could come by to get the names of those who'd purchased the artworks.

He was hesitant, of course, but in the end, Bentley convinced him by allowing Jeff to hire his company to investigate, under the guise of determining if any of the artwork was fraudulent. It was a clever twist that the police wouldn't have been able to use. Bentley and I could now contact those buyers, and honestly say we were hired by the gallery to investigate the authenticity of the paintings. That would prevent any issues, especially since

Jeff said he'd reimburse anyone if the art didn't prove to be authentic.

Jeff had all the provenance details stored on his computer, so he was able to get us that information quickly, after Bentley and I provided him a list of the art pieces in question. Bentley assured him that if the art pieces weren't hiding stolen artwork, the buyers' information would remain anonymous.

The next day, Bentley and I began contacting the buyers. It was painstaking work, as each owner had to be contacted individually, so as not to alert anyone who might be hiding stolen art to get rid of the evidence.

As the first, then second week went by, I felt myself warming up to Bentley. He wasn't nearly as intimidating as he'd been when he'd met us at Jeff's gallery that first time. Mainly he was professional and thorough. Had I not been trying to save my and Jeff's ass, I would've really enjoyed working with Bentley. Hell, he and I seemed to even have that synchronized rhythm you always dreamed of having with your partner.

I'd wanted that while on the force, someone to be friends with that I also worked with, but all the guys I'd been teamed up with, weren't with me long enough to develop that kind of relationship. It was funny that I'd already begun feeling that with Bentley.

Luckily, there were just a dozen paintings that could've hidden the art. I wasn't sure how Bentley had estimated that number, but when I asked, he said that was confidential. Confidential? I'd just put my life and my friend's life on the line, and *that* information was confidential?

His comment almost brought my walls back up, but no… that wasn't fair. He was doing his job, and if he still thought I was dirty and Jeff was guilty, he'd want to keep all those cards close to his chest.

Besides, there was nothing I could do about it. Bentley held all the cards. I was a pawn in a game that I could only pray wouldn't end with me being sacrificed.

Fourteen

Bentley

I WASN'T SURE WHAT I expected. I watched Cliff as I laid the incriminating evidence out in front of him. Most of the pictures I'd taken with him and Jeffrey in the foreground were out and out photoshopped. Sandra and Ford had gone to the gallery opening and taken photos of the art discreetly with hidden cameras. I'd basically taken those photos and added Cliff and Jeffrey in front as if the two of them were trying to be devious.

In reality, there was no evidence that Jeffrey had been involved with the transport of stolen art. All we actually knew was that the Churchills were certainly involved in the theft, if not fully responsible. We had surveillance footage of someone who looked a whole lot like Colin Churchill driving the getaway van, and video surveillance of the heist itself that revealed the inked neck of one of the thieves, which we were fairly confident matched his nephew Anderson's neck tattoo.

That, of course, wasn't enough evidence to convict the two, but combined with the organized crime arrests and corruption found in this area, it was enough for us to be involved.

Jeffrey Langston, as the gallery owner, and his friend Cliff Sparks, who happened to also be a police officer at the time, were just hunches, but knowing that the Churchills had hired Jeffrey and that Anderson had faked his uncle's death certificate, certainly indicated we were on the right path.

Jeffrey had said the Churchills had gone silent since the final gallery opening last summer. That was just when the arrests were beginning, so if they, as we suspected, were involved in all that corruption, they would've naturally gone underground.

The paintings we'd picked out were random to test our relationship with Jeffrey and with Cliff, our new asset.

Of course, we had no evidence that any of the art was hiding anything illegal, but as we cracked open each piece, I noticed a genuine fear in Cliff's eyes. He clearly had no idea about the operation, if there was one.

Jeffrey was a different story. It didn't bode well that he was so quick to give us access to his customers. Gallery owners were notorious for protecting the privacy of their clients. They usually only provided that information when a warrant was involved. If he were guilty, he would know none of the art was involved, so he wouldn't have any reason to prevent us from looking.

So, now the investigation was more focused on him. That would need different strategies to chase down, ones that would involve the Churchills themselves.

Once we finished with the last of the paintings, Cliff was visibly relieved, and surprised me when he suggested we get a drink together. "I'll buy you a pint," he offered.

Over the two weeks we'd worked together, Cliff had slowly begun to warm up to me, treating me more and more like a partner, and less and less like his enemy. The camaraderie was appealing, and not just professionally... I was genuinely enjoying his company. The man was charming and funny. Even with all the stress he was under, he seemed to always be putting me at ease, at least when I wasn't poking him with his or his friend's potential guilt.

If this wasn't all a sham to get the information we needed to solve the case, Cliff would be a perfect candidate for this job. But that wasn't a real option... no, as I had to keep reminding myself, Cliff was an asset. He's just an asset and when we were done, he'd need to go the way all assets would go. Away.

That all being said, I also knew the more Cliff relied on me, trusted me, the more likely he'd push through to the end, even if his friend was guilty.

"Sure, where do you wanna go?" I asked, accepting his invitation for drinks.

He smiled. "It's not fancy. You sure you can handle that?" he asked, clearly teasing me.

"What makes you think I need fancy?"

He laughed out loud. "You scream fancy. How many Armani suits do you own?"

I cocked my eyebrow at him. "What does that have to do with it?"

He just laughed. "So that many, huh?"

"No, I don't actually own an Armani suit," I said, but didn't mention it was only because when I tried to get them to custom make one for my tall and bulky frame, the bitch taking my order had pissed me off.

I could tell he had figured me out, though, which grated a bit. "I'm not a snob, Sparks!"

"You are *totally* a snob. You've got East Coast high class written all over you."

"And you? Isn't your grandmother a famous fashion designer and your grandfather an equally famous architect?"

Cliff stopped and looked at me. "You, of course, did research on me, didn't you?"

Fuck, I'd let myself get drawn in. I nodded. No use pretending like we didn't. I'd have preferred not to remind him of that, though.

He shook it off. "Let's go to one of my favorite bars. I used to sneak in there when I was in college. They never carded me, so I could drink there before I was twenty-one. I've been a loyal customer ever since."

"What, the cop is a customer of the local bar that serves under-age kids?" I asked, antagonizing him.

"Former cop, thanks to your buddies, and the day I became a cop again, I'll put an end to the whole under-age thing."

"Convenient for you," I said, and he chuckled.

"Forgiveness is a virtue," he said.

"Especially when your favorite bar is involved."

"Touché," he said laughing.

When we got to the little dive, I was, in fact, a little disgusted by it. It was a small cinderblock building painted an ugly chalky orange-yellow. The windows were partially boarded up and partially covered with bars.

It smelled as stale and musty as one would expect an old, half-cleaned bar to smell like. Even though indoor smoking was prohibited now, you could tell just by breathing that many decades of cigarette smoke lingering in the air had left a lasting impact that would never completely dissipate.

Cliff laughed at my expression when we sat down at a corner table. I barely fit in the chair, and it was rickety enough I wasn't at all sure it wasn't going to fall apart underneath me.

"You're punishing me for the comment about your grandparents, aren't you?" I asked, causing him to laugh out loud.

"You really are a snob. What kind of beer do you like?" he asked, and I shrugged.

"Um, do they have Guinness?"

"Probably, but if you like a stout, try their brew."

I had visions of cockroaches crawling over leaking barrels of beer, but the look of challenge on Cliff's face caused me to back down.

"Okay, but if there's bugs floating in it, I'm out of here and you're fired."

"Fired, is that an option?"

I laughed. "That depends on how bad the beer is."

Cliff ordered, and because we were literally the only people besides the barkeep in the whole place, the beers were quickly placed in front of us.

There were no floaters, which I considered at the very least a positive sign. I tentatively took a sip and immediately sat up. "That's... that's wonderful!" I said, surprised.

Cliff smiled, his face lighting up with pleasure in a way I hadn't seen since we'd met. "That's why it's one of my favorite places. Here, taste mine."

He'd ordered an amber, which, to be honest, I rarely drank, but it was good, too. Smooth and with the best balance of flavors.

"Do they make this here?" I asked.

Cliff nodded, the smile never leaving his face. "There's a cellar. A few years back, the grandson of the original owner began experimenting with his own brews. They had to completely rebuild the cellar to get the Health Department to okay it, but now they brew most of their tap beers down there."

I took another sip of my stout and enjoyed the flavor as it slid down the back of my throat. "I'd be willing to invest in them."

Cliff smiled again at that. "Don't bother. I'm a fifty/fifty owner, and Rake, the grandson I mentioned to you, refuses to do anything with it other than sell it here at this pub."

"You're part owner?" I asked.

"Yeah, they didn't have the capital to redo the cellar, and I wanted to help."

"So, what, you just invested with no chance to recoup?"

"It's not just about the money, it's the taste, the character of a place that served World War Two vets after the war. Here, come with me," he said and led me around the room showing me pictures hanging on the walls.

"Most of these guys were long gone before I started coming here, but I knew a few of the old-timers, too. They'd tell me stories of when they were in the war. This here is Jimmy Franks. Man, he was a character. He flew during the war. Was shot down twice. Can you imagine? This is Clay Mason. He just died last year."

As we walked around the room, Cliff talked about these men like they were his family. When we got to men who'd served in more recent wars, he looked at them sadly. I knew that his father had been killed in service. I even knew how he'd died, which was on a secret mission I was sure Cliff didn't even know about, but I'd known men who'd been killed in every war since then. One just didn't disrespect their kids by throwing it in their faces, not even to solve a case.

So, I watched silently as he processed the loss and moved on. When we came to the end of the pictures, we walked back over to the table. He smiled at me, and shrugged. "This place is steeped in local history. It's representative of all these men and many more. So, yeah, I sank a little money into it."

That impressed me more than I thought it would. I already suspected Cliff was innocent, but seeing him nostalgic about the men who'd served their country, then used this little run-down old bar as the place to find some ease and companionship in their final days, struck a chord with me.

He was a good guy. I'd bet money on that now, and as a result, some of the walls I'd built to keep him away from my heart began to crumble a bit.

Before I could get too mushy, though, I downed my beer. "Well, we'd best be getting back to work."

"Dude," Cliff said, with a sudden familiarity that both annoyed me and made me feel warm all at the same time. "Calm down a minute. The one thing I learned on the force is to celebrate the small victories. Even those are usually hard-won. Sit down and I'll get you another beer. There's plenty of time to work tomorrow. Besides, aren't you at least a little happy we didn't find any incriminating evidence against Jeff?

I shrugged. "There's always tomorrow."

He surprised me by laughing. "Have a little faith in humanity." His face went slack then, and he shook his head. "Listen, I don't know your background, but looking at you, I can guess you've been in and out of some serious shit. I learned early on, that shit will kill you if you let yourself start believing everyone is a criminal. There are more good guys out there than bad. It's our job…" he said, waving his hand between us. "…to make sure the bad ones don't fuck up the good ones, at least if we can."

"Even after six years on the force, you still think that?"

"I force myself to believe it, otherwise, life would get too depressing to go on."

I sighed. "Okay, I'll have another stout, then let's call it a night. I still have a shit ton of paperwork to do."

He smiled and ordered me my beer. "So, your turn. You obviously know more about me than I do you, so tell me something about yourself." I stared at him a few moments, and he laughed. "You're not going to intimidate me. The worst you can do to me is fire me, and we already know that's not gonna happen, at least not while you have something you want from me, so spit it out. You were clearly in the military, start there."

"How do you know I was in the military?" I asked, my eyebrow cocked at his insinuation.

"Um, you move with precision, your life is incredibly ordered, hell, your office is pristine, and it looks like at any moment you're going to require your office staff to bounce a quarter off a bed."

I couldn't help but laugh. "I don't make them bounce quarters off their beds."

"Because, there aren't beds in your office," he said, causing me to laugh.

After the barkeep brought over our second round of beers, I leaned back and admitted I'd been in the military. Since I'd served under a different name than Bentley Cummings, there was no way he'd be able to trace me, even if he'd wanted to.

"I served for a while, almost six years before I got out."

He nodded. "And your family? Do you have one of those?" he asked.

I tensed automatically, before forcing myself to school my expression. "No, it's just me," I lied.

I could tell Cliff knew I was lying. His expression changed then, and we sat silently for a moment.

"Well, okay then," he said, and started to get up to pay.

The trust I'd been working on was quickly being ripped away, and I needed to fix it, or lose all the work I'd been doing.

I put my hand over his to stop him, and said, "Family is a difficult subject, Cliff. I'm sorry to put you off, but yes, I have family, they're just... estranged."

I intentionally didn't bring up Sandra. If he knew the woman who'd all but gotten him fired was my daughter? No, that couldn't happen.

He sat back down but didn't move his hand from beneath mine. I felt self-conscious then, and moved it myself. He waited several moments, before he responded, "I know you already know this, but the only family I have left is sitting in an independent living facility. I just inherited her house."

"Do you have a good relationship with her?" I was looking for ways to keep our connection going, anything to keep from losing what I'd work so hard to build.

He sighed. "Yeah, in fact, once you drop me off, I'm headed over there to pick her up for dinner." His face lit up. "Hey, wanna do something naughty while making an old woman's day better?"

I cocked an eyebrow. "What?" I asked.

"My grandma is harassing me to get a man." He halted his conversation and blushed. "Wait, you're... I'm not saying you're gay. I..."

"Stop," I said, laughing loud enough that the barkeep looked our way. "Actually, I am gay, so don't get freaked out."

He looked down, his cheeks clearly burning. "So..." he said, before looking up, "...wanna go screw with a nosey old woman?"

I stared at the man across from me for several long moments, considering his offer. I liked him... more than I should as an asset. I thought of any consequences for connecting with him more, and despite my own feelings of attraction, I couldn't think of any obvious concerns so, why not? Besides, if it would endear the man to me and our case, it couldn't hurt, right?

"Sure, let's take your grandma out to dinner."

Fifteen

Cliff

As I suspected, my grandma went gaga over the sexy giant the moment she laid eyes on him. I probably should've told her I was bringing a date, but to be honest, the second he told me he was gay, my mind scrambled a bit.

I was having to work really hard at not scheming to find out all the gay facets of this man.

When we walked in, I announced that I had brought a guest. As usual, my grandma came out of her bedroom with her typical dramatic flair, dressed to the nines. However, the moment she saw Bentley, she stopped dead in her tracks.

"Well, well, what do we have here?" she asked as she looked him up and down.

"Grandma, this is Bentley, my... partner," I said, smiling.

"The police force is doing well to have you on its team," she said. I went rigid. I'd forgotten I hadn't told her that I'd resigned.

"Well, um," I said, trying to figure out how to deal with the shit I'd just gotten myself into.

"I'm a private consultant actually," Bentley said. "Your grandson is working a case with me."

"Oh, that's... whatever," she said, completely uninterested in the nuances of my work. I almost laughed out loud at the look of surprise on Bentley's face.

"Where are you two fine gentlemen taking me for dinner?"

"I thought you wanted fish and chips?" I asked.

"When I have you two escorting me? Absolutely not. You'll take me someplace nice. I'll let the two of you take me to Anthony's. I haven't eaten there in a while."

She looked Bentley up and down again. "We'll let Daddy Warbucks here pick up the tab."

"Grandma," I said, my face glowing with embarrassment.

"I think that's a lovely idea, Mrs..."

"Oh, no need for that missus stuff, you can call me Ella."

"Well, Ella, shall we go?"

"Wait, you have to have reservations at Anthony's," I complained.

"Depends on who you know," Bentley said with a smirk.

Knowing how hard it was to get into that restaurant this time of night, I just sat back and waited for him to crash and burn. I'd wanted to shake my grandma up a bit, but instead, the two of them were shaking me up, so I certainly wouldn't mind seeing Mr. Perfect humbled a bit.

A phone call to the office was all it took for him to get us in. The moment we arrived, we were met by the owner of the restaurant, who escorted us to a table that overlooked the Sound.

After being seated, I looked at our guest, as if to ask how the hell he had managed that, but he just laughed it off and didn't really answer.

Bentley ordered Grandma the drink she wanted, had the server listen carefully to the things she couldn't eat, and helped her select the best choice for her. He then graciously asked her one question after another about her time as a fashion designer.

I knew she assumed I'd told him about her, but she'd be surprised to learn, he'd researched her on his own. It was hard to remember he was supposed to be the enemy as he schmoozed the woman and worked her like putty in his big, gorgeous hands.

I was surprised that Bentley kept bringing the conversation back to me. When Grandma would say something about herself, Bentley would look up at me and wink, before saying something along the lines of, "Oh, that's where Cliff gets that from."

Although the two mostly ignored me, I felt... well, I wasn't sure how I felt. It was probably all for show, but hearing Bentley compare me to my incredibly talented and gifted grandmother, not to mention acknowledging my own skills... it all made my heart feel strange in my chest.

I was completely flustered by the time we got halfway through the appetizers. Not only had Bentley made me feel... special without even really addressing me, he'd wooed my grandmother as well.

The truth was, grandma was notorious for dressing down the men I brought home. None of them were good enough for me. Some were too unpolished, some too polished, but of course, the fake one, she was completely taken with.

As I watched him hang onto her every word, I had to admit, I was way too fucking taken with him as well. I'd never introduced a man to my grandma who seemed to enjoy her as much as Bentley was. The internal conflict between worrying about whether Bentley was a threat, and my ever-present attraction to him was warring inside me.

"If you two will excuse me, I'm going to go to the restroom," I said as I stood up.

They barely acknowledged me as I darted around the corner and into the restroom to collect myself. I had to remember everything at stake here. This man literally held the fate of my best friend in his hands, not to mention my own. He could probably snap his fingers and destroy Jeff's life and mine for good. I couldn't let my feelings get the better of me.

When I walked back out, the table was empty, and I immediately panicked. I rushed into the next room to find Bentley dancing sweetly with my grandma to one of the old songs from the nineteen forties. If I wasn't completely mistaken, it was a Frank Sinatra song.

Fuck sanity, I immediately thought. The man was too much. He was my kryptonite. Just like my grandma, I was fucking putty in this suave man's hands.

Sixteen

Bentley

Ella Montgomery was every ounce elegance and vinegar. The woman had a sharp tongue and an even sharper wit. I was smitten with her almost immediately. The fact I'd been attracted to and even impressed by Cliff, her grandson, in almost the same way hadn't been lost on me.

In normal circumstances, I'd have thought the two were ganging up on me, except that watching Cliff's reaction from the moment his grandma laid eyes on me, showed he was more put out by her reaction to me than mine to her.

I looked over toward the area that separated the dining room from the dance floor, and saw Cliff standing in the doorway. The expression on his face made my heart falter a bit. The man fiercely loved the woman I was dancing with, and his expression embodied that, but there was more to it. Hunger and need mixed with... trust? Even after all I'd put him through, I could tell he trusted me with his grandmother... someone I knew instinctively he was protective of.

That disconcerted me more than anything else. I looked away from him and continued to swing his grandma gently across the dance floor. I was an expert at deciphering human reactions. I could read a person's feelings from any distance. You learned to do that when your life continuously depended on reading your environment.

Not even my daughter looked at me with trust. Even now, even after she knew I wasn't the dangerous criminal she grew up thinking I was, she still held a small amount of wariness in her expression.

For everyone I ever dealt with, I was the big, scary Mafia guy. I was the person everyone assumed was a hitman who could at any moment go over the edge and start killing anyone around him. I wasn't someone people looked at with trust. Longing, occasionally, but trust? Never.

I inhaled and let it out slowly. The music ended and when I looked up, Cliff was gone. I assumed he went back to the table.

"He'll be as loyal as any man you'll ever meet," his grandma said.

"Excuse me?" I asked, taken aback.

She stopped and looked up at me. "My grandson looks at you like a puppy looks at his new owner." She snickered, then said, "He's totally taken with you, and if your reaction to that look is any indication, I'm betting you feel the same. I've known a lot of men in my lifetime, and I can tell you are... *worldly*."

She chuckled, then patted my hand. "Men like my grandson are unique. He loves fiercely, but rarely. You'll be quite lucky if you end up being one of the people he lets into his heart. Once you're there, he'll be loyal and completely dedicated."

I hadn't noticed I'd stopped breathing until she snickered and patted my hand again. "Okay, I'm done, you can breathe now."

I let out the breath on a nervous chuckle. She didn't say anything else about it, but as soon as we were back at the table, she turned slightly and began integrating Cliff into the conversation. Each time I'd ask her something, she'd answer and then redirect the conversation back to him.

I'd tackled combatants, crooked politicians, mobsters, hitmen... all sorts of ugly, dirty, and corrupt people, most of them sociopaths and devious in every way. What I'd never tackled before was a loving grandparent who had internally made a match for her grandson.

I knew she'd unnerved me. She knew I knew it, and there was absolutely not one damned thing I could do but roll with the punches. Ella Montgomery was my most worthy adversary. I was sure with just a few more visits, I'd fall head over heels in love with her.

I looked over at Cliff and blushed, realizing that I'd denied a very obvious fact. She was right, I did react to the way he looked at me. My hands would get clammy, and my heart would beat faster when Cliff would turn his eyes so full of desire toward me. For the first time in my life, I'd met a man who triggered my desires and longing for more than a roll in the hay. Considering he was my asset, that could end up being a very, *very* dangerous thing.

Seventeen

Cliff

AFTER DROPPING MY GRANDMA off at her home, Bentley drove me back to the office and my car. We rode in silence. I had to assume my grandma had worn the poor man out.

Seeing him with her made me realize I'd gotten too close. Too close to the edge for what could happen. He was too dangerous for me and my friend Jeff to allow my heart to get any further involved.

The moment we got back to the parking lot, I got out of Bentley's car and was headed to mine. I was almost there when I heard Bentley call my name.

"Cliff?"

I turned around to see him coming toward me. "Thanks for tonight. Your grandmother is... special."

I smiled despite myself. "She's that and so much more. Thanks for taking her out and spoiling her. She loved tonight so much."

Bentley took my hand then. "I enjoyed it." He looked back toward the office before facing me and saying, "Have a good night, Cliff." And he dropped my hand.

I nodded. "You, too, Bentley."

He turned and walked toward the building and, using his key, opened the door and slipped inside.

"Okay, that was intense," I said to myself, before getting into my car and driving away. Time for a cold shower and some mind-numbing TV. Maybe copious amounts of alcohol. Something, anything, to get my mind off my dream guy, a guy I would never be able to have.

I wasn't very successful. That night as I lay in bed, not for the first time, I imagined what it would be like for that large, muscular frame to pin me down to the mattress, skin on skin as his body moved against mine. I could almost feel what it'd be like as I reached down to stroke myself.

I actually called his name out as I came. As I cleaned myself up, I chuckled. *Cliff*, I thought to myself, *you're a mess, man... a gullible mess.* Mess I might be, but I was all in for Bentley. I just had to hope he wasn't unscrupulous and didn't destroy my life, because I was so into my attraction for him now, I doubted I'd be able to keep the necessary guard up around him.

———

"Um, hey, Cliff. It's me, Jeff."

I looked at the clock. "Jeff, it's 4 a.m. Why are you calling me this early?"

"I think I found something. Can you come by the house?"

I sighed inwardly. "Sure, I'll be right over."

Jeff wasn't one to exaggerate or be off about important things, so even if it was still the wee hours of the morning, if he said he'd found something, I was inclined to believe him.

I threw on the same clothes I'd worn yesterday and drove the twenty minutes it took to get from my house to his. He opened the door and put his finger to his mouth, telling me to be quiet. Paul was probably still asleep.

"What's going on?" I asked quietly.

"I'll show you but leave your phone on the table."

I looked at my best friend like he'd lost his freaking mind, but did as he asked. It was too damned early to argue anyway.

He left his phone with mine and I followed him to the back of the house where he had his home office.

As soon as I sat down, he turned the screen toward me and pointed to an invoice.

"What's this?" I asked.

"It's a Vickey Matheson, nineteen eighty *signed print*," he said, emphasizing it. "The print was titled, *In the Western Sky*."

"Jeff, man, tell me this means something."

He gave me his annoyed look. "A Vickey Matheson isn't very valuable, but she's one of my favorite artists from the early eighties."

"And?" I asked testily.

"And she didn't make signed prints of this collection. There were four original paintings, each representing the four directions. They were sought after when they came out, and it was a big deal when she refused to make signed prints. I did all the necessary research and found *no* evidence of there being prints made later. The only thing I could find was that the four original paintings were all sold to the same buyer and there's no evidence they've ever been sold professionally since then."

"What does this prove?" I asked.

"I-I didn't sell the print, Cliff. I remembered thinking it was strange that there was a signed print all of a sudden. If she'd made them after the fact, there would've been more information in the art community. We have to keep track of provenance and she wouldn't have just made it without alerting the rest of us..."

"Jeff..." I said, demanding he get to the point.

"Dude," he said, clearly exasperated, because Jeff never used that word unless I'd pushed him to the edge. "Don't you see? I refused to sell it without documentation that Vickey had actually signed it. So, Anderson Churchill told me to return it and gave me an actual address to have the print sent to."

It took a moment for the information to sink in. "Wait, so you think that's the address where he's storing the stolen art?" I asked.

Jeff nodded. "I mean, I can't know for sure, but it would certainly be worth investigating."

"Is that the only artwork you've sent to that address?" I asked, naturally wanting to get as much information as possible.

Jeff nodded again. "I sold everything he listed with me except for that print."

"It's a good lead, I'll tell Bentley." I looked at Jeff and could see the dark circles under his eyes. "Jeff, have you been sleeping at all?" I asked.

He shook his head. "No, I'm on the verge of losing my reputation, which means I'll lose the gallery, and if I'm found complicit, I could lose my freedom as well."

I reached over and pulled him into a hug. "It's okay, Jeff, it's not going to come to that."

"You don't know," he said as his tears began to wet my shoulder.

I pulled back a little. "Listen, if they had evidence against us, they would've already arrested you *and* me. None of the art we checked out had anything illegal in it, or any evidence they ever did. I'm fairly certain we've been pulled into all this as much to test us as to accuse us."

He looked at me funny. "What do you mean?"

I stood up to pace. "Well, let's start with those government agents. How often do you think an FBI agent voluntarily walks around with a CIA officer?"

Jeff shrugged and I laughed. "It's a turf thing. Local PDs hate when the FBI gets involved. The FBI would hate it when Homeland Security gets involved, and I'm almost certain that

the CIA and FBI wouldn't be that happy to be hanging out with one another."

"So, what? You think Bentley is scamming us?"

I shook my head. "No, I think it's all legit. My Chief wouldn't have sent him my way if he wasn't. No, I think we were being played. I think we're still being played."

Jeff's eyes opened in shock as he got what I was saying. "You think they were phishing us?"

I touched my nose to indicate yes.

"So, Bentley showed me a lot of pictures when this all started. Several of them were of you and me standing in front of various paintings. At the time, I couldn't remember whether I was at your gallery events or not, and you know all these paintings look alike to me... don't tell Paul." I chuckled.

"But the night you had the Churchill opening, was I there?"

Jeff thought for a moment, then he shook his head. "No, you didn't come to that one, because you were working that night. Also, you'd told me a long time ago, you weren't into 'old people art.'" He laughed. "I figured you'd think of this as old people art."

"You know this all means Bentley was playing me all along."

Jeff sighed. "This just keeps getting weirder."

"Yeah, so, tell me why you wanted to leave the phones in the other room?" I asked.

He blushed. "I don't know... I'm so strung out, I'm becoming one of those conspiracy theorists and I thought they might listen to our conversations."

"You know, the good guys don't do that without a warrant, but I honestly think they'd listen in on us, too. I thought that before, but I don't mind them hearing anything we are saying. You're innocent, I'm innocent, but I don't think the Churchills are innocent."

"No, me either. Like I said, that family is obsessed with art. Now that I know Colin isn't dead and Anderson faked his death certificate, I'm almost sure Anderson is looking for ways to make extra cash."

"Do you think Anderson stole the paintings from Colin?" I asked.

Jeff shrugged again. "It's possible, but it's also possible they were just testing the waters to see how far I'd go. That's why I remembered the print. After I refused to sell it, their work with me quickly dried up. I haven't heard from them since. The art they sold through me wasn't what you'd call fine art. Most of it was recent, from the last forty years. None of it priced over five thousand dollars."

I waited for him to continue his thoughts. Five grand was a lot of money to me, but I knew that wasn't the case with art.

"Up until now, I thought they'd stopped using my gallery, because I pissed Anderson off by refusing to sell the print. Your guy, Bentley, said he thought it was because of the arrests that took place in Seattle lately. Now, I'm thinking he might have stopped working with me, because I did my homework."

I smiled as I nodded. "Jeff, I think you could be right. So, where's this address?" I asked, feeling hopeful for the first time since this whole thing started.

He printed off an address on Shaw Island, of all places. The little island was run mostly by nuns in the middle of the San Juans. I guessed if you were going to hide a bunch of art, doing so under the nose of a load of nuns was the way to do it.

Jeff also printed other documents for me, including the invoice to ship the print, before putting all of it in a large envelope.

I hugged my friend and told him he did good. "Now, Jeff, go get some rest. If this works out like I think it will, you're off the hook."

He nodded and I watched as his shoulders literally slumped in front of me.

I rushed home with the documentation and began my own research. Did the Churchills own land on the island? An easy search of the county's property records gave no indication they did. However, the address Jeff had given me was a property owned by the monastery. I opened Google Earth and found a picture of a small house.

I drilled down further online and hit paydirt.

I found an article about the property that read: Upon the death of Levy Kraybill, the property in question was donated to the monastery to act as a refuge for Kraybill's family to visit when they came to worship on Shaw Island. When the family was not using the property, the monastery would be able to use it for other things.

I then found Levy Kraybill's obituary that ran in a newspaper in Vancouver, BC. It noted he was survived by a daughter, Alana Kraybill Churchill, and her son, Anderson Churchill.

"Fuck!" I said out loud. "Finally, some progress."

I quickly printed all of my finds, including Kraybill's obituary, stuffed them in the envelope Jeff had given me, and made the call to Bentley.

"Hello?" he answered, his gravelly voice almost making me back out of what I was about to do. I shook off my momentary lust, and said, "Bentley, I have something you're going to want to see. Can you meet me in half an hour at your office?"

I knew the guy wasn't used to people asking him to do things so directly. He was the boss. He'd always been the boss, from what I could tell. I liked that authority in him, but I also wanted to keep him off balance, too, especially right now.

When he agreed, I drove over to the office to meet him. His staff weren't due to show up until nine, and it was still only seven thirty, so the office was empty and quiet.

He showed me into the conference room and after we sat down, I went through all the paperwork. I showed him the invoice first and explained exactly what Jeff had told me. Then I handed him the address.

His interest was clearly piqued. "So, you think this is where the art is stored, just because the print was delivered there? Anderson could've sold it himself."

I smiled without responding and handed over the article that stated how the nuns inherited the property and the obituary linking it all to Anderson Churchill.

Bentley's smile grew as I went along. "Yeah, I think that's where he's storing the art," I said.

"That's great, Cliff. Good job."

I nodded. "You should go get your FBI and CIA friends and recover the art."

"Let me make some calls, and then we can do that today."

"No, not me, Mr. Cummings," I said, purposefully using his formal name. "You've been playing me and Jeff throughout all of this. I'm not sure if you intentionally got me fired or not, but I don't want to know, 'cause I've decided not to hate you, and if I knew you did, I might change my mind. I understand why you've done what you've done. I hope to God you recover the art and return it to its rightful owners, but I'm out."

I stood to go, and Bentley stood as well. "You aren't out of this. There's evidence..."

"There's evidence you made up," I countered, cutting him off. "I wasn't at the gallery opening the night you supposedly took my picture with Jeff in front of the incriminating art. Not that the art was incriminating. You've been phishing. Now, if you don't mind, this fish is going to unhook itself from your line, and if you're a man of integrity, now that my friend has given you the lead that might help you solve this case, you'll leave him alone as well."

Bentley's expression went blank, which was all the confirmation I needed that what I'd said was accurate.

I didn't have any company property since I'd only worked here a short time, so all I had to do was walk out the door, which I did without another word.

Eighteen

Bentley

B USTED. HE TOTALLY BUSTED me. I was still confused why Cliff Sparks wasn't intimidated by me. Usually, people stammered around or were afraid of my responses, but Cliff never showed even an indication. Had I been my father or grandfather, I'm sure he'd have been killed over such lack of fear.

For me, it was that much more of a turn-on. I'd never wanted people to fear me. I knew I was a big man, I knew my reputation was intense, but I had never played for the bad guys' team. Sure, I did what had to be done, but a small injury was never as bad as death.

I watched Cliff leave, and I had to give him credit. He'd figured me out, given me what he knew I needed, and left. I really didn't need him or his friend for the investigation any longer, so his resignation was actually a good thing in that sense, but my heart stung with the rejection. Cliff might've been the first man who made me feel... hopeful that my love life would ever be anything other than nonexistent, especially after such an incredible night we had shared with his grandmother. My lonely heart felt broken... like it was disappointed I'd let my rational brain take charge, and let something so promising and precious, a potential love match I might never find again, slip through my fingers. *Stupid heart*, I thought. There was nothing to be done, though.

To distract myself from thinking about this any further, I called Sandra and Ford, and told them to meet me at the office as soon as possible. When they arrived, we began the process of making a good enough argument to gain access to the island property Cliff had mentioned.

After a grueling three days, we were still no closer to getting access to the Shaw Island Monastery. The judge flat-out refused the warrant, saying our evidence wasn't significant enough to support one. I guessed I already knew the answer would be no. A gallery owner sending a print with an allegedly forged artist signature wasn't enough.

Regardless, I did have another route, albeit a precarious one. I phoned the abbey back home in Boston where my mom's late cousin, Sister Clarissa, had lived, and asked to speak with Mother Olive.

Unfortunately, she wasn't available, and I decided it was best I talk with her in person anyway. So, I asked the woman I was speaking with to set up an appointment with Mother Olive and Father Thomas. I told her my name and heard her gasp. *Damn,*

I thought, *this woman sounded too young to know me, yet she still seemed to recognize my name.*

I hadn't been back to the abbey since that fateful day all those years ago when I was marched off in handcuffs, but in our research of the Shaw Island Monastery, I'd seen a connection between the same order my cousin served in – the Poor Clares – and the nuns on the island, and besides, it was time to put this last demon from my youth to rest.

Nineteen

Cliff

"**Y**OU QUIT?" JEFF ASKED.

"I quit, and with the information you gave me, plus what I found, I think we might be done with all that now, once and for all."

Jeff looked relieved. "Cliff, I can't thank you…"

I put my hand up. "Don't get gushy. One, I don't know for sure whether it's over or not, and two, you found the document, and if this works, it's entirely on your shoulders for getting us out."

"Paul!" Jeff yelled toward the back of the house. "We're going on vacation!"

"What?" Paul asked, coming from the kitchen, and wiping his hands on a towel.

"I think we've seen the last of Cummings Security, and I need a vacation. Wanna go to Maui?"

Paul laughed. "It's my brother's birthday party next week, and you've got two gallery openings next month. You don't have time for a vacation."

Jeff moped. "Maybe just a tiny one?"

Paul came over and kissed his husband. "I can call Beth and see if she can put us up in her B&B for a few days. We can explore the national park."

Jeff nodded. "Perfect." He turned to me then and smiled. "Wanna come with? It's quite lovely up in Port Angeles this time of year."

I shook my head. "No, I think I'll hang out here and see if I can find myself a legitimate job."

"Suit yourself, but you should at least come up for a day or so. Daniel and Joseph would welcome you. You also need to meet Beth. The woman is nonstop."

I laughed. "Maybe, but for real, I do need a job. I can't survive much longer without one."

Jeff looked at me seriously, and I knew he wanted to challenge me to use my parents' trust-fund money, but no, that was a last resort.

I took my leave and headed back home. I still had a few of my grandma's items to go through and send off to their designated places, before I could tell her I'd fulfilled her wishes. Then, when all that was settled, I'd decided to begin doing some refurbishing. Little changes I'd always wanted to make, like opening the kitchen and the dining room up, so it was more of an open floor plan. Even though my mom had tastefully updated the kitchen many years ago, it was still tiny, which was popular when my grandfather originally designed it, and I couldn't remember when we had ever used the dining room as a dining room. Usually, it was covered with my grandma's design patterns.

I didn't sew, but I did like to cook, so installing a nice, large kitchen, and transforming the small pantry into a walk-in just made sense for my lifestyle. It would also open the kitchen up to the very large living room that looked out over the water.

I worked the rest of the day, and by evening, when I hadn't heard from Bentley or his stooges, I was feeling confident that I really was off the hook. I just wish that didn't make me feel so... disappointed. I'd finally found a gay guy that pushed all my buttons, who I was not only physically attracted to, but also shared my interests, and even liked spending time with my grandma, and he was off the table.

I drove to the UPS Store before they closed, and sent off the remainder of my grandma's designs, just as she'd asked. I sadly watched as the boxes containing the last of her award-winning designs were tagged and tossed back in the pile of packages. Sure, she'd kept a few for her own use, but I'd decided once she was gone, I'd have them professionally cleaned and placed in protective coverings before storing them in her bedroom, along with her current furniture. One day, I had no doubt, people would want this home to become a museum to honor her and my grandfather. For now, it was my home, but I wanted to ensure there would be enough of the original left for a museum when I was done with it.

The sadness I felt each time I thought of losing my grandma was threatening to force me down an ugly spiral, so I decided to go to one of my favorite places, and spend some time with the guys there instead.

I grinned as I saw the bar's parking lot was full. I slipped into the building and was greeted by several of my favorite people, before I made my way to the table I considered to be mine. Larry, the barkeep, brought me my usual amber beer, and I talked with my buddies throughout the night.

More than once, I looked over at the empty chair in front of me, and couldn't help but think of the man who'd occupied it just a few days before. How his dark brooding eyes had lit up in surprise at how good the beer tasted, and the appreciative smile he gave me while listening to my stories of the soldiers whose pictures adorned the walls. These little reminders of him, which I wouldn't forget anytime soon, were now sprinkled throughout the place. "In a different life and a different time," I said into my beer before taking a drink.

There would be years to fantasize about having that imposing man's delectable body entwined with mine, but for now, I needed to be happy he wasn't investigating my friend Jeff any longer. At least, I could let the fantasy keep me company at night.

Twenty

Bentley

I STEPPED INTO THE abbey's office and felt the muscles in my neck tense. I hadn't been in this building since that fateful day decades ago. That was also the last time I'd seen Sister Clarissa, a woman more of a mother to me than my actual mom was.

I didn't have to wait long before Mother Olive stepped out of her office and approached me. She was much more weathered now than the last time I'd seen her.

Her smile was the same, though, and I immediately felt at ease.

"Hello, Mother Olive," I said.

"Hello, Bentley. Come with me," she said, and led me back to her office. She closed the door as I went to the chairs that sat across from her desk.

"Bentley, son, it's so nice to see you after all these years. Look how well you've turned out."

I smiled, but I knew exactly what I looked like, a beaten-down Marine with multiple scars – mostly internal – to show for it.

"So, how have you been?"

I looked around and asked if Father Thomas was going to join us.

"No, love," she said, her face taking on a sad expression. "Father Thomas is no longer capable of joining in on the affairs of the abbey."

"Oh, I'm sorry," I replied.

She smiled and patted my shoulder before walking past me, and sitting behind her desk. "I know he'd have been proud to see you here today, Bentley. We spoke of you often before his mind began to drift."

"Alzheimer's?" I asked.

She nodded. "Fairly progressed. I would take you to see him, but he doesn't do well with visitors any longer. They seem to upset him."

I took a deep breath. "I understand. I'll light a candle for him on the way out."

She smiled. "He'd like that, Bentley, I'm sure."

Mother Olive turned in her seat, then pulled out an envelope from her credenza, and placed it in front of me.

"What's this?" I asked.

She looked stunned for a moment. "I assumed that's why you came. It's Sister Clarissa's final correspondence to you."

I was overcome with emotion, and sucked in a breath before I could control it. "No," I whispered when I'd regained my composure. "I didn't know this existed."

She looked sad. "I guess I shouldn't be surprised. Word was passed through your mother and father that when you finally came home, Sister Clarissa had wanted this given to you."

I nodded and wiped at the errant tear that had managed to slip past my defenses.

A large part of me wanted to open the envelope and see what she'd written. After I'd been sent away to join the military, it'd been radio silence. I'd lost her, just like I'd lost the rest of my identity.

Instead, I placed the envelope on my lap, unable to let it out of my grip even to discuss the job at hand. It was just too precious to me.

"I'm here on another matter, although, this is a very welcome surprise."

Mother Olive nodded and prompted me to continue.

"I've taken on the role of contractor for law enforcement, not only in this country, but even occasionally for Interpol. As such, I'm in the middle of an investigation into stolen art."

I wouldn't usually be so candid with someone, but if Mother Olive was anything like she'd been twenty-plus years ago, I needed to either put my cards on the table, or go on my way. She could smell a lie or half-truth a mile away.

"I have reason to believe the art is being stored on Shaw Island, at the monastery there."

"I see," Mother Olive responded. I could tell she was thinking about the situation. "You're wanting me to help you get access?" I nodded. "Well, I don't have a close-enough relationship with the sisters there to get you in, but the order has been pushing us to visit one another. We have a large order here, with more recruits than we can house, so I've been feeling some pressure to visit our less-desirable assignments so I know them firsthand, and can encourage our younger sisters to consider them."

The nun was thinking out loud, and I decided to keep quiet to allow her to work things out.

"I could visit and say you're coming to the island to have lunch with me while I'm there. What excuse would we use for you visiting me?"

I looked at the envelope and swallowed hard. As the Abbess pondered the issues, I came to terms with the fact that this was indeed the best excuse to meet me, to give me this information. I just wondered if maybe my coming here would cause that excuse to be questionable.

I knew it was very possible one or more of the nuns at the Shaw Island Monastery might be involved in the Churchills' criminal activity, so it had to look and feel real. This was the most valid-sounding pretense.

"Mother Olive, I have the perfect excuse."

She stopped speaking and looked at me.

I placed the envelope, something that already meant more to me than anything I'd ever possessed, on the desk.

"You could be giving this to me."

She smiled and nodded, but when she saw my expression, the smile fell from her face.

"But you don't want to part with it, do you?"

I shook my head. "No, I can't hardly stand the thought."

She tapped her tooth, a habit she'd had even when I knew her before, then nodded. "If you would trust me, I'll make a copy of the contents, and have the originals couriered to your home. That way, it wouldn't be the originals you were coming to pick up. If someone looks at the contents of the package, it'll still justify your presence."

There were more holes in all of this than I liked. Such as, why she hadn't sought me out before now, given my home base was in Boston, the same city as the abbey.

But, I honestly didn't have any reason to believe the Shaw Island Monastery was intentionally involved. I'd researched them in every way possible, and nothing indicated they were anything other than a benevolent organization.

Regardless, bad actors could always be taking advantage of their generosity. The envelope with Sister Clarissa's information might just be enough to keep any potential suspicions at bay.

I reluctantly left the precious envelope with Mother Olive, and made my way out of the abbey. Everything in me wanted to go back and retrieve it, but I'd chosen to trust Mother Olive, and hopefully, the contents of that envelope would be in my hands soon.

Twenty-One

Cliff

I WAS STUNNED BY how disappointed I was that a week had passed, and Bentley hadn't come to retrieve me. I knew I was a ridiculous queen with Disney dreams, but I'd imagined the ruggedly charming man charging in on his stallion, throwing me over his shoulder, and hauling me off to do delightfully naughty things to my body.

I remembered some song from the nineties, where the lyrics went something like, "Fantasy never becomes reality." Even in my youth, I'd been told not to chase fairy tales, but I couldn't quite let go of the hope.

I headed over to my grandma's with the list of to-dos she'd left for me. When I showed her the list with my check mark next to each item, she shook her head. "I was supposed to be dead before you did all this."

"I didn't want to wait until you were dead. I'm guessing when that happens, I'm not going to be in a fit state of mind to be running around mailing off taffeta, or whatever that see-through crap is you used too much of."

She looked around like someone was listening, and said in a hushed voice, "Careful what you say. If you keep up that Neanderthal shit, the gay police are going to come and strip your membership away."

I laughed. "I'm not a Neanderthal, just 'cause I don't like all that fabric stuff."

"That fabric stuff kept you well-fed, young man, so I'll not hear you disparage it, you hear me?"

I smiled. She must have been feeling more like herself, because this was one of her favorite ways to get onto me.

I kissed her cheek, then flopped down on her uncomfortable loveseat. "I never had any interest in sewing, or anything like that, but I'm glad you loved it. Oh, before I forget, the New York Textile Association sent a card thanking you. I forgot to bring it, sorry."

She waved her hand dismissively. "Like I said in my will, you should save anything like that in my scrapbook. My great-grandchildren might want those someday."

I almost spat out the coffee I'd just sipped. "Great-grandchildren?"

"Yes, that man you were all snuggled up to, he's a family kind of guy. He'll be wanting babies, I'm sure."

"And how the hell do you think I'll be making them for him?" I laughed.

"You're a creative person. I'm sure you'll figure something out."

I shook my head. "You're feisty today. What happened, you run over a small child, or something?"

"Oh, Grandson, let's watch that show."

"Ugh, no, Grandma, I just said that to—"

"Never mind why you said it," she interrupted me. "You said it. Now we're watching it."

I smiled, knowing we were about to watch her favorite movie. Well, second to *Nine to Five*. She adored Dolly Parton, and at some point during the movie, I knew she'd look down at her boobs, and make some comment about having work done.

I was keeping a list of things to do with her that would cheer her up, now that she was in independent living, and I hadn't even thought of watching *Steel Magnolias*, but I'd add it to the list now that we were doing it.

After the movie, she wiped her eyes, and we had lunch at the little cafeteria down the hall. She said the breakfasts and dinners here were on the same level as a meat smoothie, but the lunches were decent, so we both had hoagie sandwiches, which were far from great, but not bad.

I walked her back to her apartment, and she sent me on my way, saying she needed a nice after-lunch nap. I kissed her and left after that. My strong, powerful grandma never would've taken a nap, even if she hadn't slept in days. This was another difficult sign that times had changed. My heart broke a little more every time a new sign showed up.

I'd hired an architect, the grandson of my grandfather's apprentice, to meet me at the house later that afternoon to help redesign the kitchen/dining room to stay true to the architecture of the house.

He was fifteen or more years older than me, and was now a part-time professor at the university.

I already knew he was going to try to talk me out of the remodel altogether, and I honestly looked forward to the debate. I was pretty sure I was going to update the kitchen/dining room, but at least I knew this guy would force me to remain true to the home's original design, at least as much as possible.

Unlike my grandma, I was never averse to a nap, so I came home and took my own. I woke up just in time for the architect to arrive. I threw water on my face and cleaned myself up as much as possible, and came downstairs in enough time to meet him.

Our appointment time came and went, which was strange. I knew the architect from a variety of places, including the ceremonies where my grandfather had been given awards posthumously. I couldn't understand why he wasn't here.

I called his office and his secretary apologized, saying he had been held up. "Would he like to reschedule?" I asked, and after she paused a moment, she said he'd get back in touch with me later.

"Okay, that's weird," I said out loud after I'd hung up. I immediately called Jeff. "Hey, do you remember Evan Tinkle?"

"The architect that's always harassing you at those parties?"

"That's the one."

"Yeah, why?"

I told him about how Tinkle had missed his appointment to help me remodel the house, and Jeff was as surprised as I was. "Well, give him another chance. I'm sure whatever happened must have been a big deal."

"Okay, well, if it doesn't work out, try to use that artsy-fartsy brain of yours to help me find someone who can design my remodel, without destroying the historical integrity."

"Oh, Cliff, I'm so proud of you. You're even using the right terminology."

"Shut up, dweeb," I said, and he laughed. I was so far from artistic, which had always confused him. My grandfather was a famous architect in Seattle, my grandma was a nationally renowned fashion designer, and I was... well, I was a cop, or at least I used to be.

I dismissed the weirdness of being stood up by the architect, and busied myself with a job search. As I pursued the job-listing sites, and uploaded a few resumés, I couldn't help but wonder why I didn't inherit artistic genes. My mother had even been an amateur painter, but I couldn't even draw stick people. I knew good art when I saw it, but I had little love for it. I certainly didn't understand why people like the Churchills obsessed over it and stole it. If you loved it so much, buy a print, right?

I also understood it on some level. I absolutely loved law enforcement. I loved knowing I was helping keep the innocent safe. I knew law enforcement as a whole was far from perfect, but, despite its faults, protecting the innocent would always be an honorable profession.

I took a deep breath and let it out slowly. I guessed I didn't have to be a cop. When it all got boiled down, I liked helping people. I also liked helping people find justice. At one point, I thought about becoming an attorney with the intention of being a judge, but no, I wanted to play an active, hands-on role.

Too bad Cummings Security didn't work out. The more time I spent with them, the more I liked the idea of working alongside law enforcement—still solving crimes, but without the badge and the negative connotations.

Ugh, every time I thought about that job, or the potential of one like it, I thought of Bentley. I tried to force thoughts of him out of my head, but the more time passed, the more I struggled with feelings of lost opportunity when it came to that man. It was disconcerting that it wasn't just attraction that caused me to feel so disappointed.

Bentley was smart and made me laugh. He was intimidating at first, but the more I got to know him, the more I realized he was more than his appearance.

I'd felt my hard resolve to hate him melt as the time we spent together passed. Our last night at the bar, right before I invited him out to go meet my grandma, I'd basically begun to think of him as... *what?* I thought, interrupting my own thoughts. *That's the question, right?* What was I feeling? Friendship? No... although we were friendly now... what I felt was more than friendship.

I shook my head trying to shake out the frustration. I wished I could call what I felt for him simply an emotional response one might have toward a captor, like Stockholm Syndrome, except he hadn't held me captive, and now he seemed just a bit *too* happy to let me go, not that I really knew how he felt. I'd walked out. He just hadn't tried to stop me...

I needed to stop with this destructive train of thought. Not only did I have feelings for the man now, but I'd probably never meet another gay man who I was this attracted to. Why did life have to be so cruel as to put him in front of me, just to take him away?

Twenty-Two

Bentley

I OPENED MY FRONT door just as the courier stepped up to it, my security sensors having alerted me to someone's presence long before the woman even got out of her car.

She smiled, handed me the envelope containing my precious letter, and left.

As soon as I was back inside, I stared at the envelope. Was I strong enough to read what my beloved Sister Clarissa had written for my eyes only all those years ago, a message that had sat undelivered for the past two decades?

I finally steeled my resolve enough to open it, and began reading.

Dear Bentley...

The letter was six pages long. Six pages that ripped me into small shreds of grief.

You are as much a son to me as a birth child could've ever been. I'm so proud of how you've turned out.

She spoke of specific things I'd done. *Letting little Michael beat you in an arm-wrestling challenge. Keeping the boys from picking on Alejandra Lopez.* I remembered the young immigrant girl from Guatemala, who as a new student at our Catholic school had been bullied by a few of our classmates.

These were things I'd forgotten, most of them I had no idea Sister Clarissa had seen. I knew now she'd seen it all, even when I didn't know she was looking.

I broke down and cried, tears coating my face as I remembered this remarkable woman—my guide, and as she said, my parent.

Life will always throw challenges at you, Bentley. It's your lot in life to overcome them. Please, remember you don't have to walk that path alone. You have a soul mate out there, someone who will stand by you, even when the world seems to be on your back. Knowing you, he's already shown up and you've chased him off with a stick, like you did that Doberman Pinscher that wandered onto the playground and was growling at the other kids, when you were in the second grade.

I chuckled, both at the accusation and the memory. I had been so scared of the dog, I'd peed myself, but I'd stood up to it and kept it from biting any of the other kids. The fact that I'd found a branch that'd fallen off the tree next to the playground, and was lunging at the poor creature with it, might be why it decided to go in the other direction, instead of attacking me.

I wiped away tears as I read her final paragraphs.

I'm most certainly dead or you wouldn't be reading this letter, but, young man, I'll always be watching you. Remember, I'm a nun. I'm sure that will get me special privileges in heaven, and the first thing I plan to do is talk Saint Peter into giving me a free pass to keep my eye on you. No doubt they'll all be wanting to keep you on the straight and narrow, so I don't think I'll have to work hard to convince them. So, please, understand I plan to be watching and tweaking your ear every time you get out of line.

I automatically reached up and rubbed my left ear, the one she always went after when I screwed up. Even after I towered over her, she could still somehow get ahold of that ear and twist it.

Please, stay good, dear boy. You are meant for great things, and your brave acts throughout your life, not the least of which was saving all those young women your father held captive, makes you a hero. You are a hero, Bentley. Never forget that.

I love you with all my heart.

Sister Clarissa.

I took the letter, and folding it carefully, put it away in my safe, the one I had hidden behind the front safe. My father had taught me one very valuable lesson: always give the thieves a decoy safe to find. That way, they wouldn't get to the one you really wanted to keep hidden.

Of course, since my father was the most likely culprit to rob me, I wasn't sure that advice still held the same weight, but I guessed that was why I had more than one decoy safe with various papers and money in them.

This safe was the one I had buried behind a false wall that led to a secret room, that had another false wall that led to a closet, which had a secret compartment in the floor. I hid Sister Clarissa's letter there. It was with my daughter's birth certificate, and the judge's order that granted me full custody of her. I also had a rosary Sister Clarissa had given me on my confirmation when I turned fourteen. Until now, it was all I had left of her, and the only reason I still had it was, because I'd had it in my pocket to recite the rosary the day all the crap involving my family hit the fan.

Now, Sister Clarissa's letter was among my other most-prized possessions.

I closed the safe and walked back into the main room, then into my own chambers. I thought of the words she'd written about finding someone to walk with me through this life. She'd thought I'd see that letter long before I did.

I wondered if maybe I had seen it earlier, I would've considered allowing myself to have a companion. I immediately thought of Cliff Sparks, then of his grandmother, and her telling me he was fiercely loyal.

I'd fucked that up for sure. If I'd have known him better before I presented the fake photos to him, I would've known he'd have figured out they were photoshopped. Not that my photoshopping wasn't top-notch. More than once, experts I'd hired had looked at my doctored photos, and sworn they were originals.

Luckily, none of them had ever been used in court. I wouldn't allow that. I was, as Sister Clarissa had said, one of the good guys, and that would've been allowing things to go too far.

However, Cliff had figured it out, because he knew himself, knew his friend, and therefore knew I'd made the photos to trick him. I was sure, to him, I was no different than the dirtbags he hauled off the streets as a cop.

Not that I could blame him, but there were times for such measures. I definitely didn't think he was involved with any crime. I couldn't see any evidence that incriminated his friend either. In fact, his cooperation was a good sign he was innocent. Regret engulfed me, and my breath hitched a little as I thought about Cliff, and how any possibility of having him – in my bed, or in my life – was lost now, but I was in no position to be anything to him or anyone, despite what Sister Clarissa had said. If I wanted to be a good person, I had to step out of his life and let him go forever. That was what it meant to live the life I lived. It just didn't matter whether I'd chosen that life, or if it'd been chosen for me.

I packed my bags that night, and flew back to Seattle. Mother Olive had told me she was able to secure her time on Shaw Island for the coming weekend. She used the excuse that she didn't want to wait to visit until fall, when the cold weather would upset her arthritis. Apparently, that had worked.

I would go to the island the day after she arrived, and hopefully, she'd be able to get me access to the Kraybill home. I called Sandra when I got back to Edmonds, and told her to meet me at the office the following morning, so I could fill her in on all I'd found out.

Saturday morning came, and I crossed over on the ferry to Shaw Island. Sandra and Ford had come across the day before pretending to be tourists, and were staying in a B&B there. I'd planned to go to the monastery at a certain time, and Sandra and Ford had both planned to tour the monastery then as well.

There was nothing amiss on the trip over. The ferry ride was enjoyable, the vistas breathtaking. When we pulled into port, I drove my car off and up to the monastery. When I walked in, one of the nuns smiled, and said, "You must be Mr. Cummings. Mother Olive said we should be expecting you."

"I'm guessing my size gave me away?" I asked, and she chuckled.

"You do stand out a bit, Mr. Cummings."

I was left in a hallway that smelled of wood polish. The place was as immaculate as you'd expect in any monastery. A few minutes later, Mother Olive came out with a young woman at her side.

Mother Olive approached me and shook my hand. "Thank you, Bentley, for coming to the island. I would've brought the papers to you, but—"

She stopped short as if she'd just remembered the young woman was with her. "I'm sorry, Bentley, this is one of the order's aspirants, Lucia Kraybill. Lucia, this is Mr. Bentley Cummings. He's one of our abbey's more charitable friends."

Lucia nodded, but didn't take my hand.

Mother Olive handed me the envelope, and thanked me again for coming out.

"If you don't mind, Mother Olive, I'd like a tour of the monastery. Would you join me?"

The Mother looked stunned. *Good acting on her part*, I thought, and turned to the young woman. "Do you mind if Mr. Cummings joins us on our tour?"

The girl shrugged. "I can't see why not," she said. "The other tour is going on right now as well, so maybe we can join them. Sister Harris knows significantly more than I do about the history."

"I know a little of the history of the order," I said, and began to spout off what I'd learned. Lucia's eyes glazed over, which was perfect for what I'd planned. I could also use the fact that she had the same last name as the person who'd donated the home in question to the monastery.

We followed the tour, and I spotted Ford and Sandra, although we didn't acknowledge each other.

As we were taken around, I noticed we turned away from where the home sat. "Lucia, your last name is Kraybill?" I asked the girl. She nodded. "Didn't a Kraybill donate property to the monastery a few years back?"

"My grandfather did, yes. That's why I decided to come to this order," she said, and I could see she was indeed proud of her family's past.

"I'd love to see the property. I read that the home was designed by the famous architect Mitchell O'Keefe."

"You do know your history, Mr. Cummings. I can ask if we can show you the home. It's usually not open to the public, and my family are the only ones who use it, but I'm sure they'll let you if I request it."

I nodded and smiled. Sure enough, the girl got the keys and led us to the house. I noticed Sandra and Ford had pulled away from the group, and were sitting under a shade tree where they could see us entering the home.

There were several boxes stored around the living room, and I knew instantly that these were the stolen art pieces. I asked if I could take pictures, and the girl shrugged, as if she couldn't care less. So, I pulled out my phone and began taking photos of the home's interior, making sure I caught the boxes.

"This is fantastic," I said as we walked out. Lucia locked it back up and proudly led us back to the monastery, talking about what she knew about her grandfather, and recounting the times she'd come to visit him on the island.

I thanked her, as well as Mother Olive, profusely, as a student of architecture might before I headed out the door. I made eye contact with Sandra and Ford, letting them know I was done, and walked to my car and left.

I drove slowly, giving them time to catch up to me as they followed me to the B&B.

We all went inside, and I showed them the photos. "This should be enough for a warrant," I said.

Both of them agreed, and talked about how it looked suspicious.

I forwarded the pictures to my contacts with San Juan County, then called them asking for the warrant.

"It won't be until tomorrow," I was told. "Maybe even later. Can your FBI guy sit on it?"

"Seriously, no. If your guy can't do it, then I'll go to a federal judge."

"I'm sorry, Mr. Cummings, our judge isn't available. He's on vacation at least until—"

I hung up before he finished and called my contacts with the FBI in Seattle. "Bring us what you've got, and since you're a witness, you come, too. We'll appeal to the federal judges here," he said.

"I can do that," I confirmed. "They have a ferry leaving in a couple hours, I'll be on that, but just so you know, I won't be there until late."

"It doesn't matter. No judge is going to give you a warrant to search a monastery without the person who saw the stolen merchandise himself. It's not likely he'll even go on your word alone," he said, the last bit under his breath.

I wasn't offended. I knew I wasn't law enforcement. In fact, in the eyes of most judges, I was, at best, a high-end security guard. I was persuasive, though, if given a chance, especially since I held higher security clearances than most regular FBI or even CIA agents.

I told Sandra and Ford to watch the property while I went back to secure the warrant. "If you see anyone, don't approach," I said, and looked my daughter in the eye. "Do *not* approach. Document, and try to see where they are going."

I stared at her until she nodded, which she did reluctantly.

When it came time for the ferry, I boarded, and got out of my car with the few other passengers to go up to the waiting area. This time of night wasn't busy, not that Shaw Island ever was. The island was still fairly unsettled. There weren't a lot of tourist sites like the other islands comprising the San Juans had, its biggest attraction being the monastery.

The sun was already down when the ferry left, and I was more than a little disappointed. The view coming out had been spectacular. I would need to come back to the San Juans sooner rather than later, to see the sites as a real tourist.

I was staring at the pictures on my phone, when two men sat on either side of me. "Mr. Cummings, I presume?" Another man stepped out from around a corner and stood in front of me.

All three men were showing me they were armed.

"To whom do I owe the pleasure?" I asked.

"Follow us, and we'll tell you."

I had to think quickly. If I followed them, they'd probably kill me. If I didn't, they might still kill me, but people would see it. I saw two of the men carried semi-automatic Glocks. There were maybe fifteen or sixteen people on board, counting the crew. I doubted anyone was armed. They could easily take out everyone on the ferry.

I stood to go with them, figuring it would probably be better if I didn't give them an excuse to hurt anyone but me.

We walked down the stairs and toward the back of the ferry, where I saw the attendant who'd guided us onboard lying in a pool of blood next to the controls.

"As you can see, this is where our little charade comes to an end."

"Who the hell are you?" I asked, already recognizing the man from his photo, but determined to give myself time to assess the situation.

"Why, haven't you guessed, Mr. Cummings? I'm Anderson Churchill, and you've tampered with my business enough. Shoot him, boys."

The two men with him weren't professionals. The first was about five six, and I could tell by how he handled his pistol that he didn't know what he was doing. One wrong move and his dick would be toast. He was also fidgety, a sure sign of an amateur.

The other appeared to be tweaking on meth or something. I decided he was my weakest link, and I reacted before either man could draw his weapon. I throat punched the tweaker, sending him back against the wall, and immediately turned to the amateur. I had just punched his face when I heard the gunshot. It missed, but I felt it whizz past my right ear. Just then, the tweaker got his senses back and charged at me, knocking me back toward the safety chain that blocked passengers from falling into the water. A second shot was fired, but instead of hitting me, it struck the back of the guy charging at me, knocking him into my arms. I tripped backward into the chain and managed to throw the dying man off me. I looked up to see the barrel of a gun aimed right between my eyes. When I looked past the gun, I saw the arrogant face of Anderson Churchill at the other end.

He pulled the trigger, but a spent cartridge had jammed the ejection port, blocking it from firing. I didn't have time to do anything other than react, so as he cleared the jam, I forcefully pushed myself backward and immediately hit the cold water. I took a deep breath and swam down as deep as I could to get out of his view as I heard the sound of bullets whizzing past in the water surrounding me. My lungs were on fire when I returned to the surface and gasped for air, and I saw the ferry pulling further away from me. I was alone in the middle of Puget Sound with no chance of rescue.

Remembering my water survival training from the Marines, I quickly struggled out of my wet jeans, tied the legs together in a knot and flipped them over my head to fill them with air. I stuck my head through the legs of my makeshift flotation device and took a moment to survey my surroundings. I could just make out a few lights on an island to my south, so I began paddling in that direction, periodically stopping to reinflate my jeans.

Exhaustion was quickly settling in, and hypothermia wasn't far behind. I swam as fast as I could, while keeping my makeshift life preserver inflated.

When I heard the sound of oars in the water, I immediately knew it was my only chance for survival.

The night was dark, and I knew no one would see me unless I called out. "Help!" I yelled.

No one responded, so I yelled again. "Help! Is anyone out there?" The sound of the oars hitting the water stopped, and I yelled louder. "Help me!"

"What the hell?" I heard a man say. Luckily, that meant whoever was in the water was close enough to actually help me.

"I'm here!" I yelled. "I'm here!"

I kept repeating myself as I heard the oars moving closer. Finally, I made out the silhouette of the boat.

"Damn!" I heard someone else say, and the next thing I knew, two sets of hands reached over the side of the boat and began to pull me in.

"Who the hell are you, man?" he asked. "Is this one of the giants your people used to believe in?"

"My people don't have stories about giants," the other man argued.

"I thought they had legends of orca giant people."

"My God, you're an idiot."

As they continued bickering, it took all they had to help me out of the water and into the boat. I wasn't at all sure how they managed to keep the rowboat from tipping over from my weight, but I was fucking happy they had.

"Damn, son, you're about to turn blue. Throw this over you."

I could just make out enough of their faces to see they were both older than me. The blanket one of them tossed me was scratchy, but I didn't complain. I pulled it around me as the man behind me rowed us back to the shore. At least, I hoped that was where we were headed.

I began fumbling with my pants to see if I could get to my phone, as I needed to alert Sandra as soon as I could, but the phone wasn't anywhere to be found. *Fuck,* I thought, *it must've fallen into the water.*

I was still freezing, but being out of the water and under a blanket helped at least. I pulled it tighter around me, trying to warm myself up.

The two men didn't say much, other than what they needed to for navigating. They had a very low light, but it didn't do much other than illuminate what was in the boat. They seemed to be navigating by the stars. What the hell was going on with these two?

Now that I was in the boat, I could see the lights in the distance much better than I could before. Luckily, I'd been swimming toward land, because it only took the two men a few minutes before we hit the shore.

They helped me off the boat and up a staircase to a nice-sized cabin on a hill. "Where are we?" I asked.

"Guemes Island," both men said at the same time.

"I need a phone. I've got to call—"

"Yes, you can use mine," one of them said. "But, first, you need to hand me your clothes, so I can wash and dry them."

The other guy disappeared and came back in with a pile of blankets. "You can wrap up in these until you warm up."

I quickly began stripping, intent on getting the phone to call Sandra and tell her we'd been set up. I hadn't noticed the men until I got to my boxers, but they were both watching the show with a great deal of interest.

"Um…" I said, "Can I have the phone?"

"Sure," the guy said, handing me his phone, and apparently waiting for my wet clothes. I quickly dialed and put the phone to my ear as I stripped the rest of the way down. If the two Daddies wanted to check out my package, it was the least I could do after they'd rescued me.

Sandra picked up immediately and, in a whisper, asked, "Dad, where are you?"

"I was attacked on the ferry. I'm on Guemes Island. A couple of the locals rescued me."

"We've been tagged here, too. There are people watching the B&B. Ford and I are on one of the trails that lead around the coast."

"Have you called in backup?"

"Ford has, but they're having to come in by boat. It'll take them a while to get here."

"The paintings will be gone long before anyone gets there. Sandra, it was Anderson Churchill that attacked me. I know two men were killed. I don't know what he's done with the rest of the passengers."

"I'll have Ford contact Anacortes officials."

"Good, Sandra," I said, and paused.

"Yeah?" she whispered.

"Be safe, okay?"

"I will. Can I call this number to reach you?"

The two men had left the room to give me privacy, but I yelled out. "Can my daughter use this phone to reach me?"

"Yes, that's fine," one of them answered.

I let her know, and she hung up. I quickly wrapped my body in the blankets they'd brought me. The first blanket had been tossed over the back of a chair, and I could tell it was old. It was mostly an off-white color with two orange borders running along the edges, and I guessed it must've been one of the Native-American dog-hair blankets that I'd read about.

While researching Shaw Island, I'd run across a website about the Native Americans of this area that included an entire section about how dog hair from a now-extinct breed had been used to make blankets. I'd had a strange obsession with dogs, ever since I dealt with the animal that'd come onto our schoolyard when I was a kid, the same dog Sister Clarissa had recalled in her letter to me.

I much preferred the softer modern varieties, but beggars couldn't be choosers, and after being pulled from the water, I needed warmth, and needed it fast. If this blanket was a precious artifact, as I suspected it was, I knew I owed even more to my rescuers. In their shoes, I doubted I'd have used such an important historical piece for practical purposes, even if someone was freezing.

After grabbing a newer, softer blanket, and securing it around me, Roman-gladiator style, I went to find my rescuers.

The two men were sitting in their kitchen, across from one another. "He's lucky he didn't get eaten by a sixgill."

"You've been told repeatedly that sixgills aren't known to attack humans in the Sound."

"You were there when it came after me."

The other man laughed. "Just goes to prove you aren't human."

I cleared my throat to announce my presence.

"Ah, you're done with the phone then?"

"Yeah, thank you."

"So, you able to tell us why you were swimming in the Sound in the middle of the night?"

"I was thrown off the ferry. Thank you two for saving me."

Both men nodded, and surprisingly, didn't push for more information.

The man on my right said, "Have a seat, son. I'm John Griffin, and this idiot over here is my cousin, Phil Walden."

"Nice to meet you," Phil said with a side-eyed look toward his cousin.

John got up and poured me a cup of coffee. "It's decaf, sorry, us old guys can't do caffeine this late at night, but this'll warm you up, though."

I nodded my thanks, and declined anything to go in it. I didn't love the flavor of decaf, and neither milk nor sugar would improve it, if experience was any indication.

I sipped the bitter drink, and enjoyed the feeling of warmth coming back into my bones.

"I don't know much about Guemes Island," I admitted.

"Not much to know," Phil chuckled. "Our ancestors settled here long ago. We inherited the land together and built this cabin. Since we're both sworn bachelors, it just made sense to do it together."

"Bachelor my ass. I'm still looking to catch me some handsome young man," John replied.

"My God, what are you going to do if you catch one?"

"Play hide and seek with his ass," he said.

"Like you can get it up—"

I almost spat out my coffee. "Are you both gay?" I asked, and both men looked at me.

"Oh, sorry, we don't have much company these days who don't already know us. Yes, we're both homosexuals. I'm sorry if we made you uncomfortable."

After having them both check me out, I decided it was best not to come out, quite yet. "I'm completely good with your sexuality, gentlemen, just curious."

"And you?" John, the cousin who'd just admitted he was still looking, asked.

"I'm still looking to catch some ass, too," I commented, causing both men to laugh out loud.

John got up and refilled my coffee, before asking, "So, I'm afraid you're stuck on the island for tonight. The ferry leaves tomorrow morning. Your clothes should be done washing by then. We can drop you off in time to catch it."

"My wallet..." I said, and Phil got up, grabbed my car keys and wallet and put them in front of me. "I'm guessing that key fob won't be working anytime soon. You probably need to take it apart and let it air out. Your wallet's pretty wet, too."

"At least I have it. My phone must've fallen out."

"So, by the look of your improvised life vest, I'm guessing you've had some training on survival in the water."

I nodded. "I have."

"Not really excited to share that information with us? Well, that's okay," Phil said. "I was in the Marines myself. That tattoo tells me you were FORECON?"

I nodded. My tattoo was concealed on the front of my right shoulder. I seldom took my shirt off in public, mostly to keep that part of my life secret, but considering I was stark naked in front of these men just a moment ago, I figured there wasn't much about my body to hide.

Phil rolled up his sleeve to reveal his own tattoo. "Raiders," I said, and immediately began to harass him companionably, like the guys used to do when we worked with the Marine Raiders in the field.

Phil relaxed into the conversation, and got up to refill his own cup.

"So, we heard a bit of your conversation before we came into the kitchen. You were attacked on the ferry?"

I nodded. "I'm guessing—" Phil continued, "—you're not really at liberty to discuss the attack?" I shook my head, not letting my eyes leave his. "You know we should contact the authorities to let them know we've found you, but from the conversation I heard, I'm guessing you're part of the authorities. Is that true?" I nodded again. "Okay, just a couple more questions. Does this have anything to do with the whole crime bust mess that went down in Seattle?"

I thought for a moment. "No... and, yes," I said, more to put the older man off track than to answer.

"And do you want the authorities notified?"

I sighed. "If it would make you feel comfortable, sure. I've already let my team know."

Both men nodded. "Good, 'cause I hate the new sheriff. The man is a total dick, and not in a good way."

"I swear the guy's so anally retentive," John added, "I wonder how he shits?"

Just like that, we were back to the banter. I realized a mixture of things had made the men trust me. My tattoo, my candor, and maybe my ass. Occasionally, even now, I'd catch John's eyes wandering to my crotch.

"So, why were you out on the water in a rowboat? And no light?" I asked, suddenly feeling suspicious myself.

The two men looked at one another and I could tell Phil was giving John permission to tell me. "Through our grandmother, we are both descended from the Samish people who occupied the island until the white settlers came along. We were doing something to umm... honor our ancestors."

"When I was getting into the boat, I thought you said something about John's people," I said, confused about the conversation.

John snickered. "Yeah, my mother married a member of the Cowlitz Tribe, but Phil's mom married a scoundrel. Our grandmother was too far back and not documented, so he's jealous that I'm an enrolled member of a tribe."

"And you're jealous—" Phil immediately came back, "—that I got away with anything I wanted."

I sat back and listened to the two men go at each other. It was surreal to be here. Just a few hours ago, a bunch of really bad men had tried to kill me. Two men had been killed, and I was sitting here listening to two cousins go at it.

John's phone rang then, and when he saw the number, he handed it over to me. "I think this is for you."

"Hello?" I answered.

"Dad, are you still okay?" Sandra asked.

"Yeah, just fine. Why?"

"Things are bad. Churchill escaped in the chaos, but three people were dead on the ferry. Churchill must've slipped off the boat when it was docking. The police found the bodies and your empty car, so they're searching for you."

"Can't Ford get them off the scent?" I asked, alarmed.

"No, and it's probably best to keep it on the down-low. Your house in Boston was trashed. Some of your guys are missing, too. Dad, this seems to be bigger than just the art robbery."

"Are you safe?" I asked, then stood up to go into the other room.

"I am... well, I will be, because the agency will keep me safe, but you aren't. Right now, you're presumed dead, and you need to stay that way, at least until we can get to the bottom of who's really behind all this."

I sighed. "I'll need an alias and credit cards to check myself into the resort here on the island. I'll need clothes, too, Sandra."

"No problem, I'll see if I can get some of our operatives to sneak stuff to you."

"You can stay here," Phil said from behind me.

I turned toward him, and he nodded. "You're welcome to stay. No one knows you're here, and we're secluded even from the other islanders. Your people can drop stuff off to you at the dock, no one will be any the wiser."

"Sandra, hold on," I said, and turned to the older man.

"The people who are after me are dangerous. We don't know how dangerous yet. You shouldn't be putting yourself in the middle of this."

"Is it better to put families in danger at the resort?" he asked, and I was stumped.

"Besides, they won't find you here, unless the phone call is being traced."

I shook my head. "No, not this one. The line I'm being called from is secure."

"Then, you are welcome to stay here. We've got more than enough room, and John and I are beyond tired of each other's company."

I chuckled. "Okay, and John is good with it, too?"

"As long as you show more of that sexy ass of yours, I'm more than happy for you to stay."

I cringed. "Is he always like this?"

Phil smiled, but shook his head. "No, he's usually worse."

I was laughing when I turned back to Sandra. "I'm going to stay here. You can ping this phone and trace where I'm located. They have a dock that should accommodate your guys. They can slip in and drop off supplies without anyone noticing."

Sandra was distracted. "Shit, when?" I heard her ask. "I've got to go. Someone is shooting up Langston's home."

"What? Is he hurt?"

She listened to someone talking. I couldn't make out what they were saying, but I could tell it wasn't good. "They don't know. The Edmonds Police are headed there now to check it out. I'll let you know when I learn more." I could tell she was walking away from whoever she was talking to, probably to hide my identity. "Dad," she whispered, "Be careful, and don't contact anyone you know, okay?"

"Wait, Sandra. Mother Olive..."

"She's safe. She's agreed to stay on the island for now. We'll keep guards here until we figure out what's going on."

"Thanks, San…"

"Keep that phone on you. I have to go, but I'll call you as soon as I find out what's going on with the gallery owner."

I hung up and looked at the concerned faces of the older men in front of me. "Well, what do you two do around here for fun?"

They both laughed, and John said, "Pulling you out of the drink was the most fun we've had in ages."

I moaned. "Do you play cards?"

The two men looked at each other, and a wicked grin crossed their faces. "Do you play poker, young man?" Phil asked.

I nodded. I didn't dare tell them I'd been trained at an early age to cheat, twist, and manipulate every turn to win.

"Then, Texas Holdem it is."

We played until the wee hours of the morning. When John handed me my warm, folded clothes, I put them in the bedroom he'd shown me was mine, and without changing, went back out to play another game. I'd been wearing the blanket toga the entire evening. What could a few more hours hurt?

"You've been taught to play," Phil said. "Military?"

I shook my head. "Nope, let's just say I was trained by my family."

"Okay," they both said, and chuckled. Of course, they probably thought I meant cousins. No way in hell was I going to tell them it was an illegal gambling ring in the basement of a community center run by my dad's men.

The two men were card sharks in their own right. If I hadn't known the tricks they were playing, they'd have mopped the floor with me. As it was, we were neck and neck throughout the game. It was also more fun than I'd had in a long time.

I'd all but forgotten someone wanted to kill me, and had almost pulled it off. We were just about to call it quits when the phone rang. "Dad, are you alone?"

"No, but I can be. Hold on."

I excused myself and went out the back door. "I'm alone now. What's going on?"

"Jeffrey Langston was nicked by a bullet, but not seriously hurt. Ford has him packed up and headed for his brother's place in the woods around Port Angeles. But, Dad, they are going to go after Cliff Sparks, too. I feel like I'm responsible—"

"Sandra, listen, don't go down that road. You were following a hunch, and you were right. The players aren't what you thought, but you still helped us find the art. So, can you stash Cliff somewhere safe?"

"No, he's refusing to go, saying he needs to be close to his grandmother."

I stamped down the unusual panic that engulfed me at the thought of Cliff being in danger. I shook it off. *No*, I chastised myself. *You need to keep your head on straight.* I thought for a moment, before responding, "Sandra, he has to go, and it's best if the perps don't know he's got a grandmother. If they do, they'll use her against him. In fact, Sandra, she's not safe either. I would normally take both of them back to my place in Boston, but that's apparently been compromised."

"How about where you're staying? Can they keep you and Cliff's grandmother, too?"

I looked at the large home, and knew there was more than enough room. Would they want to keep an elderly woman and another guy here, as well as me? That was what I didn't know.

"I'll ask then call you back. Sandra, I need to know what you know. I can't figure out who's behind this, if I don't have all the intel."

"Let's get all the assets safe first, then I'll fill you in," she said.

I went back into the house and sat across from the two men, who had incidentally stolen several of my tokens while I was gone. Ignoring that, I asked, "So, I can't tell you everything that's happening, but I'm not the only person in trouble. Are you open to having more company? We can pay."

"We aren't really kid people."

"No kids, a man and his grandmother. I need to keep them safe for a while."

"How long?" Phil asked.

"No idea, not more than a couple weeks, but if it's longer, they can transport us somewhere else."

"No problem," John said, and Phil shrugged. "There's plenty of room. My room is on the third floor and Phil's is on the second. You can let the woman stay in the room we put you in on this floor, and you and your friend can sleep in the one next to Phil."

"Wait, together?" I asked.

The two men smiled. "I mean, you could bunk with me," John said.

"Um, I think my ass is safer with him."

"Definitely," Phil agreed, and they both laughed.

"Okay, if you're certain, I'll let them know."

"This old home used to house huge family get-togethers. Now our family is scattered like sand in the ocean. It'll be nice to have her full again."

I moved my things up to the second-floor bedroom, and was pleased it was private. There was a nice king-size bed in the room, which meant Cliff and I could share without being uncomfortable.

With my and Cliff's size, the king-size was still going to be snug. The sudden thought of being snug with Cliff un-nerved me. The blood began flowing into my cock at the idea, so I quickly dashed out of the room to call Sandra before I turned in.

"Cliff won't be happy, but yeah, he and his grandmother can stay with us here on the island. The owners have agreed."

"That's good. I'll work on Cliff. The fact that his grand-mother and friend were in jeopardy, I think should help persuade him. Get some rest. I'm not sure how all this is going down, Dad, so you'd better be rested in case it goes bad."

"Agreed," I said, and after reminding my daughter once again to be safe, which was ludicrous considering she prob-ably knew every trick in the book that I did, I disconnected.

John said no one ever called him, so I could keep his phone until he needed it back. I appreciated that, because I wanted to know Sandra could reach me if she needed to.

I returned to my new bedroom and crashed in the big and much-more comfortable bed than I'd have guessed, and immediately fell into a fitful sleep. Dreams of being shot at, dead men falling on top of me, and trying to swim in the frigid water plagued me all night.

Despite that, I woke up feeling rested enough the next day to enjoy most of it with John and Phil. Midafternoon, we met the boat carrying Cliff and his grandmother as it came up to the dock.

John and Phil stood watching as the private yacht pulled up to their property, and Cliff and his grandmother climbed out onto the dock. Mrs. Montgomery was grinning from ear to ear, but her grandson looked like he could strangle me with his bare hands. "Boys!" she yelled back at the men, who I knew for a fact worked for the CIA. "Bring my bags up to the cabin." She then turned to me. "Oh, you handsome devil, what did you have to do to get this one to spring me?" she asked, clearly thinking this was a vacation.

"Oh, you know, bribe him," I said.

She looked me up and down. "I'm sure that wasn't hard to do." And she laughed when I blushed.

She made her way to the stairs, and I helped her as she climbed them one by one. I could feel her determination to get up them on her own, and when I glanced back at the men behind me,

Cliff was still glaring, and the CIA officers were grinning. She must've entertained them all the way from the home to here.

I was ignoring the glare from Cliff. Although his expression clearly conveyed that he was pissed, his glare was also giving off smoldering vibes. Considering we would be sharing that king bed tonight, *and* for several nights to come, it was best not to think of the ways I could use that smolder to both our benefits.

Twenty-Three

Cliff

I GOT A CALL early in the morning from Paul, yelling into the phone that Jeff had been shot. The cops were already on their way, but he didn't know who else to call.

I rushed over to their house in time to see it surrounded by policemen and an ambulance. Jeff's wound was treated while I consoled Paul.

"First my brother, now this. Cliff, what's the world coming to?"

Paul's brother, Daniel, had been stalked and eventually shot by a psychopath who'd come after him a few months before. Now Jeff, his husband, was being treated for a gunshot wound, too. I could understand why he was freaking out. Hell, I was freaking out myself.

"Paul, it's okay, we'll figure it out," I assured him.

Because, a couple of the cops recognized me from my time on the Seattle PD, they let me hang out and get some information about the gunman. He'd fired directly into the bedroom, and must've shot at the shadows as Jeff was getting ready for work.

Amateur work, at least. If it'd been a professional hit, they would've waited for Jeff to come out of the house, and killed him as his car backed out of the driveway.

Of course, one couldn't rule out that this was just an errant bullet. Still, after all that'd happened to Paul's brother, and the whole issue around the art theft, I didn't have it in me to give Paul that kind of news, whether he'd take it well or not. We needed more evidence before I said anything.

Just to be safe, I phoned Bentley's number to see if he knew anything. He didn't answer, so I left a message telling him someone had shot at Jeff and even nicked him, and that I needed to know if this was something related to the art theft.

In the short time I'd known him, Bentley had always answered his phone, or at least responded soon after. So, thirty minutes later, when I hadn't heard back, I tried again. The phone went directly to voicemail, and I was beginning to get concerned.

If someone had gotten to him, there was no way I would know. My mind began making up all sorts of scenarios where the art thieves were trying to clean up the mess they'd left behind.

Paul was headed to the hospital to pick Jeff up, so I headed over to Cummings Security to speak to them directly.

I walked into the office to see panic. The secretary was speaking to a couple men I'd never seen before, so I walked up to the desk and waited for them to finish.

Margarette Jeffers, their HR person, stepped around the corner. "Cliff, what are you doing here?" she asked.

"Looking for Bentley, is he here?"

Concern crossed her face, and I immediately felt a tightening in my gut. "Margarette, what's going on?"

She looked at the men and secretary, who'd just stopped talking. They were listening to our conversation. "Come back to my office, Cliff."

I looked back over my shoulder at the three people behind me. I couldn't read their expressions well, but the energy in the room alerted me to the fact that things weren't good.

"Tell me about Mr. Langston," Margarette said, the moment I walked into her office.

So, she knew about him. That was enough to throw up some red flags, but right now, I needed to know what was going on.

"We're not sure, just that someone shot him through his window this morning and nicked his arm. It should've been a lot worse. I'm concerned if something isn't done soon, it *will* be a lot worse."

"Hold on," she said, and picked up the phone. "Sandra," she said a moment later.

"Yeah, I know you've got a lot going on, but there's stuff happening here, too. Mr. Sparks just came into the office. Someone shot at and even nicked his friend Jeffrey Langston. Yes, I can put the phone on speaker."

"Cliff, this is Sandra. We met before."

"Yeah, I remember. What's going on?" I asked.

"Bentley is indisposed," she said, and I could tell in the way that she paused, she was debating whether to tell me more.

"Mr. Sparks, someone tried to kill him. There were three bodies found on the ferry he disappeared from. If they shot at Mr. Langston, you and he are likely in danger as well."

"Margarette, are Chuck and Ed still there?" she asked.

"Yeah, they were about to leave, though."

"Tell them they are being reassigned. They need to stay on Cliff and Jeffrey Langston until we are sure they are safe."

"I understand. I'll go let them know now."

She got up and walked out, leaving me in her office. Adrenaline still pumped in my veins from the events involving Jeff, but I couldn't deny I was also dreading what was happening with Bentley. "Sandra, is Bentley okay?"

I heard her inhale deeply, and when she let it out there was a momentary hitch that caused me to wonder if there was more to their relationship than being colleagues. "We don't know, Mr. Sparks. Hold on..."

I heard her say something to someone before coming back on the line.

"Mr. Sparks, I've got to go, but we are going to put you and Mr. Langston in a safe place. If you can stay at the office, I'll work with my contacts to figure out where to put you."

"O-Okay," I said, confused and concerned.

She hung up after that and Margarette came in with the two men from out front following her. She introduced me to them, and even though they didn't wave badges at me, I understood they were law enforcement in some way or another.

"I need to call my friend Paul and check on him and Jeff," I told them, just as the secretary came in and pulled the two men out of the office for a phone call.

I spoke to Paul, who'd just arrived at the hospital. "Paul, I'm at Bentley Cummings's office. Someone tried to kill him, and it looks like these things could be connected."

One of the men came back in and asked if I had Mr. Langston on the line. When I told him it was his husband, he asked to speak with him.

I flipped my phone onto speaker, and he proceeded to identify himself as Special Agent Chuck Zimmerman. "We've been asked to secure you and your husband. Where are you now?"

Within an hour, the two men had collected Jeff and Paul, and we were all sitting in the front conference room of the office.

The moment the men left the room to speak with who I assumed was Sandra, Paul and Jeff asked if we could trust these people.

"I don't know any more than you do, but I'm guessing if they were the ones shooting at you this morning, we'd all three be dead already."

"We're going to go to Daniel and Joseph's. It's a lot more secure than any place these guys would stash us. Besides, it's

Daniel's turn to play concerned brother after all he put us through."

Jeff snuggled into Paul, but was strangely quiet. Jeff had gone into a completely different profession than I had. It wasn't unusual for my life to be in jeopardy. I knew the first time I dodged a bullet how impacted I had been, so I understood what he was processing.

When the men came back, Paul told them they were going to go stay with his brother. The men acted like they were going to argue, until they heard where the cabin was. They used the computer in the room to look the location up on the GPS, and seeing it was surrounded by forest on every side but the coast, and the road leading to it was clearly not a main road, they nodded in agreement. "That's probably as safe as we can get," Special Agent Zimmerman said.

After Paul made the arrangements with his brother, and I'd agreed to stay at the office until we got orders from Sandra, the men left with Paul and Jeff to take them to Port Angeles.

Less than an hour later, Sandra called and was put on speakerphone in the conference room. "Mr. Sparks?" she asked.

"Yes, I'm here."

"Good, I'm sorry, I've got some bad news. The people who attacked Bentley are likely the ones who shot at Mr. Langston. We believe they are likely to be after you as well. We'd rather be safe than sorry. Bentley is at a safe house, and we'd like to take you and your grandmother to stay with him there."

Anxious relief washed over me. Not only because Jeff and Paul would be safe, but hearing Sandra assure me that Bentley was safe. *Good... good*, I thought. *Wait...* "My grandma? What? I'm sorry, Sandra, my grandma is in independent living."

"And she's at risk. I'm sorry, Mr. Sparks, if she stays there, she could be in danger. It's only temporary while we figure out what's going on."

"There's more to this than you're telling me," I countered.

She chuckled. "You were a cop, Mr. Sparks. You know there's always more than we can tell you." Her demeanor changed then. "I'm very sorry you were dragged into all of this, but luckily, we are making headway. That's why the cockroaches are coming out."

"Very dangerous cockroaches. So, can these people care for an elderly woman? She has needs that have to be met."

"With your permission and hers, we will set up the procedures for her care. I promise we won't let anything happen to her. As far as she's concerned, this is just a big vacation."

"Where is the safehouse?"

She hesitated. "I'm not able to say, just somewhere in Washington is all I can tell you."

"Can I go back home to pack?"

"No, someone will pack for you. I'm sorry, it's just not safe."

"Fuck," I said out loud. "Okay, but you let Bentley know he owes me big time!"

She chuckled. "I'll let you tell him yourself."

"I'm sure," I said, knowing everyone around Bentley seemed to cower before him. If I had any sense of self-preservation, the giant would probably intimidate me, too. But, as much as it pissed me off to admit it right now, all I saw when I looked at Bentley was a very solid, perfect-sized jungle gym to climb. A jungle gym I had yet to stop fantasizing over.

As Margarette removed the SIM card from my phone, replacing it with one she apparently had lying around, I thought about Bentley. I mean, I knew I already had feelings for him. My heart, as well as my cock, yearned for the man.

No, if I was being honest, my heart seemed to be winning out. Ugh, this was so frustrating. Was he even someone who'd ever be able to return my affections? And why was I thinking about this now? *Geez, Cliff,* I chastised myself internally. *Get a grip.*

I'd already called my grandma from the office to let her know Bentley was whisking us off on some mysterious vacation. I didn't even have to persuade her. She was one hundred percent gung-ho the moment I mentioned it.

"Bentley is sending some people over to pick you up, and to speak with your care staff to know what we've got to do to keep you healthy."

"I don't need babysitting. My God, *I* checked myself into this place."

"I know, Grandma," I said, chuckling. "But, let Bentley spoil you."

I knew that was the way to my grandma's heart. If she saw the care as a way to spoil her, she'd be totally in, especially where

Bentley was concerned. She'd been head over heels in love with the man from the moment she'd laid eyes on him. Not that I could blame her, he *was* very nice to look at. Luckily, I hadn't had the heart to tell her there was no Bentley in my life. Not in the way she thought anyway.

I guessed, though, once things were finally settled, I could tell her what had happened, and why he was truly in my life. I dreaded that day. My grandma wasn't one to nail a person, but when she was frustrated with you, she could dress you down in a way you would never forget.

Bentley's men picked her up, along with what looked like her entire wardrobe, and drove us in a limousine to the Port of Everett, and loaded us onto an impressive boat. The men were incredibly amenable as we navigated the insanely beautiful scenery around us.

It took a good part of the day to get to wherever we were going, but the crew served us and chatted with my grandma about the different sites we were seeing. I was still frustrated with our situation, but my grandma's excitement was definitely influencing me.

When we sailed through Deception Pass and around Fidalgo Island, I knew exactly where we were headed. I wasn't surprised when we pulled up to a small dock on the north side of Guemes Island. I'd been obsessed with this area since I was a teen. A couple of buddies and I would come up here when we were in college, and explore every island that had a ferry running to it.

I'd hiked every available public space on this island, and knew it well.

Bentley met us at the dock and helped my grandma—who had still not stopped chattering—up the multitude of steps to a cabin on the hill. There were two older guys watching us as we came in. Grandma was treating the agents, or officers, or whatever they were, like servants, which I could tell they were amused by. I took some of her luggage to help out.

Bentley basically ignored me, which was for the best, considering just seeing him made me angry, not so much at him or the situation as at myself, because it had taken over a week for me not to think about him, or wonder if he was ever going to call. I was like a freaking high-school kid pining over a new boy who'd just started school. Ugh, it just irked me that I was so attracted to him.

The cabin was beautiful. Modern yet rustic. You could tell it was well kept. The two men who'd watched us come up the stairs greeted my grandma, and one of them was answering her questions.

When I helped drop her things in a first-floor bedroom, I turned to see Bentley give me a meaningful look. He turned then and introduced us to our hosts, Phil and John, the cousins who owned the home, and were gracious enough to allow us to stay.

"This is Mrs. Ella Montgomery and her grandson, Cliff Sparks," he said, and both men shook my hand.

"Well, I can't see why you were so hesitant to share a room with this one, he's even hotter than you," the man I'd just been introduced to as John said, causing me to look at Bentley.

"We're sharing a room?" I asked as harshly as my quickening heartbeat would allow.

"Yes, why don't I show you to our room now," Bentley said, and I forced my expression to remain hard. No way was I going to let this be easy on the man.

"Oh my. Lovers' quarrel. Mrs. Montgomery, why don't you come with us?" John said. "We'll get out of the way before the shrapnel starts flying."

"More like the semen," my grandma said, and all four of us turned toward her. "What? I'm the straightest thing in this room. It's not like you two weren't thinking it."

Laughing, Phil and John took my grandma by the arm, and led her outside onto the deck as the men who'd brought us set down my pitiful luggage that someone I'd never met had packed for me, then left.

"So, what the hell, Bentley?" I asked in a quiet voice, then I quickly shook my head. "First, are you okay?"

He nodded. "Just barely. If it wasn't for those two, I'm not sure I'd have made it ashore."

"What happened?"

Bentley sighed. "Not here. Let's get your luggage and take it up to the room, and I'll explain it all there."

Twenty-Four

Bentley

"**I**'LL SLEEP ON THE floor," I said as soon as we walked into the room.

Cliff turned to me as he put his suitcase into the closet.

"You can sleep wherever you like," he said angrily, before he plopped down into a chair next to the bed. "Now, tell me what the fuck is going on."

I sat on the edge of the bed. "I'm sorry, Cliff, things got out of hand. We found the art where you thought it'd be. I was headed back on the ferry to be a witness with a federal judge to get a warrant and was hijacked on my way in."

"I heard people were killed. It's all over the news."

"I imagine it is. That's about all I know," I said, leaving out the break-in at my home in Boston.

"Pffft, I doubt that. Are you sure my grandma is safe here?"

I shrugged. "I think she's a hell of a lot safer here than in her retirement home."

"I guess that's good enough. What about Jeff and Paul? Are they safe?"

"I honestly haven't spoken to Sandra about that. She said they were going to stay with Mr. Langston's brother-in-law."

"Yeah, it's way out in the middle of nowhere. The only way in looks like an old, abandoned logging road."

"Then, they'll probably be safe enough. Sandra said it didn't look like the assassin was a professional."

"Thank God, no. I'd come to the same conclusion."

"Then, they are probably fine. If whoever wanted them dead had really wanted them dead, they would be."

He nodded, and I could see his face turn green at the thought.

"Who is Sandra to you?" he asked, completely surprising me.

"She works for me..."

"And what else?" he pressed.

"Why?"

"Bentley, you have the most precious person on the planet to me sitting downstairs on a deck with two men I've never met, brought here by three men I'd never met before. Two men I'd never met before picked up and delivered my best friend and his husband to a small cabin in the woods on the Olympic Peninsula. For once in your goddamned life, *answer the fucking question.*"

I looked at him for several moments, trying to rationalize why I shouldn't just tell him. I had several clients who knew Sandra's identity and who she was to me, but someone had just broken into my house in Boston, a fortress guarded with the most modern technology. There were only a handful of people who could've done that without getting caught. I didn't feel comfortable putting her name with mine... not until I felt safer.

"I understand," he said, and stood to go.

"Wait, you *don't* understand, but I'll answer your question. She's the most precious person on the planet to me."

Cliff sat back down and sighed, compassion reflected in his expression. "I get it, Bentley, but that means you must understand how scared I am."

He was right, I did understand. Sandra hadn't asked me if she could or should join the CIA. I knew she'd been brought in to this case because of me, and that bothered me, made me feel responsible. At twenty-four, though, she'd shown time and time again she could hold her own in most situations. Yes, she was still too impulsive, but that usually mellowed with time. Most twenty-something field agents were impulsive. Still, I worried about her all the fucking time.

"This is the safest place for now."

"How do you know these men?" he asked.

I shook my head. "I don't. Not really. They pulled me out of the water after I'd jumped in to avoid being killed by Anderson Churchill, then they rowed me back to their house and put me up. We needed a safe place, and they offered."

"That isn't giving me much confidence," he said.

"Sandra and Agent Ford checked them out before you arrived. They're pretty clean."

I thought for a moment about the intelligence Sandra had given me on the two. I decided I should trust him with it.

"So, Phil, he's been quite a live wire. He was in and out of trouble growing up, but ended up joining the Marines and then went to Vietnam. That had a major impact on him. He retired from the Marines eight years ago at sixty-five. I doubt he'd have retired then if they hadn't made him."

"Wow, people stay in the Marines until sixty-five?" he asked, stunned.

"Well, *he* did."

"What about the cheeky one?"

I laughed at that, because he had no idea. "John is only a year older than Phil, but he had a very different life. He graduated from the University of Washington in seventy-one, and worked in a variety of positions, none of them suspicious. They are both sitting on significant amounts of money that they've saved over the years. There's never been a history, that we can see, of them getting any huge payments, or having been involved in anything concerning."

"So, they appear clean. Why were they out in a rowboat after you'd been almost killed?"

"Good question, I've not gotten a full answer yet, but it's something to do with them honoring their heritage."

"Doesn't that concern you?" he asked.

"No, they covered me in an old blanket I believe was Native American-made when I first got into the boat. That supports their story."

"I'm going to want more information than that, but for now, I'll take your word for it."

I smiled. "Okay, so, this situation," I said, pointing at the bed.

"What?" Cliff smirked, his eyebrow raised. "Don't think you can keep your hands off me?"

"Wow, you're sure of yourself," I said, my nerves overtaking me. Damn, what was I, a teenager again?

"Why pretend? You know you want me."

I did want him. I wanted him with every fiber in my being, but that was a bad idea. It wasn't time to be rolling in the sheets with someone who had this much power over my thoughts and caused me to feel so much need.

Now was the time to focus on keeping everyone safe, not lusting over a man I couldn't get out of my mind. There was nothing I could say, so I just shook my head, and walked out of the room.

Twenty-Five

Cliff

T HE HEART-TO-HEART WITH BENTLEY had made me feel vulnerable, which I knew was a bad idea, considering how I was already feeling about him, so as soon as he mentioned the bed, I switched the conversation to teasing him. Of course, I had no idea that would cause the large, tough guy to run away. *"I would so be doing more of that,"* I chuckled to myself, as I followed him downstairs.

We arrived to find the two older men sitting with my grandma, and from the sound of the conversation, they'd found common people. "I haven't seen her in so long!" my grandma exclaimed.

"She was a real friend to me through some tough times," John said, and shook his head. "You do know she moved to the island over twenty years ago now?"

"No, really? I thought she'd retired back to New York."

I half-listened. Long ago, I'd stopped trying to engage with my grandma's conversations. I did glean enough information from this conversation to know some woman my grandma used to know who made "just the most amazing fabric designs" now lived on the island. John was apparently one of her best friends.

I got up to go outside and was followed by Phil. When I sat down, Phil asked if he could get me a beer. "Looks like you could use one."

I smiled and nodded. He didn't ask what kind I wanted, just went into his kitchen and came back out a few minutes later with a bottle in hand.

"So, this, I'm guessing, wasn't your choice of a vacation."

I looked at the guy for several long moments, before I took a drink. "I'm not here by choice, no. I'm guessing you hadn't planned on having guests either," I said, hoping to get a reaction.

"Oh, this old island has a way of attracting the people who need it. I long ago stopped trying to figure out why or how or even who."

"I'm a bit more concerned." I looked at my grandma through the big windows that lined the front of the cabin.

Phil followed my gaze and when he looked back, he said, "You're very protective of her, I see that. I was the same with my mom."

I nodded and turned toward the water and a view that could melt even the coldest of hearts.

Phil came over and sat next to me, but didn't pry.

"Why were you and John on the water in a rowboat when you found Bentley? I know I should be grateful for what you're doing for us, but it doesn't make sense to me."

Phil took a long drink and set his beer on the deck's railing, before answering, "John and I are some of the last of a very long line of people who still honor the old ways. I know I don't look it, but my ancestors were the first inhabitants of this island. There are traditions those ancestors held very dear. We were simply carrying out one of those traditions in the ways that we still can."

"So, you didn't know he was out there?"

Phil laughed. "No, son, we weren't expecting to run into a seven-foot-tall man swimming in the water when we went out."

I took another sip of the beer. "Has he told you what's going on?" I asked. I saw out of my peripheral vision that he was shaking his head no. "He should've told you, 'cause we're into some dangerous shit!"

"I figured as much, but I've been in dangerous situations before, and I'm not concerned too much. This land is protective of those it cares about. Trust me on this one."

I shook my head. "I doubt even the ancestors can stop gunfire, Mr..."

"Walden, but Phil is fine."

"I was on the Seattle police force. Muscle Bear in there is somehow involved with the government, although I'm not one hundred percent sure how much or even how for that matter. We're here because where we live isn't safe. Someone tried to kill my best friend this morning, and the powers that be are convinced they would like to kill me and possibly my grandma as well. Is that what you've signed up for?" I asked. I was tired of the fucking intrigue. If someone was putting their lives on the line, they should have a fucking choice.

Phil stared out at the water. "Like I told you, the island chooses her own people. Muscle Bear, as you called him—" Phil chuckled at the name, "—was being brought by the current right to our place anyway, and the fact that *we* found him when we did? Son, we were fishing during a ceremony that was designed to bring prosperity. Finding him when we did, how we did, it would be seen by anyone, even those not of Native descent, as an omen."

"And John, does he know?"

Phil nodded. "He knows something is going on, but we both decided to invite you and your grandmother to the property."

"Even though we're strangers?"

I hadn't heard John come out, but he stood on the other side of me, and said, "You aren't strangers now, and you're welcome here."

I turned around to check on my grandma, and when I didn't see her, John added, "She said she needed to lie down before dinner."

I nodded. "So—" John continued, "—please feel welcome here. We love having guests, and it's been way too long since we've had anyone here. Besides, your grandmother is a true delight. I can't wait to reunite her and Patricia."

I couldn't help but smile. "My grandma would really love that, I'm sure."

"So, the plan is, after Ella rests, we'll all go down to the resort for dinner. They have a Friday night fish fry that can't be beat. Your friend already said it should be fine."

"My friend?" I asked, confused.

"Mr. Cummings," he clarified.

I laughed. "I'm not sure you'd call us friends, but good. Yes, fish sounds good."

John clapped me on the back and walked back inside. Phil finished off his beer and said, "My advice, for what it's worth, is just to lean into the experience. Let Guemes work her magic on you. I promise it'll be worth it in the end."

I nodded but didn't respond. I didn't believe in magic. I just hoped we were secluded enough we wouldn't be found. Despite that, I was going to have fun screwing with the big boss man. Who knew being stuck in the middle of nowhere, on an island I've known and loved since I was young, not to mention sleeping in the same bed, could lead to some significant fun? At least until reality found us, then we had to hope none of us got killed.

Twenty-Six

Bentley

THE EVENING WAS ENJOYABLE. Sandra's men had brought me a new phone and some clothes that I could change into. I recognized them as the clothes I kept tucked away in the office for when I needed them. All my clothes were custom made. My body was too big to buy anything off the shelf, so I'd learned long ago to make sure I had spare clothing packed and ready. And this was far from the first time I'd *needed* them.

That evening, we went to the island's resort. It was quaint, and everyone knew Phil and John, so as their guests, even though we'd pushed ourselves onto them, we were welcome as well. Islanders greeted us and told us about things we should see while we were here.

I'd been surprised to learn that Cliff had been here before. He'd said as a young man, he and his buddies had hiked and kayaked around the different islands.

John and he talked about the areas on the island he should go back to. I just listened, even if I didn't go out and hike the trails. In a situation as precarious as ours, it never hurt to know your surroundings.

Mrs. Montgomery was still fully enjoying her vacation. She was the bright light in an otherwise dark time. I loved listening to her engage our two hosts and meet the islanders. When people learned she knew Patricia Gomez, they immediately seemed to embrace her as one of their own.

John had already stated that he was taking her to meet Mrs. Gomez the next day, or I'd have figured out how to do so myself. Watching her and her brooding grandson, I could see where he got so many of his ways. She was gracious and accommodating, but she was also fiery and had little room for nonsense.

I looked over at him and felt my desire for him move inside me. He was in full-out protection mode. Even with me here, he had scanned the room repeatedly, making mental notes in his head – a maneuver I knew way too well. Of course, if my daughter was who I was protecting, I'd be as vigilant as him. No matter who else was supposed to be protecting her.

That night, the five of us sat on the front deck as the waves crashed gently upon the shore. The evenings were still cool here, so the guys brought out a blanket for Ella, who had once again instructed me to stop referring to her as Mrs. Montgomery. We played cards, spades and rummy, rather than poker like we had the night before.

Ella turned in around nine, saying it was an old woman's bedtime, but she kissed her grandson and waved happily at the rest of us before leaving. I could feel as much as see how happy she was to be here.

The guys turned in shortly after that, and it was just Cliff and me sitting out on the deck, sipping the last of our beers. Finally, Cliff asked, "Are you paying them for letting us stay? If not, I want to…"

"It's all handled. They refused money, so I agreed to have a crew come out and do some work on the cabin as payment."

He nodded. "That's great, and if something happens to us, they'll still come out?"

I looked at him. "What do you think's going to happen?" I asked.

He turned toward me, and in a voice so low only we could hear, said, "I'll fight to the bitter end to keep my grandma safe, and now that these two have allowed us to stay here, I'll do the same for them. People want to hurt me and tried to kill you, so it's a real possibility, is it not?"

"How would they find us? I mean, our phones have been changed out, no one but Sandra's people know where we are. Besides, they think I'm dead."

"How did they know you were on Shaw?" he challenged angrily, but still in a quiet voice.

I shrugged. "I'm not sure we've figured that out yet."

"So, until you do, you can't tell me we aren't at risk here."

I couldn't disagree with him. There were still too many unknowns.

"Cliff," I finally said, "I've been in and out of situations where my life was in danger most of my life. I'm not saying you shouldn't be cautious, but you also need to learn to enjoy what you have while you have it. We're as safe as we can be right now. If that changes, we'll find someplace safer. But for now, enjoy this amazing place we're being allowed to stay in."

He nodded, and I noticed some of the stress went out of his body. That made me feel, well, better than it normally would. This guy had definitely gotten under my skin. And for whatever reason, I had no problem with that.

"I'm gonna turn in," Cliff said and stood up to go. When he turned back around, he had a huge grin on his face. "Gonna come join me?" he asked.

I felt the desire to do just that fill my whole body. "No, I think it's best if I sleep on the couch. Luckily, the one in the living room fits me. I've already tried it out."

"Suit yourself," he said. Then, loud enough that I could hear, he said under his breath, "Chicken."

No doubt I was a bit of a chicken. I had a feeling I'd probably have better luck facing Churchill and his bullets than coming out of that situation unscathed.

Twenty-Seven

Cliff

THE BIG GUY BEING too afraid to share a bed with me caused me no small amount of amusement. *Good*, I thought to myself, *Keeping him off-center is exactly what I want to do.*

I mean, I'd be lying if I didn't admit the rejection stung a little, but I knew when a man wanted me, and he had to know I wanted him. Taking one look at him, one had to know he could have his choice of men.

Tall, giant-sized, muscular, grumpy. All those things combined caused me to want to cream myself every time I looked his way, but I knew for a fact I wasn't the only gay man who liked a Daddy Bear.

Regardless of his desires, or lack thereof, I slept like a kitten on the big comfortable bed. Although I'd admit, I didn't think I would. Seriously, my world had just been turned upside down, and I'd really prepared for a night of staring at the ceiling. Hell,

I hadn't even been given the chance to grab a book from home before coming here. Since I'd been unemployed, I'd caught up on my to-be-read list a lot faster than I ever thought possible.

Regardless, a book wasn't necessary. I woke up the next morning refreshed and ready for the day. I came downstairs to a kitchen filled with my grandma. A woman who flat-out refused to go into a kitchen most of the time. When she did, it was to use the quickest, most modern food preparations possible.

Today, though, she stood across from John, chatting away as she cooked bacon. "Well, this is a first," I said, coming into the room. Both of them turned to me, confused. "You cooking bacon. I've never seen you do that before."

"Oh please, honey, I know how to cook bacon."

"Um, knowing how and doing are two very different things."

She smiled and began turning the bacon without responding.

"Good morning, Mr. Griffin," I said as I walked over and kissed my grandma on the cheek.

"Good morning, and you can call me John. The whole mister thing is for my father's generation."

"Then good morning, John. And how are you this morning?"

He winked at me. "I'm well. I was just telling your grandmother that Patricia has gotten back to me, and we're going to head over and say hello and get these two reacquainted. Do you want to come along?"

I looked at my grandma and almost choked from the expression she was making. "Um, I think my grandma would prefer to get reacquainted without her grandson tagging along."

"True enough," she said. "You'd be bored anyway. Why don't you take your handsome man on a nice long hike? He looks a bit rough for wear after last night on the couch."

She leaned over and whispered, "You should let him off the hook for whatever he's done that landed him on the couch."

She turned to John and said loud enough for the entire home to hear, "If I had a man like that in my bed, I'd never let him sleep on the couch."

"Grandma," I said, and heard chuckling behind me. I turned around and saw Bentley standing behind me, looking mussed, tired, and sexy as fuck.

I smiled into the coffee John had just placed in front of me. "Morning, Bentley. Sleep okay?" Grandma asked.

"I slept fine, thank you. Mrs. Montgomery, um... Ella, did I hear you're going out for a visit this morning?" Bentley asked, and I looked up from my cup to see his expression. If she wasn't safe going out, I probably needed to go with her.

When his expression seemed to be neutral, I settled a bit. "So, Bentley, you think today is a safe enough day for traveling alone? I mean, the storms this time of year can be intense."

Anyone who knew anything about the Pacific Northwest would know storms this time of year were unusual, but I also knew he'd catch my drift.

Of course, my grandma cocked an eyebrow and John stifled a smile. "No storms on the forecast for today."

"Good, then do you wanna take my grandma's suggestion and go for a nice long hike?"

Bentley looked at me and I could see the frustration on his face. "Sure, why not," he replied, and shrugged before walking past us to fill his coffee cup.

Grandma and John resumed their chat about fabrics and people they both knew, and I followed Bentley out to the deck. As soon as we both sat in the Adirondack chairs, I looked back to see if we were alone and asked, "You're sure she's safe?"

"As safe as she would be here. Let her go visit her friend. I already looked, and her friend doesn't have social media, so it's not like she's going to start posting to Facebook or Twitter revealing where we are."

I chuckled. "No, that's unlikely."

"So, there's no harm in her going. Besides, Sandra has assured me they've got agents hidden around the island keeping an eye on us. They're all disguised as tourists, but we've got some backup if it's needed."

"What else did she tell you?"

He looked hesitant. "Well, not good stuff, I'm afraid. They recovered most of the art, except the three most expensive pieces. Those were taken off the island during the upheaval. All three of those are international paintings, so that means..." He hesitated again and shrugged. "It means there are a lot of angry people."

I chuckled. "Doesn't matter if you're a beat cop or CIA apparently, there are always people above you who are angry."

Bentley laughed. "That's true enough."

"There are some leads on who else is behind this. I, well, I have a history in Boston, one I've been fighting since I was a kid. It appears it might've caught up with me."

"I see," I said, although I didn't really, but men like Bentley always had a history. I'd assumed when I learned he was a contractor with the government that his history was somehow tied up with the military, but I couldn't say I was surprised his family was involved as well. When you scratched the surface, Bentley had a distinct wounded kid look about him. Unfortunately, that look was something I'd seen way too often while patrolling the streets of Seattle.

"So, does that mean you aren't as concerned about us?" I asked.

He shrugged. "Still unclear, and your Mr. Langston was shot at, so better safe than sorry. I've been told to stay here and to stay inconspicuous. My contacts are investigating just how much danger I'm in, and how much danger I'm putting others in, then the powers that be will put me wherever I need to be."

I nodded. "Okay, well, then let's finish our coffee and go take that hike. You can't get much more inconspicuous than wandering over the trails of a small island in the San Juans."

Twenty-Eight

Bentley

S ANDRA HAD CALLED ME in the wee hours of the morning, waking me up from the horrible, fitful sleep I was enduring.

I knew the men who I'd helped put away all those years ago were getting out, but seriously, most of them were in their late sixties at this point. I mean, they had kids, but those kids were scattered around the globe. I'd been watching them since I'd returned to Boston, and there was no indication anyone was putting the gang back together.

I guess I'd missed something, because according to Sandra, that was who was behind the break-in of my home. Her contacts at the CIA and FBI thought the art robbery and the break-in were somehow connected.

It seemed too far-fetched to believe. Why would a group of gangsters in Boston have any contact with art thieves in the Pacific Northwest? But stranger things had happened.

When I saw Cliff come down the stairs and cheerfully kiss his grandmother, I decided I wasn't going to keep any of this from him. He had a right to know my past might be what was putting him and his grandmother in jeopardy. I would've wanted to know.

As soon as Phil came down the stairs, John and Ella left for their visit.

I eyed him for several long moments, trying to size him up again after Sandra had given me another piece of interesting information. She deliberately didn't tell me who, but she'd said, "Someone in that house with you is former CIA. Their codename was HBFASH." Then, she chuckled. "No, it's not Sparks," she'd stated, before I had time to ask.

The only other plausible person in our group was Phil. As she went through the detailed history of the former special agent, I could see how Phil fitted that description. Strong, brave, fearless, and certainly not someone to be trifled with.

The things he was able to accomplish were, well, they were remarkable, and he'd managed to save a hell of a lot of lives in the process.

Phil was a self-admitted hater of all things morning, and I chuckled as he grumpily moved about his kitchen.

I'd liked him and John the moment I met them. Not just 'cause they pulled me from the water and an inevitable demise, but because there was good there, CIA or not. Another thing I'd learned over the years was to trust my instincts when it came to people. Phil was a good man, and now that I knew more about his history, I'd stake my life on it.

Cliff and I skirted around him, leaving him in peace as we took our hike along the trails of Guemes Island.

"Wow, this is stunning," Cliff said as we stood looking out over the Sound. "You forget how beautiful it is up here."

I just nodded and continued to walk up the mountain trail. I wasn't really in the mood for scenery. I hadn't had enough sleep, I was developing a headache, and I was stuck on top of a freaking mountain on an island, instead of figuring out how to handle my own affairs—something I wasn't used to doing.

Luckily, no one else was on the trail, because when we got to the end, I unceremoniously plopped down onto a bench and leaned my head back, letting the sun beat down on me.

"You okay?" Cliff asked as he came up and sat down beside me.

"I'm fine," I replied.

"Yeah, you look *totally* fine."

"What do you want from me, Cliff?" I asked, frustrated. "I'm stuck here with no way off 'cause the people I usually control are now controlling me, and all while my world is collapsing around me!"

"Hey, don't bite, man, I was just trying to be supportive."

I looked over at him and suddenly... fuck it all. I just wanted to take him and... and what?

Fuck if I cared at this point. I stood up to walk away before I really did something to screw things up. He'd slept in the fucking bedroom last night, and I could go back there and sleep now.

I started walking back down the mountain when Cliff came up behind me. "Hey, why are you upset with me?"

"I'm not upset with you," I argued.

"Feels like you're upset with me."

I wheeled on him. "I'm not fucking upset with you."

Usually, when I came at someone, and I seldom did, they would cower. Not Cliff, he stood his ground and fuck if he didn't turn that smug face of his toward me.

"Go ahead and kiss me. You know that's what this is all about."

I knew he was teasing me, but fuck if he hadn't hit the nail on the head. I didn't need to be asked twice. I stepped up to him and pulled him into a kiss unlike I'd ever given in all my life.

At first, he was shocked, but that changed quickly enough. Cliff's hands slipped around me, pulling me into him, demanding more from me, more than I'd ever let myself give another man.

Fuck, I shouldn't be doing this when I was on edge. That was what my brain was saying somewhere in the background of my consciousness, but my body was now fully in charge.

Had we not heard a car coming down the road next to the trail, I thought I'd have stripped him naked and fucked him right there on the ground, but the disruption forced some space between us.

Cliff pulled back. His face was red from the bristles of my beard and that, just that, almost put me over the edge.

"I haven't..."

Cliff nodded. "I know, me neither."

"Wanna get back to the cabin?"

"Yeah, but you're not sleeping on the couch any longer," Cliff said, and that was when I accepted that things were moving to the next level between us.

We all but ran the mile back down the mountain to the cabin. Luckily, when we got back, there was no sign of anyone. We both raced up the stairs, slinging our clothes off as we went.

As soon as his shirt was off, I was on him. I wanted, no, I fucking *needed* to have my skin on his. To feel his body pressed under my own. I attacked his mouth as I continued ripping off my own shirt, then as we both stripped the rest of the way down, I moved him to the bed.

As he fell backward, I straddled him and ground my hard cock into his. "God, I've wanted this since I met you," I admitted, and found perverse pleasure in his moans as I forcefully rubbed my cock on his.

"Tell me you want it," I demanded.

"I want it."

"Say please," I said, and laughed when he stopped and looked up at me.

"*You* say please!" he retorted, and I was surprised when he flipped me onto my back and straddled me, taking control.

"Fuck," I said as he ground into me this time.

"Say it," Cliff demanded, his expression both playful and demanding at the same time.

"Please," I relented, and couldn't help but smile. Cliff pushed all my buttons without even trying.

"Good. Now say my name," he said, in a way that caused the smile to fall from my lips, and sent shivers up my spine. It was almost like he was claiming me.

"Cliff," I whispered, suddenly understanding the emotional impact of what we were doing would have on me.

He attacked my mouth then, savoring it, savoring me.

Pulling open the drawer next to the bed, Cliff pulled out lube and a condom. With a wicked grin, he showed them to me. "We should kiss the hosts for this!"

I laughed out loud. "You kiss John, but be careful. You know you'd be putting your ass at risk."

Cliff ground his cock onto me again, bringing me back to our sexual escapade. With expert skill, he sheathed my cock before leaning forward and kissing me while he lubed us both up.

"I've wanted you inside me since I laid eyes on you, Bentley Cummings."

All I could do was groan as he moved his hand up and down my aching cock.

Moments later, he lined me up to his hole and slowly lowered himself down. I was surprised he hadn't done anything to prepare himself, but I was so horny for him. I wanted him so much, so deeply, all I could do was stare at his handsome face.

Once he'd worked my cock all the way inside, he began to move, sending me into fits of ecstasy. "Fuck, Cliff. Fuck..." I moaned as his movements got faster and faster.

Finally, I couldn't stand it any longer, and I began bucking into him, thrusting my cock deeper and harder into his ass.

He leaned back, giving me more access, but it wasn't enough. I wanted to have all of him. I wanted to control my movements, so I could maximize the experience for both of us.

I flipped him onto his back, causing him to laugh out loud. "Controlling much?" he teased, just as I lifted his legs and quickly shoved my cock back inside him, causing him to suck in a deep breath before moaning with pleasure.

At first, all I could do was pound into him, thrusting myself deep, enjoying the sensation of his tight ass as it drew me in time and time again.

Then, I saw his face, flushed with desire, and suddenly I couldn't resist kissing him. Kissing his luscious mouth. I slowed my thrusts and leaned over him, putting my hand behind his head as I drew him to me.

His eyes opened just as our lips met, and he purred as my desire and unexpressed feelings for him poured out of me and into that kiss.

"You are so... so much," I said as I pulled back and looked at him.

He smiled and quickly leaned up and kissed me again. "Show me how you feel, Bentley. Show me."

The emotions swirled through me, and I wanted nothing more than to do just that. At first, the fucking, the slamming into him, had been pure lust, just the need to empty my seed and quench desires I'd had for him for so long. Now, though, it was more.

Cliff's body was perfection, and he had an amazing bubble butt that I'd spent way-too long ignoring. "Get on your knees," I demanded, wanting to see that part of him. "Give me your ass, and I'll show you all I feel for you."

Cliff smiled as he obeyed. This time, I let my cock slowly slide into him and wrapped my arms around his toned body, thankful that my height allowed me to embrace him while fucking him.

He leaned back against my chest and turned toward me, letting me kiss him from behind as I slowly worked my cock in and out of his ass.

Realization suddenly overwhelmed me, causing me to falter for a second. I was making love to Cliff. I'd been so... so desperate for him, but now... this was more than just a fuck.

I should've known it would be more with Cliff. Maybe that was why I'd been so reluctant to get romantically involved with him in the first place.

Cliff's moans of pleasure snapped me from my thoughts as I pulled back from our kiss. "More, Bentley, I need more..."

I was helpless to do anything other than comply. I'd give this man anything he wanted at this point.

I leaned back from him, and began to pound into his prostate, knowing I was sending him into fits of ecstasy. His moans grew louder and louder, and he began calling out my name.

His desperate cries spurred me on, reverberating in my heart unlike sex with any other man had ever done before.

"Fuck!" he yelled. "I'm gonna come!"

"Yeah, baby, come for me. Come for me," I repeated.

Cliff tensed around my cock as I continued to thrust into him. Suddenly he leaned up, and cum poured out of him and onto the bedsheets.

The sensation of his ass tightening around my cock caused me to climax moments later.

I poured into the condom as I held Cliff tightly to me. I thrust into him repeatedly until I was spent, then I fell over to the side of the bed, shortly followed by Cliff, who lay on top of me in my embrace.

We both fell asleep in the afterglow of our lovemaking.

I woke up some time later, removed the condom, and tossed it in the wastebasket before rolling Cliff over and spooning him from behind. He nuzzled into me, barely missing the wet spot we'd created. We'd have to figure that out later, but for now, all I cared about was having this amazing man in my arms.

Twenty-Nine

Cliff

I ROLLED OVER AND looked at the sleeping form next to me. This was the first time since meeting Bentley that he'd looked at peace. Unfortunately, the moment I moved, he jerked awake. "Shh, I'm just getting up to pee," I said, and he settled again.

When I came back, he was watching me. "You okay?" he asked.

I laughed. "Um, I'm about as okay as you can get. Why? You okay?"

He shrugged. "Been a long time since I've done that."

I crawled back on top of him, kissing his grizzled face. "I think we should do it again. What do you say?"

"Cliff..." my grandma called from the first floor, "...we're home."

Bentley laughed out loud. "Maybe later," he said.

I smiled and kissed him. "I'll take you up on that. Why don't you rest now, and I'll go entertain the troops? I want you rested for later."

He winked at me as I got up and went to the bathroom to clean up. When I came downstairs, my grandma was grinning from ear to ear. "I see the two of you made up."

I was confused about what she meant, until I looked over and saw one of Bentley's shoes flung into the dining room, the other on the stairs, and his shirt hanging over the railing. I thought we'd stripped in the bedroom.

I just smiled and asked if I could fix anyone something to drink.

"No," Grandma said. "But I could use a little rest before dinner."

"What are we doing for dinner?" I asked John, who had just come around the corner. He, too, was smiling knowingly at having seen the strewn shoes and shirt.

"Phil's taken the ferry across to Anacortes. He said something about bringing back dinner. We'll just wait and see."

I smiled and thanked him when he handed me a beer.

After Grandma went to rest, John and I sat on the deck and enjoyed the remarkable view. "I think I'd love it here," I admitted.

He sighed. "It's a special place. I was never able to settle here permanently, since I've always had a nervous streak in me. I enjoy it more now, though, than I used to."

"You live in the city?" I asked.

"Yeah, downtown Seattle. I live in the home I grew up in."

"Phil lives here year-round?"

John nodded. "Ten or so months of the year. He and his friend Peter sail down to San Diego every September and October."

"Really? Isn't that dangerous?"

John laughed. "Yeah, but Phil likes danger. He and Peter used to sail all the way to Hawaii and back, but that was a while ago."

"According to my mom, when my grandfather was still alive, he and my grandma would take Mom out sailing. It was his thing, though, so they stopped after he died."

"Hmm, I wonder if Peter is around? He usually rents his boat out to the Park Service this time of year for scientific study. It's possible Phil can talk him into giving you all a ride."

"Really?" I asked, thinking of my frail grandma. "I'm not sure. Grandma might be a bit too..."

"Too what for what?" she asked accusingly as she walked out the door.

"Too stubborn and nosey," I said. I got up and kissed her cheek as I walked past her to put my bottle in the recycling bin. "I thought you were napping."

"I can't sleep. I'm having too much fun. Besides, you know I always know when someone is talking about me."

I laughed, and after dropping the bottle in the bin, filled a couple glasses of water for us, and came back out to sit with them on the porch.

"Your grandson was telling me how you and his grandfather used to sail around the islands."

"Oh dear, that was a long time ago."

"Mom said you used to enjoy it," I added.

She smiled up at me from the chair I'd just vacated. "I did. I mean, I would lie on the bow sunning myself while Elvin did all the work," she said, snickering. "Then I had your mom. Oh, those are good memories, though."

We spent the rest of the afternoon with her telling us stories of the places they sailed. I was surprised to learn they'd even sailed up to Alaska before my mom was born.

That night, when Phil made it back home, we all ate the pizza he'd brought back and reheated for dinner. When John told him about our conversation, he texted his friend Peter and arranged for us to go sailing the next day.

"Wow, how did you manage that?" I asked, surprised.

"Peter lives on his boat, and he owes me from our last poker night, so I told him I'd forgive his debt if he'd take the lovely Mrs. Montgomery on a sail around the islands."

John chuckled, and I knew there was something up about these poker games. "Maybe we should have a poker night," I said cheerfully.

"Not with these card sharks," Bentley said, joining us for dinner.

I'd somehow thought that after having sex with Bentley, I'd lose some of the sexual buzz that had been building in me since I'd first laid eyes on him. Damn, I couldn't have been more wrong. If anything, I wanted him more now... if that was possible.

"Hey..." Phil said, distracting me from my thoughts. "...let's play for pennies, then if you take us, none of us will lose much."

"Deal," John said, and before I knew what was happening, he'd pulled everything off the dining table, flipped the top, and just like that, we were all sitting at a poker table.

"Damn, Grandma, I think we're screwed," I said.

"Speak for yourself there, Grandson. I've got a few tricks up my sleeve."

I ended up getting taken out within the first few games. The total bet was twenty bucks, and my twenty left me quickly enough. To my surprise, Grandma played the three obviously great players and won as often as they did.

By the time everyone was ready for bed, she'd walked away with a little more than she sat down with. I honestly didn't know she even knew how to play poker. I knew she and her girlfriends used to play cards every week, but I always thought it was old-lady card games, not poker. *Goes to show what I know.*

Thirty

Bentley

After Cliff left our room, I'd slept like the dead. I was more tired than I thought, and sex always did relax me. To be honest, I think knowing Cliff was here watching out helped, too. No, I didn't usually trust people, and would never trust them to do a job for me, but I knew he was vigilant when his grandmother was involved. If something happened, Cliff would be ready.

I shrugged to myself, though. I hated to admit it, but I was guessing the truth was that finally having sex with Cliff had more to do with me relaxing around him than just trusting him. I'd trusted my Marine buddies, but I'd remained vigilant in times of crisis, only sleeping lightly, so as to be able to move at a moment's notice. I didn't really like admitting my feelings for Cliff were dictating my actions at the moment.

As we made love, it was like an emotional dam had opened up inside me. He surprised me with how he embraced my love with no difficulty as all my emotions poured out. Cliff rocked me in so many ways. I'd never felt like this before. I'd never wanted to feel like this before... I'd never been so completely entrenched with someone that my entire being relaxed knowing he was near. What was it Sister Clarissa had written in her letter? *You have a soulmate out there, someone who will stand by you even when the world seems to be on your back.* Not only was Cliff standing by me, but he had my back, too.

Somehow, I'd fallen asleep with these thoughts, and when my phone rang with a call from Sandra, I was surprised that I'd slept at all. "Dad, we have news."

"Yeah?" I asked.

"Anderson Churchill and his uncle Colin were both found dead at Colin's island estate about an hour ago."

"Okay," I said, concern flowing through me. "Any leads on who killed them?"

"None yet, but we found the remaining stolen paintings at the estate. So, whoever killed them didn't do it for those."

A familiar frustration fluttered to life inside me as I realized what this really meant. As much as I didn't want to accept it, I was likely once again dealing with my father's gang of thugs. I braced myself for her answer, before asking, "What about Boston?"

She hesitated. "Dad, it's not good. People are dropping like flies out there. People that once were part of the gang... Your father..."

Sandra had never referred to my father as her grandfather. She'd had visitation with him while I was away in the military, but the moment I got custody of her, I ended all visits. She had always called him Leo or even Mr. Cummings, always maintaining that emotional distance.

"Is he dead?" I asked.

"No, but he's missing. Your mom, she's worried."

"Did you talk to her?" I asked, the bile in my stomach beginning to churn.

"Yeah, I'm the only person she'd speak to. His enforcers, Joey and Christopher, they got out last month."

"So, what? You think they killed him?"

"No, Dad, I think they're looking for you."

"So, you think my father has rebuilt the gang, and is now coming after me?"

"That's what it's looking like. I'm sorry, Dad."

The fact that Sandra was only using Dad to refer to me now should've warmed my heart. Instead, I kept thinking of my own dad, and how bad my relationship with him had been, if non-existent now. It caused me to feel sick, like I was somehow tainted by the darkness that came from him.

I loved Sandra with all that I was. I'd stand in front of bullets to block them from hitting her, but our parental legacy was like an endless pit of tar. My own father was, and always had been, the most dangerous thing I'd ever faced.

"Listen, Sandra, I need to get back into the system. I know them better than most, so if someone's going to take them down..."

"It'll be someone besides you," Sandra interrupted. "Again, Dad, I'm sorry, but this is from the highest officials. You're too valuable to the government to lose. Besides, you're too emotionally invested. Your orders are to remain where you are."

I laughed. "My orders? Honey, I don't work for anyone. I'm my own boss."

"Dad, they'll pull your contracts in a minute if they think you're compromised."

Fuck, she was right. "I'll stay put for now, but Sandra, you tell KOPATICAL-" My codenamed CIA contact. "-I will not sit tight long. They need to shut this down, or I will."

"I don't really think you want me to tell them that."

"If you don't, I will. Sandra, I've been in this business a long time, don't assume you know more than I do. I love you, but remember, at the end of the day, I don't work for your agency!"

She was silent, and I knew I'd pushed things with her. She was a loyal foot soldier in the CIA world, a good one *and* a dedicated one. I never wanted to force her to choose loyalties, but right now, my hands were tied. I'd tried texting my contact multiple times, and had been ignored each time.

If it wasn't for Sandra, I'd have already gone after the sons of bitches myself. I knew her job depended on my being compliant. But there were limits to that compliance, and I needed her to understand that.

Once she'd hung up, I forced myself to calm down and went downstairs to join everyone for dinner. Phil had brought back pizza, which was surprisingly good for having traveled across on the ferry. The positive thing in all of this was the people here were easy and fun to be around, especially one of them.

We played poker through the evening, and to all our surprise, Ella was a card shark herself. Poor Cliff was whipped almost immediately, but he sat back and enjoyed the show. In fact, even though none of us gave anything to her, we all enjoyed watching the woman kick our butts.

That night, I was ready to have Cliff back in my arms, but I didn't want the intense fucking we'd done earlier. Tonight, I wanted to show him more. Thank him for making all this easier for me.

I took my time with Cliff that night.

As he came into the room and lay on the bed, I moved over him and began taking off his shirt, kissing his neck, then chest.

"You make me feel so much," I said, before I began undoing his pants. "I've never..."

Cliff put his hand on my cheek before tilting my face up to kiss me.

"I know..." he whispered, and I could see my emotions mirrored in his expression.

I moved back down his body and removed his pants, determined to show him tonight just how I felt. All the emotions that had been stirring in me since I'd met him, emotions that I'd always had inside me, but were left unexplored and locked away. I'd always longed for love, but had been afraid of it, afraid I would destroy anyone I dared to care about so deeply.

I wanted Cliff to understand that through him, I was beginning to unlock my heart.

When we first made love, he showed me he could handle anything I gave. Somehow, that gave me permission for the first time in my life to take chances that might lead to love. Maybe it already had...

I took Cliff's cock in my mouth and as he bucked back, I used my hand to massage his chest. He moaned as I savored him, loving how I could make him feel this way.

I edged him twice before I moved back up his body, licking my way up his sexy stomach and nipping his chin before lying on top of him, and grinding my cock into his. "I want to fuck you from behind... can I?" I asked.

Cliff moaned with pleasure, and although he didn't say it with words, I knew that was an affirmation.

I rolled off him and he got on all fours. Then I lubed myself and him, before putting my condom on.

Cliff moved under me, receptive to my thrusts and moaning deliciously when my cock hit his prostate. When I pulled him up toward me, he came willingly and met my mouth with his as I continued to take him from behind.

"God," I said as I held him in my arms. "You are so amazing, Cliff... I've never..."

Emotions rushed into me as I continued to make love to him, and recognizing it, he lifted his left arm, embracing my head and taking my mouth again.

"Fuck me now, show me your feelings..." Cliff said, when he leaned forward again.

I could do that. I could show him... even if I couldn't tell him. I pounded my cock into him, adjusting myself until I hit his prostate, then I thrust into him harder, letting all my emotions pour through me and into him.

I could hear his climax coming on as his moans increased with intensity. We came at the same time, and I couldn't help but bite down on his muscular neck as I thrust once, then twice again, while I emptied into the condom.

I fell onto the bed then, and as Cliff cuddled into my side, we both slipped into an afterglow. I thought of how I'd never made love before, not like I did just now, and not with anyone I cared so much about. I just hoped Cliff understood how much that, and he, meant to me.

Thirty-One

Cliff

W HEN WE WALKED DOWNSTAIRS the following morning, a man I hadn't met before sat at the kitchen table across from Phil.

"Wow..." I said, assuming this was Phil's friend Peter, "...so, you do have mornings in you." Of course, I'd have been alarmed if there wasn't a giant sailboat mast sticking up from the dock below.

Peter laughed. "No, my friend Phil is not, nor has he ever been, a morning person. Hi, I'm Peter," he said.

As I introduced myself, Phil gave us both the stink eye over his coffee.

"You should've seen him in Nam. The poor man could hardly move before ten."

"Okay, enough talk, let's get Junior here to help get your boat put together, so we can send you all on your way."

As Phil walked out the door, I looked at the man, and laughed. "He really isn't a morning person, is he?"

"Damn, man." Peter clapped me on the back. "He's barely a night person."

Bentley came down the stairs and stopped short upon seeing Peter. I eased the tension, by stating, "This is Peter. He's the guy that's taking us out on his sailboat today."

Bentley visibly calmed, although I could tell he was still on alert. "Pleased to meet you," he said, and extended a hand. "I'm Bentley Cummings."

Peter wasn't a little man. He was toned from working his sailboat, but even his hand was dwarfed by Bentley's bear paw. He didn't seem put off, though. Instead, he dragged us out to the boat, and started giving us instructions about what needed to be done to prepare for the day's sailing.

Grandma was happier than I'd ever seen her. She had to have help up onto the bow, which was where she demanded to be, and where she leaned back against the mast, and just enjoyed the wind blowing through her hair.

I hadn't seen her this content in ages. You could almost feel the memories as they flowed through her. Yeah, we were in a dangerous situation, but at least she had this.

It became obvious after a few minutes that, for the most part, we were better off staying out of Peter's way, so when Bentley sat down, I sat next to him and cuddled in.

"You okay?" Bentley asked as he wrapped his arms around me.

"Oh yeah, you?" I asked.

He smiled at me and kissed me warmly in answer.

Occasionally as we sailed across the sea, Bentley would snuggle his face into my neck, or he'd cuddle into my side. It was so uncharacteristic of his personality that it seemed to make it that much more... sweet.

The sea has its own aroma, and the breeze today was consistent, meaning that Peter worked the sails the entire time we were out.

It was as beautiful to watch him maneuver the sails as it was to look out over the intensely beautiful scenery.

John and Phil had packed a lunch for us, so around noon, Grandma announced she was hungry and went down into the cabin to prepare it for everyone. I followed her down, because I knew for a fact that she sucked at preparing food, and would need assistance.

As soon as I was downstairs, I saw her wipe a tear. "Grandma, you okay?" I asked.

"Oh, honey, ignore me. I'm just being nostalgic. I should've made peace with your grandpa years ago. Can you imagine I've deprived myself of sailing all this time, because, well, it doesn't matter why. It's just silly."

I went over and put my arm around her. "I'm sure it's not silly, but I'm glad you came out today. I can tell how much you're enjoying it."

She nodded. "I really am enjoying it. Now, let's get some food into Peter. I swear he's working like two men up there."

Peter pointed out various sea life as we sailed, and at one point, he pointed out a cabin up on a hill as we sailed out past Port Angeles, and said his friend lived up there.

I recognized it immediately. "That's Joseph and Daniel's place."

Peter looked at me funny. "Yeah, do you know them?"

I laughed. "Daniel's brother-in-law, Jeff, is my best friend. They're up there right now, actually."

"Well, let's go pay them a visit," Peter said, and steered the boat in their direction.

It amused me how shocked Jeff and Paul were as the sailboat docked and we all piled out. They were all four sitting out in Daniel's new sitting area he'd built next to the water. I hadn't realized how much stress and worry I'd been carrying around, until I laid eyes on my best friend and his husband. I couldn't help but sigh with the relief at seeing them happily sitting out by the water.

After Jeff and Paul introduced Bentley and my grandma to everyone, Joseph asked, "What brings you all here?"

"They said they knew you, and I figured why not give everyone a pee break that didn't involve a small bathroom or hanging off the side of the boat," Peter said.

Joseph laughed. "You came to find out if I'm going to take the job."

Peter smiled. "Yeah, that, too."

"What job?" Paul asked.

Daniel chuckled. "We weren't going to tell you until it was official, but we did just get word that the grant has been accepted, so…"

Joseph smiled. "I've been offered a position as assistant investigator for a fifteen-year scientific-research grant here in Olympic National Park."

"And if the primary investigator that was in charge of the grant retires, which he's already said he's going to, and Joseph gets his Ph.D. before that happens, he'll be first in line for the job."

"No way," Paul said, and grabbed his brother and brother-in-law into a hug.

Peter was smiling as he watched. "So, I guess that means I'm going to be working for you now, huh?" he asked Joseph.

"That's what the grant says," he chuckled.

"What about the Ph.D. part?" Jeff asked. "Won't you have to come to Seattle to get that?"

Joseph shook his head. "No, I'm already enrolled online for the degree I'll need for the position."

"That sounds perfect," Paul said. "I mean, really perfect."

I turned to Daniel then, and asked if he was still working on the new Seattle-based home-renovation TV show. His boss had gotten a contract with them last year, which, of course, was a big deal.

"Yeah, I'm surprised you knew about that."

Paul blushed. "Well, I, um, told him. Cliff sort of knows Bennett and Les."

I blushed as well. I had been the officer in charge of the investigation that involved Bennett when his ex-partner ended up stabbing him about a year ago. In the end, I was also involved in the investigation that brought down a crime syndicate in Seattle that included Bennett's dad.

"Yeah, I don't know them that well yet—" Daniel said, "—but Joseph's dad is now the official furniture maker for the show. So, I'm guessing I'll work with them a lot more now."

"In fact," Joseph added. "Dad was just invited to a big party to reveal the home they're about to finish next to Lake Washington. They need a significant crowd for the show, to fill the lot the home sits on, so if you know them, you should come with us."

I blushed again. "I'm not sure they'd want me there, but thanks."

"I'll ask," Daniel said. "I'll be talking to them tomorrow to finish up a couple of last-minute item designs that Les's mom wanted."

I shrugged. "Make sure before they invite me, they speak to Bennett and Les."

"They won't mind," Bentley finally said. "You were doing your job, and they know that."

I looked at him funny. I had no idea why he would have an opinion, but I didn't press. Instead, I turned my attention back to the group.

We left after just half an hour, with Peter saying we needed to leave if we wanted to get back before sunset.

We sailed mostly along the coast, and Peter had just announced that we needed to keep an eye out for orca when a pod showed up right next to us. A huge whale swam alongside the sailboat, and fuck if I wasn't intimidated. "It's almost the same size as your boat," I said, causing Peter to chuckle.

"That guy right there is a buddy of mine. I've been sailing these parts since he was a little one. Now he's the leader of his pack. This pod has about six members, but it's growing."

Just then, a smaller whale breached the water's surface about five hundred feet away from us. "That's the youngest in the group," Peter said, laughing. "Joseph is convinced it's a male, because of how flamboyant it is."

"Nah, that's a young female stretching her wings," Grandma said as we all watched with wonder as the young whale breached again and again.

"They must have just eaten," Grandma said. "I read once that the little ones were more playful after they'd eaten."

Peter nodded. "This group of whales eats only fish, and now the dam near Port Angeles has been removed, the salmon are more plentiful in this area. You can see this pod over fifty percent of the time you sail through here."

Peter talked a bit about the plight of the fish-eating orca in this part of the Strait of Juan de Fuca. Luckily, the changes taking place were beginning to have a positive influence, such as with this small family.

Grandma went below and rested, and Peter, Bentley and I chatted all the way back to Guemes Island. John and Phil had laid out quite a spread for our arrival, and after eating, Grandma hugged Peter, which was something she never did with strangers, thanked him, and went to bed.

Bentley and I went shortly after, both of us confessing how tired we were, but Peter seemed to have all the energy in the world, like he hadn't done anything other than leisurely hang out with friends all day. I heard the tell-tale signs of a poker game starting, and I couldn't help but chuckle and hope poor Peter knew what he was getting into.

Thirty-Two

Bentley

I DIDN'T THINK I could remember a day that I'd had that much fun. Having the matters of my security company taken out of my hands was driving me insane, and even with Cliff cuddled into me, it took a good portion of the morning before I was able to relax enough to just enjoy the experience. Coming up to Jeff and Paul's hiding spot seemed strange, but serendipitous.

I did some inconspicuous surveillance of the place with the computer Sandra's crew had brought me, and, from what I could tell, I had to agree with Sandra's assessment that it was about as safe as it could be.

I didn't mean to, but I let the cat out of the bag a bit about knowing Les and Bennett. I never let my guard down, and certainly never enough to expose my familial relationships. My slip just went to show how relaxed I'd gotten.

This, of course, just reminded me that I needed to ask Sandra to make sure someone was monitoring that side of the family. It was no secret nowadays that they had been the ones to hide me back when I was young.

That got my mind stressing about things again, and I was just about to go down into the cabin and start making calls when we came upon the family pod of orca whales.

My God, they were fantastic. The male was definitely interacting with the boat, and when Peter said he'd known him since he was little, I could see that had to be true. Otherwise, I didn't think those wild creatures would've come that close to people.

I actually forgot about my family and didn't think about them again until the next day when I was woken by Sandra's morning phone update.

I slipped out of bed, trying not to wake Cliff, and rushed down the stairs and onto the deck where I could speak with her privately.

"So, what news do you have?" I asked.

"Your dad is in the area," she said.

"Damn, in Seattle?" I asked.

"No, he was seen in Anacortes."

"Fuck, you've got to have a mole, Sandra," I said, frustrated that he would have known to come up here.

"No, not necessarily. He could just be chasing the lead from the paintings."

"Fuck, so you think he might come to the island?"

"Dad, there's no way to tell where he'll go. My guess is he'll show up on Shaw Island."

"So, in the event you do have a mole, who all knows where I'm at?"

"No one, besides our team and the men who dropped off Cliff and Mrs. Montgomery."

"What about Ford?"

"No, I haven't told him."

"Can you trust your team?"

"Yes, Dad, most of them are your guys. The men who dropped Sparks and Mrs. Montgomery off aren't from here. I only had access to them, because they were in Seattle and had a boat. They're somewhere north of here by now, so no, I doubt we have a mole. At least not on the CIA side."

"I hope you're right, Sandra, 'cause I'm hunkered down with civilians here."

"I know, Dad, but we all still think it's the safest place for you and the civilians."

I'd heard that before, but of course, never from my own daughter. "I reminded her to keep Les and my cousin safe in Seattle and then sighed, before saying, "Okay, I trust you, but please, let me know if it looks like my dad or his men are coming this way. I want to have enough time to get everyone off the island if there's a problem."

"Of course, Dad," she said, and hung up just as I heard someone start asking her questions.

A few moments later, Cliff came down, looking sexy and ruffled. Just seeing him eased the stress inside me. How was that even possible? I once again recalled Sister Clarissa's written words about meeting someone who could help me navigate life's rough waters.

Again, I wondered if Cliff was that person? I mean, as I watched him pour his coffee and the happy face he made when the caffeine hit his system, he certainly made my heart beat faster, but just being with him, whether it was on a sailboat or in bed, and being close to him eased the stress that would normally be eating me alive at this point.

He came over and squeezed into the space next to me on the deck. As I nuzzled his hair, I thought, *Yeah, he could be the one Sister Clarissa was talking about.*

"You're quiet. What are you thinking about?" Cliff asked, interrupting my thoughts.

"You," I admitted.

He smiled and kissed me. "I've been thinking about you a lot as well. Anything in particular?"

"Oh, just how cute you are when you have your first sip of coffee."

"Mmm, I do love my coffee." He snuggled closer, causing me to chuckle, because seriously, he couldn't get much closer than he already was. "I love this, too."

"The island?" I teased.

"Yeah, the island."

We sat like that until the rest of the household began to wake up. "You know, it is beautiful. If I didn't have the home in Edmonds, I could see myself living out here. Think I could get a job as a deputy in the Sheriff's Office?"

"You wouldn't be bored?" I asked.

"Nah, too much to do. I might take up deep-sea fishing, or sailing, and there's plenty of islands to hike."

"I'd give you a reference."

"Psht, for the five minutes I worked for you?" he asked, making me laugh.

"You were a very good employee for those five minutes."

"I like this..." he said, waving his finger between us, "...more than I did being your employee."

I kissed his head, but didn't respond, because as disconcerting as it was, I liked this, too.

We hung around the cabin the rest of the day. Phil had to run errands, and John said he'd ordered a salmon he needed to pick up from the ferry. After a long day on the sailboat, Ella was still tired and wanted to spend the day watching TV or reading.

That was a perfect day as well. Just hanging out. Phil let me borrow one of his John Grisham books that Cliff said was good. I chuckled at the worn pages. Clearly, this was one of his favorites.

For a while, I'd been all into Tom Clancy's novels, but I thought that was more because it was fun to find the parts that were far-fetched and far from reality. Clancy's books were thrilling. The reality was, well... most of the time, working in intelligence was boring as hell.

The salmon John had ordered was remarkable. It'd been smoked, and John had created some sort of sauce using raspberry jelly and mustard. I thought it was going to be nasty, but damn, it really wasn't.

In every way possible, this had been a real vacation. I was relaxed and I really liked our hosts, Ella was more fun than I'd ever imagined possible, and learning Cliff's body, not to mention personality, was like taking a long sip of cold water after working all day in the heat.

Thirty-Three

Cliff

EVERY DAY SEEMED MORE and more wonderful than the next. The island seemed to open its arms and pull us in. One day, John and Grandma had a party at her friend Patricia's house, and Phil showed Bentley and me around the island. Another day, he introduced us to several of the inhabitants that, as he said, "...don't get out very much."

Most of them were well over the age of eighty, so I understood what he'd meant. The day he'd been running errands had been him delivering food and supplies from his ferry run the day before.

For the most part, island life was about doing whatever the hell we wanted to. There was a woman on the island who owned a rather big farm that Phil took us to meet. She ended up working us half to death weeding and fixing chicken pens, all of which we later found out was important, since her small farm provided food for a good portion of the island's residents.

But, work or leisure, I hadn't been this happy in a very long time.

Part of that was because of Bentley, of course. The man really was my type in every possible way. It sucked that I was a big man who desired men bigger than myself, because there weren't very many of them around. I chuckled as I thought about that now.

With few options, I'd had to go out with guys that weren't quite my type, so it was no surprise when those relationships never went very far. If any did approach the point Bentley and I were at now, I'd be getting antsy and ready for them to end.

But, there was more to Bentley and me than just attraction. I guessed that was the scary part of this. I wouldn't have thought he would also make me feel... well, I sort of thought he and I were also getting closer... emotionally? Yeah, ugh... I hated thinking about that.

I knew this would end eventually. We were only here because we were being hidden to stay safe. Once that was done, this, whatever it was between us, would be over. I needed to keep it just about sex, just about satisfying a need, or else, when he was gone, I would be a freaking emotional basket case.

I sighed inwardly as I caught sight of my grandmother laughing with John about something... I mean, this experience had also been great for other reasons. I had gotten to know sides of my grandma I'd never seen, and she and John were quickly becoming best friends.

John and Phil were fun to be around, and I could tell they were enjoying the distraction. When we'd first arrived, the two of them were at each other's throats all the time. Now, they hardly bickered, and if they did, it was mostly just in jest.

I guessed the reality of having the crew of people around us meant we were forced to get to know each other. If it wasn't for that, I knew for a fact, I would only be getting to know parts of Bentley better, but maybe not his personality.

Friday nights were a big deal on the island, and the fish fry we'd been to at the resort seemed to bring in all the locals. Naturally, John and Phil pushed us to go, but for some reason, Grandma wasn't feeling well, so she said she'd be happy just sitting home.

I was worried about her. Just a week ago, she was in an independent living facility, one she had moved herself into. Now, she was running all over the place, having parties with old friends. I wondered if maybe it was all too much.

When I pushed her to let me stay home with her, she flat-out refused. "You missed the part about not having my grandson underfoot," she said, and then patted my hand.

"Go, I'm fine. Stop mothering me so much and have fun with your man."

"You sure you're fine?"

She just nodded and walked back to her bedroom.

I couldn't help but laugh. My grandma was never one to take someone hovering over her. I just hoped she didn't have some sort of health issue she wasn't telling me about. At best, if she had an emergency, it'd take an hour to get transported off the island.

We went to the resort, and like last week, the food was delicious and the camaraderie even better. Even in just one short week, I was recognizing faces I'd met during our time here. People came over and greeted us. Mrs. Thompson, the farmer, told John she had his eggs in the car, and when he offered to pay, she shook her head. "No, your guests here covered the cost of eggs in free labor."

I chuckled. "See, we were worth something for all the effort."

John smiled. "We've enjoyed you all more than we can say, especially Ella. I hope she's feeling okay."

"Me too," I said, concern wafting through me.

Mrs. Ellefson and her son, whose name I couldn't remember, came over and asked if we'd all like to come over for a bonfire later that night. John and Phil immediately agreed, but when they saw my face, they said, "Oh, we should get back to Ella."

"No." I laughed. "If she thought you skipped out on a party just to keep her company, she'd skin you alive."

John chuckled, and nodded. "I think you're possibly right."

I noticed then that Bentley had gotten a text and had gone all rigid again. I assumed it must be bad news, but right now, I needed to go check on Grandma.

"I think I'll head back. Do you mind dropping me off?" I asked.

I would have walked, but John and Phil lived on the opposite side of the island from the resort.

"No problem," Phil said as he got up, and led the way out of the restaurant.

Bentley whispered in my ear once we were in the back seat of Phil's Jeep. "I'll stay with you."

The implication of his words sent chills up my back. I'd been thinking about all the things we hadn't yet done and was determined to try them out. I all but pulled him out of the Jeep.

"See you guys later," I said, and shut the door to their laughter.

Thirty-Four

Bentley

WE WERE JUST FINISHING our meal when I got a text from Sandra telling me to keep my eyes open. My dad was seen getting on the ferry to our island.

Sandra, why didn't you tell me sooner?

She texted back immediately.

Needed to verify!

Shit. No, she needed to tell me. I texted back.

Get us off the island.

I smiled at our hosts. It would do no good to get them upset, until I had a safe way for us to clear out.

When we got back to the cabin, I pretended like I was wanting to sex up Cliff, which, of course, I did, but first I needed to get everyone safely secured.

We went in, and Ella was lounging back against the couch, sound asleep with her book lying on her chest.

Cliff put his fingers up to his lips to indicate we should be quiet. I pointed around the cabin to show Cliff I was going to do some surveillance. He nodded and pulled me into a kiss, before whispering, "I have another idea first."

I allowed him to pull me up the stairs and onto the bed. God, I really did want everything this man would give me, but for now, I knew his safety was more important than my libido.

"I need to just do a quick scan of the perimeter. I'll be right back."

Cliff sighed and fell back against the bed. "Okay, but hurry."

I chuckled, feeling the same desire as he felt to get back soon.

I dashed down the stairs and slipped out into the night. Sandra's men had provided both Cliff and me with a gun after we'd first arrived. Cliff left his sitting next to the door of the cabin. In a conversation we had early on, Phil had requested that we leave it handy, in case he needed to help keep things safe.

I slipped my gun holster on and headed out to check the perimeter.

As I suspected, there was no one around. My dad might be coming for me and somehow knew I was here, but I had to believe, if there was a mole, Sandra would have kept my specific location to herself.

I was just about to go back into the cabin when, to my horror, I saw my dad and his two enforcers, Joey and Christopher, waiting for me by the door. What terrified me more than anything was the fact that Dad was holding a gun to Cliff's head.

Thirty-Five

Cliff

I'D DECIDED TO SNEAK out to lure Bentley down to the dock and make love to him there. However, when I walked outside the cabin, I came face to face with three men I'd never met before.

The shadows were deep enough that I could barely make them out, but one of the men had features that were impossible not to recognize. This had to be Bentley's father, and I had no doubt they were here for him.

The man pointed his gun at my head, and motioned quietly toward the side of the cabin and slightly behind as the other men followed, guns drawn.

I wanted to call out for Bentley, but I instinctively knew if I did, we'd all be dead. I looked up and into the cabin, thinking of my grandma there on the couch, and tried to think of anything I could that might at least save her.

Just then, Bentley came around the corner of the cabin, and stopped dead in his tracks.

"Well, well, fancy meeting you here," the man I assumed was his dad said in a really thick Boston accent.

"How did you find us?" Bentley asked.

"Well, you don't really need to know that, now, do you? What you need to be thinking about now, son, is how long I'm gonna let you live. First, why don't you take that weapon you have and put it on the ground? Don't want you getting any ideas, now do we?"

Bentley reached behind himself and slowly removed the Glock from the holster at his back, and put the gun down on the deck, kicking it toward his father and the men.

"Now, let's talk about your future, son!"

"You're here to kill me, Dad. There isn't much to talk about, is there?"

"Oh, I don't know. Word is you've got some good connections. I'm open to letting bygones be bygones if you're open to some negotiation."

"That's what this is all about? You're wanting to use my government connections to build your organization back?"

Bentley had a look of resignation on his face, which was strange to see on him. If I weren't already anxious that my life was about to end, his expression would have turned my insides cold.

"It's only fair since you're the reason it went away," his father said. "Or, we could just kill you." He aimed the gun and, having seen more than one person set on killing another, I understood. There wasn't really an alternative to death on the table.

Thinking fast, I asked, "You're gonna kill your own son?"

"Now, who's this?" the man said, turning his gun back on me. "This must be your faggot boyfriend. I think we'll kill him first, so you can watch."

Things moved fast then. I was dead either way, so I decided the least I could do was rush the son of a bitch. Just as I was about to leap, I heard three rounds fire, one right after the other.

Almost like you'd see in the movies, all three men collapsed in front of us. Dead on impact was my first thought, then as I'd been trained, I instantly began searching for where the gunfire had come from. *Determine if there's a threat...*

Bentley rushed forward to kick the guns away from the men, then checked for a pulse that I knew wasn't there. Ignoring him, I ran toward the back of the cabin, and saw my grandma... holding my Glock in her hand.

"Grandma?" I asked.

"Sorry, Bentley," she said to him, ignoring me. "I couldn't let them kill my grandson."

"You did the right thing," he assured her. "He was going to kill us both."

Bentley walked away then and made a phone call.

I went up the front steps, took my gun away from my grandma, and laid it on the table. "Grandma, how did you learn to shoot like that?" I asked.

"That's a long story," she said, but didn't add more before she pulled me into her arms.

Adrenaline still coursed through me as tears streamed down my face while I held my grandma. "You saved us."

"I know, sweetheart. I know."

It didn't take long for three boats to show up and moor at the dock. Judging by the speed at which they arrived after Bentley's phone call, I assumed they must have come from Anacortes. The bodies of the three men were photographed, bagged, and put on two of the boats. The gun used to kill them was bagged, and their blood splattered across the cabin's exterior was cleaned up. Then, after a few moments of the crew members speaking with Bentley, the two boats with the bodies were gone.

"What the hell?" I asked, when Bentley came up the stairs.

"My dad and his men can't be found on this island, and sure as hell not at this cabin," Bentley said. "Cliff, more bad people will come, and..."

I put my hand up to stop him. "I don't have the security clearance to know this, Bentley, but how the hell did they know we were here?"

"A mole," he said. "But, we know who they are, or at least we think we do. HBFASH, you certainly live up to your reputation."

Grandma, who was now sitting on the edge of the Adirondack chair, blushed. "Been a long time since someone called me that."

"Thank you," Bentley said. "Someone will come to collect you two tomorrow and take you back to your homes. You should be safe now."

"You said bad men will come if their bodies are found here," I said, ignoring their exchange, but still concerned for my grandma's safety.

"Yes, but no one will associate you with their deaths now. The men who collected them will ensure nothing can be traced back to you, or your grandmother."

He hesitated a moment and looked at me. I saw the longing in his eyes, but I knew this was probably going to be the last time I saw him. "Bentley..." I said, and he stopped me before I could say anything else.

"I have to go... My being here will put you and your grandmother at risk. I'm sorry Cliff..."

I wanted to run and hold onto him, not let him go, but there was something in his expression that forced me to stop.

He looked over at my grandma and smiled. "Can you thank John and Phil for me?"

I wanted to scream, rant, yell, *Tell them yourself, you asshole*, but then again, he'd just watched my grandma shoot and kill his father and two other men. I gripped the deck railing and kept my mouth shut.

When he climbed aboard the last boat and disappeared into the darkness, I thought I'd crumble, not just from the slowing of adrenaline, but from the loss. Out of everything, the loss of Bentley was more than I could handle.

Grandma came up and put her hand on my shoulder. "Son, he's going to be buried in paperwork for weeks. Give him time."

"What's HBFASH?" I asked.

She shook her head. "Something I never thought I'd hear again."

"You were an operative?" I asked, overwhelmed by what I was learning. "You never told us."

"Couldn't, and shouldn't have told you now. Bentley did that, though."

"Did you know what was going on here?"

She shook her head. "No, I suspected, when CIA men showed up at my door, but when no one explained the mission to me, I figured it had to do with your man and not me."

It dawned on me then. "That's what happened to Grandpa, isn't it?" I asked. "And Dad?"

"Well, it's what happened to your grandfather, yes. He didn't have a stroke. He was on a mission that went bad. Your father was killed exactly like we'd been told he was, and Cliff, he was a hero. I wasn't supposed to know what'd happened, and I still can't give you specifics, but your dad and your grandpa were both heroes."

"Dead heroes."

"Yeah, that's how it usually works out."

I shook my head. "This is more than I can handle. Are you okay?" I asked.

She nodded. "Yeah, go on up to your room, I'll wait for John and Phil and let them know Bentley had to leave." She looked at me, and quickly added, "Never mention those men. Not them, my codename, nor what happened here tonight. I've only ever seen the CIA move dead bodies like that and clean up the scene once. Trust me, there are ugly things at play here, and we need to keep this under wraps."

I nodded. "Grandma, are you sure you're okay?"

She smiled sadly. "Sweetheart, this isn't the first time." I understood what she was saying. This wasn't the first time she'd had to kill someone. Hell, I'd been on the police force for six years and had never shot anyone. I almost did once, but luckily, the person backed down before I had to.

"Want me to stay here on the couch?"

"No, I'd prefer to be alone," she said. So, I hugged her, then headed up to the bedroom. I crawled into the bed that still smelled like Bentley, and let myself cry it out. It'd been a long freaking time since I'd cried this hard and this long. Being a cop had trained me to knock all the emotional stuff to the side quickly, but too much had happened tonight. I might not have inherited my mom's or grandparents' artistic talents, but clearly, I'd inherited other family traits. Maybe that should've consoled me, but tonight it just made the overwhelming emotions more intense.

Had I been a stronger man, I'd have stayed downstairs with my grandma, no matter what she said, but I just wasn't able to. I heard Phil and John come in and Grandma talking to them. I got up and closed my door to block hearing her explanation. I just didn't want to hear her leave out all the details of why

Bentley had left. I knew he'd left the island to ensure our safety, and I'd understood he'd leave me when this case closed anyway, but all of that was cold comfort right now lying here in this king-size bed alone.

All night, I stared at the ceiling, and thought about all that'd happened. Jeff being almost implicated in art theft and being shot, my losing a job I thought I'd be in for the rest of my career, and meeting and falling for Bentley. Yeah, I'd fallen for him. No, not the instalove stuff of movies and romance novels, but the kind where you knew, if given more time, that you would fall in love for real, and it would last.

I guessed those dreams were cut short, and done so in a massive blood show. Bentley's father had wanted to kill him. That was clear from the conversation before they were shot, but he was still his father. He had to be hurting, but there was nothing I could do.

Thirty-Six

Bentley

I HADN'T EXPECTED TO walk up on my father. I also hadn't expected to live to tell about it. My father didn't leave witnesses. That was the thing he'd said over and over when I'd been a kid. Yeah, he was tempting me with an offer, but fuck if that was real. He intended to kill me, and had it not been for Ella, he would've.

Sandra had found the file on Ella, but hadn't told me who she was until I pressed her a few days before. Up until that time, I'd assumed it was Phil. I was hoping if he was the one, I could get him to divulge information to me. Unfortunately, Ella wasn't going to be able to help me in that way. Her file had been inactive since the death of her husband, another operative who'd been killed in Europe while conducting a covert operation for the CIA.

If things had been different, even slightly different... if Ella had gone with us to dinner, or John and Phil stayed after dropping us back at the cabin, both Cliff and I would've been killed, instead of Dad and his two long-time enforcers.

I stared out the front of the boat as we rode toward Anacortes. One of the operatives who'd picked me up told me that Sandra was lying low until I got to her. When I went to call her, he shook his head and said she wouldn't be able to answer.

"What happened?" I asked, worried.

"I can't tell you. She will, though."

With nothing to do but wait until we reached shore, my thoughts drifted to the man I'd just left behind. I wanted to hold Cliff, comfort him, but I was too overwhelmed. My dad was dead, and if the operative's vague responses to my questions were any indication, my daughter was probably injured. I needed to get as far away from Cliff and his grandmother as I could, before they ended up getting hurt because of me, too.

Cliff had watched me go, and I could see the look of rejection on his face. That was harder to experience than watching my father be killed in front of me. Even in the short time we'd been together, I knew Cliff really cared for me, and I cared for him. Had we been giving more time... well, there was no use thinking about that. My father had taken everything from me since I'd been born. This was just his latest, and, if I was lucky, his final accomplishment.

Once we docked in Anacortes, a car met us at the dock, and I was whisked away to an airport and flown what appeared to be east. When the plane landed, I knew I was in DC. I'd used this airport several times in the past, and recognized it.

I was being taken toward Langley, but before getting to CIA headquarters, we veered to the right and ended up at a nondescript building just outside the complex.

When we entered, I was asked to surrender my weapons, and as we walked through the big doors in the front, I could tell this was some sort of private hospital.

Within moments, I was led into a room where I saw Sandra hooked up to machines. I immediately rushed to her, and when I got to her bed, she looked over at me. "Hi, Dad," she said.

"Sandra." It took me a moment to catch my breath. The sight of her lying there scared me more than I'd ever been scared in my life.

"I'm okay, Dad. It was just a little bullet."

"Fuck! Who?" I knew my anger was probably palpable as I digested this latest information.

She shook her head. "They'll tell you, but, Dad, don't be a fucking cowboy, okay?"

"Cowboy? What?"

A moment later, I heard someone come in behind me. I turned to see a stranger, though I had my suspicions of who she was. "KOPATICAL?" I asked, and she nodded.

"Can you come with me? Let's let your daughter rest."

I kissed Sandra's head and turned to follow my CIA contact out the door. If she was here, that meant things were more serious than had been anticipated.

I followed the woman down the hall and into an office that sat behind the nurses' station. "Have a seat, Mr. Cummings," she said as she sat across from me behind the desk.

I did as instructed, eager to find out what was going on.

"Our operation was infiltrated by someone who was very close to your daughter. Does the name Finn Degnan ring a bell?"

I shook my head. "No, but I know the Degnans. They're related to me."

She nodded. "Finn Degnan is the son of Alec Degnan, the man who was supposed to take your dad's place in the organization."

"Son of a bitch! You were infiltrated by Alec Degnan's son?" I asked, ready to storm out of the building and take the SOB out myself.

She waited for me to calm down. I took a deep breath and let it out to calm myself, before asking, "How the hell did this happen?"

"It's twisted. Alec changed his son's name at birth, and he grew up with relatives we weren't tracking. Apparently, he slipped through the cracks. He's been posing as Kevin Ford."

"The FBI agent who was assigned to work alongside Sandra."

She nodded. "The Degnans have been planning this for a while. Sandra caught Finn searching her phone and knew we'd been compromised, and when she went to warn us, Finn shot her and left her for dead. She managed to get to a landline and call for backup."

"How serious are her injures?"

"Barely missed her heart," KOPATICAL said.

I closed my eyes for a moment to gather myself before re-acting, all the fears I'd ever had about my daughter living the same life as me suddenly becoming reality. "So, what now?"

"They want you. Now that they know you aren't dead, they'll be coming after you, or, more accurately, they'll be coming after you *again*."

"So, how was my father involved in all this?"

She sighed, reached into her briefcase, and pulled out a transcript of a phone conversation. As I read it, I could see how things were coming down. Dad had officially assumed leadership of the organization now that my grandfather was dead, and Alec—the next in line—was suffering from cancer. So, they were waiting for the last of the gang to be released from prison. None of them had gotten life. Dad's guys were the last to get out, so the moment they were, the ball was set in motion.

Dad's job was to kill me, then come back and cede his position to Alec's son. Dad had readily agreed.

"Well, shit!" I said, frustrated. "Are the folks in Washington safe now that I'm gone?"

"Yeah, Churchill was the only person behind the paintings. We think the Degnans made contact to exchange the paint-ings for your murder. They almost succeeded, too."

"I'm hard to kill," I said, causing her to crack a smile, something I didn't think KOPATICAL did often.

"I recommend you not be in contact with any of the people in Washington, though, not until this has all blown over and we subdue Finn Degnan and his crew."

"And how likely is that to happen?" I asked, not feeling confident.

"Mr. Cummings, we've used your services for a long time, but you have to know we didn't ignore the threat you could pose at any moment. We've made it our priority to keep track of every person in your family. We have an entire team monitoring them, and you, for that matter."

I already knew this, so wasn't surprised. "Except you missed a very important piece."

She nodded slowly. "An issue that's been firmly reprimanded, I assure you. However—" she added, "—the FBI knows the whereabouts of the rest of the old crew, where they are, what they've been doing. We've monitored those who were in prison, and we know who they've spoken to over the years. You'll have to take my word for it when I assure you, this situation is firmly under control."

There wasn't much I could do, other than nod. "So, what now?"

"You will stay here with your daughter while she recovers. There are apartments on the top floor, and as soon as she has recovered enough to be monitored remotely, she'll be moved up to be with you, but Finn Degnan thinks your daughter is dead, and we are using your father's mobile phone to communicate that you are dead as well."

"You'll have to make sure to let Cliff and Ella know that."

She smiled. "They will be briefed in the morning when our people pick them up and take them home. For all the world, you are now dead, again."

She stood then and led me back out into the hall, and pointing to the elevator, escorted me up to the top floor. I surveyed the sterile apartment as we walked in. "Pleasant," I said sarcastically. "At least my holding apartment was modern."

KOPATICAL looked around and smiled. "Well, it's better than being dead," she said, and turned to leave. "If you need anything, pick up the landline. There's always someone manning it. Ask for whatever you need, and someone will provide it for you."

After she left, I settled into the uncomfortable chair and put my head in my hands. "Fuck this day," I said to myself.

I'd had everything. Now I was sitting in an uncomfortable chair, in an institutional apartment, with a daughter who was recovering from being shot, and a horrible excuse for a father who'd been shot and killed before my very eyes.

I thought once again of everything I'd lost, and almost lost. Cliff's image came to mind, and I had to wipe at the tear that got past my defenses. How could it be that I almost had it all just to have my old man steal it away from me?

Thirty-Seven

Cliff

As Bentley had said, we were picked up the following morning by people who didn't seem to have a clue about anything that'd happened.

We both hugged our hosts, who looked miserable to see us go, and we thanked them profusely. John hugged Grandma so hard I thought she was going to break, but when she pulled back, she assured him that she'd call and set up a time to come back out and visit him and Patricia.

When we got back to Anacortes, we were picked up by an Uber driver, some kid who looked to be fresh out of high school. When he opened the door to let Grandma into the front seat, he cheerfully said that he'd been paid to drive us back to Edmonds.

We were driving when the kid turned the music off, and said, "I've been asked to fill you in on some details about yesterday."

I was shocked, and my grandma chuckled when she turned toward me. "It's never who you assume."

The guy told us that Bentley wouldn't be able to contact us again. We were not to discuss it or him, and if we did, we were to speak as if we thought Bentley hadn't made it. The official line was to say he'd been shot by his father and that it didn't look like he was going to survive.

We'd tried to be discreet in public, so I didn't think anyone knew we'd become an item, and even if they did, I didn't think they really cared. I guessed that was good, because if they were faking his death, there was still an obvious threat.

Grandma smiled at me over her shoulder and said, "You never get used to all this, but you have to learn to roll with it."

When we pulled up in front of her building, I helped get her bag out of the back of the car, and when I dropped her off at her front door, she seemed exhausted. "I'll call you tomorrow, okay?"

"That'll be perfect, thanks, son."

I was then dropped off at my house, and looked around to see all I'd been planning to do to the place that had been held up by the events of last week.

Regardless of how things ended, I still held out hope that Bentley would find me once everything was over. Based on what the driver had said, it sounded like he was basically in witness protection. If that were the case, I'd never see him again.

Despite being exhausted, I tossed and turned in my bed and ended up once again staring at the ceiling, my mind racing with thoughts of Bentley. How would I manage to be happy as a bachelor now that I'd found the man I wanted to be with more than I wanted to breathe?

Whoever said, *It's better to have loved and lost, than never to have loved at all,* must have had no idea what they were talking about. I missed Bentley deep down in my soul. I felt as if I might suffocate every time I allowed myself to consider he would be gone forever.

Thirty-Eight

Bentley

WAS IT POSSIBLE TO be this miserable after spending such a short time with a person? But not just any person. Cliff. I missed him terribly. I couldn't rationalize in my head how sleeping with him only a few times made me long for him—the feel of his full body pressed against mine, the way he nuzzled back into my chest as we spooned—every time I lay down.

I missed his body, I missed his smile, I missed his conversation. I missed him, period.

Sandra was recovering slowly, and although that was heartening to see, it also meant I was completely stuck here, bored out of my head. I watched more television than I'd ever watched in my adult life, did crossword puzzles, and even tried a few video games they had in the apartment. Nothing entertained me for long.

By the time Sandra was well enough to be moved up to our apartment to continue her recovery, I was fit to be tied.

She laughed when I told her, saying, "Read a book, Dad." Clearly, she was already tired of my whining.

I had tried that already, and I'd been too anxious, but for her sake, I decided to try again. When I asked the phone operator for books, they brought me a John Grisham. *Of course, they did.* And it was the same damned book I had been reading when I had Cliff at my side.

I almost moaned when I thought of him sitting next to me, snuggled in, reading whatever he'd found while I read my borrowed book.

The thought comforted me and as long as I imagined Cliff next to me as I read, I was able to enjoy it, which honestly saved me from going completely stir crazy.

It took six weeks of progressive recovery for Sandra, and excessive boredom for me for the case to break. Sandra and I were told the FBI had arrested all the offenders who'd joined with my dad and Alec Degnan. The only one they hadn't apprehended was Alec's son Finn, the man formerly known to us as Agent Kevin Ford.

They thought he'd gone underground somewhere in South America. When KOPATICAL gave us this news personally, Sandra sighed. "No, he wouldn't have gone to South America. They're wrong. If he left the country, he'd have gone to Russia."

Both of us waited for her to explain.

"Ford, um, Finn, spoke of having friends in Russia, but from what I could tell, most of them live in the US now. He never mentioned South America."

"But he wouldn't have if you were his asset," KOPATICAL said.

"Maybe, but Finn wasn't as clever as you all are making him out to be. Mostly, he was a huge man who looked intimidating, but once you got to know him, the façade disappeared. He told me a lot about himself over the year we worked together, not much about his childhood, but his time in college, then going through Quantico. He was really proud of that."

"So, you think he's regretting all this?" KOPATICAL asked.

"I don't know. He pulled the wool over my eyes. I would've never pegged him as following in his father's footsteps." Sandra's expression was both sad and angry. I could tell she felt betrayed. She had been, especially when he tried to kill her.

"What's going on with Alec Degnan?" I asked.

"His cancer has progressed, and he's very sick, so the judge has allowed him to remain under house arrest," KOPATICAL said. "His phone is being monitored. As far as we know, he's not been in touch with his son."

"That's unlikely, but I doubt he'll be much of a danger while he's on his deathbed," I said.

When KOPATICAL left, I went over and sat next to Sandra. "If it helps any, I understand a little about what you're feeling."

She sighed. "I'm sure, Dad, but no, it doesn't help much. Gathering intelligence is my job. It's what I'm paid to do, so I should've done a better job chasing down Degnan's history."

I chuckled, then apologized. "I'm sorry, honey, but no, you can't know everything about everyone you meet or work with. That's why you have a team. I *did* research him. I had our team trace him as far back as we could get, and we missed it. The FBI missed it, and I'm sure your superiors missed it, too. The fact is, the boy and his dad hid this well."

"You think his dad was involved all along?"

I shook my head. "I never met Alec Degnan, but no, not directly. There must have been an intermediary. Who that was? I'm not sure we'll ever know."

Sandra nodded. "Well, if I ever see the SOB again..."

I smiled. "I think he knows better than to let either of us see him again."

Thirty-Nine

Cliff

I F LOSING BENTLEY WASN'T enough to cause me to wallow in depression, the fact that I had to finally give up on the job search and start accepting a monthly stipend from my parents' trust fund certainly did. I was in no condition to begin working again until I'd had some time to work through all that'd happened over the previous months.

I didn't take much from the trust, and luckily, the interest more than covered my expenses. What it didn't cover, I could use some of my own savings to handle. It was my only consolation that I wasn't spending any of the actual principal in the account.

I spent too much time over at Grandma's, and when she'd had enough of me, she kicked me out and told me I couldn't return for at least seventy-two hours.

I could tell Jeff and Paul, who were back home in Edmonds, needed their time together, too. They were still recuperating from their own trauma around all that'd happened.

So, that meant I was alone. I went to the bar daily, but even that left me lonely every time I glanced over at what was now, in my mind, Bentley's chair.

All this was weighing on me when, of all the damned things, Evan Tinkle, the architect who'd stood me up all those weeks ago, contacted me and asked if he could meet me at the house.

My first thought was, *screw him for standing me up*, but the hope that maybe the old home's renovation could help lift me out of my funk, prompted me to agree to the meeting.

Tinkle arrived on the morning we'd agreed to meet and wandered through the house, touching the woodwork reverently, almost dramatically, as if it were a lover.

It caused me to chuckle inwardly. I knew my grandfather's designs were revered, but this was almost to the level of worship.

"So," I started, after giving him the downstairs tour. "I want to remain as true to the historical elements of the home as I can. The kitchen, however, is just..."

Tinkle put his hand up to stop me. "I'm sorry, Mr. Sparks, but I will not be helping you redesign this home. In fact, I'll be doing everything in my power to prevent you from getting the permits to do any work on it."

The statement was like a slap in the face. "What the hell do you mean you'll try to stop me? It's my goddamned house."

"Well, it's also a historically relevant piece of property. I have already begun the legal proceedings to prevent any renovation being done on the property."

"Get out!" I demanded. "And if you're telling me the truth, you should be prepared for countersuits for blocking my rights to do with the property as I see fit."

Tinkle raised his hand again, calm as a cucumber. Of course, that just caused me to see red.

"Mr. Tinkle, I won't tell you again to leave my home."

I was already reaching for my phone to dial the police, when Tinkle said, "I'll leave, and I didn't mean for this to come out the way it did, but you have to understand, Mr. Sparks. This is the only Elvin Jennings home left intact anywhere in the Seattle area. Allowing you to tear it apart would be like someone ripping apart Frank Lloyd Wright's Taliesin in Wisconsin. It wouldn't be right to allow you to do that without a fight."

"I'm the grandson and the owner of this property, you are not." I'd already pressed the button on the nine-one-one call, and was waiting for an answer when Tinkle walked voluntarily toward the door. When the operator answered, I said, "I have someone on my property who is refusing to leave."

"I'm leaving," Tinkle said then, and opened my front door. "But, I wanted to be the one to tell you we are going to fight you, Mr. Sparks."

I told the operator my intruder had voluntarily left, and hung up. Fuck, it wasn't like I didn't have enough on my plate. Fuck that arrogant, self-absorbed asshole. My grandfather had built this home for my grandma and her daughter, *my fucking mom*. Who the hell did he think he was?

As I stomped up to my bedroom, I found myself throwing clothes in a suitcase before I even knew where I was going. I just knew right now I wanted to be anywhere besides this fucking city.

So, I just let my instincts guide me. I wasn't surprised when I found myself driving toward the ferries that would take me to the San Juan Islands. Even before all this had gone down, the islands were an escape for me. Now they were even more so.

I didn't go back to Phil and John's. No, that wasn't going to help at all. Instead, I rented a kayak, some fishing equipment, and a cottage on Lopez Island. I'd kayak out like I'd done when I was in college, or I'd find a public beach to fish.

The islands were healing. Magical really. I never caught any fish, but of course, I wasn't really out there with that intention. The fishing was an excuse to be there, by the sea, allowing the waves to heal me.

I ended up calling Grandma instead of going to visit, telling her I was on Lopez and that I'd see her when I got back.

Knowingly, she said she believed that was the best place for me right now. "Son, when you get back, we need to chat, okay?"

"About what?" I asked.

"Don't you worry about anything right now, just find yourself again. When you come home, we'll talk."

I stayed in the San Juans for well over a month, moving from cottage to cottage, island to island, and beach to beach. I didn't even try to go home until the weather turned so cold I could no longer be out on the water comfortably. Fall came early on the Salish Sea.

I got home late one Friday night, called my grandma and told her I'd see her the next morning. I shaved and got my hair cut before I went over to visit her, knowing that a lot of the sadness inside me still existed, but no longer controlled me.

When I walked into Grandma's apartment, she was once again dressed in her finest clothes, and on her table was a spread like she was preparing to serve a huge party of people.

"Um, Grandma, what's all this?" I asked.

"We need to have a heart to heart, and I know you probably didn't eat enough while you were gone, so I figured I'd order breakfast from the kitchen. As you can see, when you order, they are able to actually make stuff that's edible," she said, with no small amount of disdain.

The look on her face caused me to laugh out loud. "You know you don't have to stay here, right? Why don't you come home with me? We'll hire a nurse."

I figured I'd at least get a flat-out no, but instead, she looked sad. "I'm afraid that's not going to be possible. The architect, Evan Tinkle, came by to visit while you were away," she said. I immediately bristled.

"Grandma, I will get a restraining order..."

She held up her hand. "Son, that man has a lot of influence, more than you realize. His family are sprinkled throughout the city government. He's going to make your life a living hell."

I chuckled. "You do realize he has no claim on the home, right?"

"Well, that's not entirely true," she said sadly, then went to her desk and pulled out an envelope, not unlike the one she'd shown me when I'd inherited the property. I opened it and saw a letter from Ralph, my estranged half-uncle, alerting her that he intended to sue me for the home, challenging my inheritance.

I laughed. "Grandma, this won't hold up in court. That's why he sent this to you instead of just filing. The home belonged to you, not him, and you have a right to give it to whoever you wish. Not even if a judge was in Tinkle's pocket could he expect to win an appeal."

She nodded. "That's not what this is about, Cliff. They intend to bleed you dry, fighting them in frivolous lawsuits. Neither you nor I have the money to fight them for long, and I don't want all your inheritance to be wasted trying."

"Grandma, I know a little about the law. Countersuits can be just as costly to them as they are to me. I don't know my half-uncle all that well, but I know enough about him to know he likes his money."

Grandma chuckled at that. "He does, but Tinkle and his family have been obsessed with our home since your grandfather completed it. They've been trying to get their hands on it for, well, forever."

The bitterness rose in me then, and I wanted to spit on the ground. "After this crap, I'll fight them to the bitter end to prevent them from ever owning it," I said.

She smiled. "You really are like me."

"Do I have an alternative?" I asked, unintentionally spewing venom at her. She walked over to the same desk she'd just come from and pulled out a card that looked to be several decades old.

"This is a friend of your grandfather. He, too, expressed interest in the home, but unlike the Tinkles, he doesn't want to live in it. He wants to turn it into a museum."

I stared at the card and then looked up at my grandma. "Um, is he still alive?"

She gave me her look and shook her head. "You are the most obstinate brat sometimes, Cliff. Of course, he's alive. I wouldn't have given you the damned card if he wasn't. Sometimes..." she muttered as she walked over to the kitchen sink and poured herself a glass of water, before coming back and sitting across from me.

She reached across the table, flipped the card over, and pointed to the number written there. "That's what he's offering for the property."

My eyes grew large at the huge amount of money. "Um, Grandma, that's like three times what the property is worth."

She shrugged. "No, it's twice what it's worth. You have to remember, it's a unique property. I had it appraised before I gave it to you, and when I told Mr. Rutherford that you might be interested, I made it clear that he'd have to double the appraised value if he were to have a chance of getting it."

"But Grandma, that's my home."

She studied me for several long moments, before she said, "Is it? Are you sure you're so locked into that house that you wouldn't consider relocating?"

I couldn't understand what she was asking. "Of course, it's my home," I told her. "Why would you even ask that?"

She smiled and patted my hand. "Home is where the heart is, Cliff."

I was beginning to understand. "You think I should sell up and go find Bentley?"

Her smile brightened. "I saw how the two of you looked at one another, and I know for a fact you are perfect for each other. Don't throw away your chance for love over some old pile of wood."

"Grandma, please, you love that old home."

Sadness crept up her face and overtook her smile. "No, dear one, I loved your grandpa. The house was just what I had left of him."

"Exactly, so I should keep it."

She shook her head. "I let your grandpa go that day on the sailboat. That's what I was doing up on that bow. I'd held onto my anger for him taking a mission I'd expressly told him not to. He was so fucking stubborn." She looked at me and laughed. "Maybe it isn't me you take after. I honestly don't give a damn what you do with that house. It's not Elvin. It's not your mom. It's just a house. What I *do* give a damn about is my grandson finding happiness, and the sooner you do, the better."

I looked down at the card again, then back up at her. "Really? This is what you think I should do?"

"Really, this is what you should do."

I nodded. "Then, let's call him, but you have to go with me to meet him. I'm not nearly as good at negotiation as you are."

She laughed at the truth of that.

"I'm a tough cop, I won't waver when it comes to justice and criminality, but I'd give everything away if someone acted like they needed it. It was a curse of mine. I'll come with you, but we both have to be there when that son of a bitch Tinkle finds out, so we can see his expression when he learns we beat him."

Forty

Bentley

"You're as safe as you ever are," KOPATICAL said as she sat across from me in the sterile apartment.

"What about my home in Boston?" I asked. "Did someone board it up?"

She nodded. "But, Bentley, you're not going to like what you find. They thoroughly trashed it."

I knew that already, but it stung to think about my dad's henchmen rifling through my stuff. Worse, it stung to think I'd not been able to fix it, or if I was being honest, to go after those who'd done this to me.

Sandra agreed to stay at the CIA hideout for a while longer, until I could find her accommodation. Finn, or Ford, or whatever the fuck he was called, had not been seen nor heard of, and both the government and my network were looking for him.

Sandra had said Russia. KOPATICAL had said South America. I had contacts there and elsewhere around the world. They were all looking for the son of a bitch. He should be praying the government got to him first, because not all my contacts were, well, they weren't gentle.

The limo pulled up in front of my Boston home. I chuckled as I got out, thinking about the time Cliff had called me a snob. He'd been right, of course, but I'd be damned if I took a cab after living in that crappy CIA apartment for almost two months.

My house was boarded up and tagged with graffiti in several places, something that'd never happened before.

I pulled the plywood down that covered my door and walked inside. Trashed was an understatement. Someone had knifed every fucking piece of furniture I owned. Pillow stuffing was spread everywhere, along with countless broken possessions the intruders had apparently thrown against the walls.

They'd clearly been looking for my safes because huge sections of my wallboard had been ripped out, exposing the two-by-fours behind.

I walked through the house, looking for anything that would give me a clue as to who had done this, but without a really close inspection, I knew I wouldn't find a smoking gun. KOPATI-CAL had acquired all the reports of the break-in from the cops and had forwarded them to me when I'd requested them.

The reports were completely worthless. The only real lead we had was a security camera about a block away that had captured a car with what appeared to be four people inside, parked outside the building during the break-in.

Besides that, it was anyone's guess. Of course, my guess was my dad's organization. If that was the case, the people who did this were probably already dead or in custody.

I ignored the damage and went up to my bedroom to see if they'd made it into the safe. Of course, they'd found the false wall and had literally ripped it off the hinges. They'd found the safe in the floor and had managed to pry it out and take it.

They hadn't, however, found the second false wall or the safe I had in the floor there. My dad was a jackass of epic proportions, but he at least had given me good advice about that.

I removed Sandra's birth certificate, her custody papers, and Sister Clarissa's letter, and secured them in a box I'd brought with me for that purpose.

The guns, the money, even my passports with all my different aliases didn't matter to me even a fraction as much as these things did.

I went back out to the limo that'd waited for me and had it drive me to my local bank, where I deposited the items in a safety deposit box. Then I returned to the house to collect the other hidden items that were important for other reasons.

KOPATICAL sent several of her people to collect the more sensitive items I recovered, which were to be stored by the agency until I had a secure enough place to keep them. I knew they'd gone through my belongings several times after the incident, and I could tell they'd found a lot of the documents that would've been considered national security. I'd told them where most of those were myself, just for safety purposes.

But not everything I kept was appropriate, even for a typical CIA operative's eyes. Those were the things I needed to collect on my own and deal with personally.

I took several hundred thousand dollars in cash that I kept in my home for sensitive situations to my bank, which the CIA and FBI both had a relationship with. That allowed me to deposit the amount without throwing up red flags to authorities who had lower clearance levels than me. Once the money was deposited, I took the more sensitive documents back to the CIA safe house and personally handed them to KOPATICAL.

"Is this all of it?" she asked.

I nodded. "Yes, I didn't hold anything back."

She looked at me strangely. "Are you retiring?" she asked.

I couldn't help but laugh. "You and I both know I'll never retire, but let's just say I'm taking a sabbatical. This all hit a bit too close to home. Hell, it did hit my home."

She sighed, but I knew she understood. "I'll send out a team to put your house back together. You know I can't have just any renovation company in your house, just in case you might have accidentally forgotten something."

I laughed. She knew me well enough to know I wouldn't. Hell, I wasn't even sure I could let important documents slip past me. I was too... me.

We both knew this was her throwing me a bone. She would foot the cost for refurbishing my home and make sure it got done appropriately. She would also know all my hiding places once this was done, which both of us also knew I'd never use again now that they were compromised.

No, things were changing for me. My life in Boston was coming to an end. I'd grown up here. I'd been a part of a horrible criminal organization, even though never by choice. With the death of my father and imminent death of Alec Degnan, I'd finally closed that chapter in my life, too.

Of course, as long as Alec's son Finn was still around, there was a chance he'd restart the family business. Still, neither the CIA, FBI, Interpol, nor even I would allow that to happen. Finn Degnan's days were numbered.

I thanked KOPATICAL, and after loading Sandra in my car, I flew her and myself back to Washington, and back to the small apartment she and I had shared there for over a year while we worked through the Seattle crime syndicate bust, and this most recent mess involving my dad and his cronies.

"You okay?" Sandra asked me, when we finally took off in the private jet toward what I now considered my home.

I nodded. "Yeah, or at least I will be."

"You're not coming back to Boston, are you?" she asked, shocking me. Sandra was becoming more observant now that she'd become an operative.

I looked down and shook my head. "No, it's time to leave Boston for good."

She looked out the window, staring at the landscape that flashed by below us. "I think I'll stay out West, too, if you don't mind."

"I don't mind. Honey," I said, waiting for her to look over at me, "this lifestyle you've chosen, is it really what you want?"

She didn't answer right away. Instead, she stared down at her hands. Finally, she looked at me and nodded. "It is. It's almost like this is what I was made for."

Her expression turned quizzical. "How about you? Are you going to come back?"

I nodded. "Eventually, it's what I was made for, too."

Sandra smiled then. "You know this whole thing was bad, but we ended up saving lives. We recovered all the art, too."

I nodded. "We lost a lot as well."

"Not if you don't let it be lost," she said, causing me to look at her funny.

"Please, Dad," she laughed. "I don't have to work for the CIA to know you've fallen in love. Don't let him go. Go after him."

I couldn't help the smile that crossed my face. "Honey, I think I just might do that."

Forty-One

Cliff

MY HEAD SPUN AS I went from a guy who barely had enough money to pay my bills, to a multimillionaire with the sale of the home in Edmonds.

I tried to force Grandma to take the money, because shit, it had only been my home for a few minutes, it seemed, but she just laughed. "Son, who do you think will get the money when I die?"

"You aren't going to die. You're gonna find some weird magical potion and become immortal."

"God, who would want that?" she asked, then ribbed me.

"Take the money and live a good life," she said.

Alexander Rutherford, the buyer of the home, was one of the wealthiest men in the country. Hell, the world. He had known both my grandparents back in the day. Of course, that could've been in either the art world or their spy world. Either way, I didn't really think I needed to know how he knew them.

Because all the title work on the property had been done when the home had transferred to me, the sale to Rutherford had only taken an instant. As he sat across from Grandma and me in his Seattle high-rise office, signing the final documents that would turn our home into a museum, he smiled at us.

"This will be a huge asset to the community. We've already begun setting up the trust for the museum, and with any luck, we'll be able to create parking with the acreage that goes with the home."

I sighed. "Mr. Rutherford, you may have problems with that. As I've told you, the local government might be very unhappy they weren't the ones to get this home."

He laughed. "Oh, I think you'll find I don't usually have problems with entitled, spoiled brats like Mr. Tinkle and his cronies. Trust me, the National Trust is quite intrigued with what we are planning to do with your grandfather's home. That will bring grants not just for the museum, but for the community as well."

I had no idea what he meant, but I didn't really need to. What I needed was to go say goodbye, pack my things, and make my exit from the only home I'd ever known.

While we were still in Seattle, Grandma forced me to go to Pike Place Market and get an ice cream at my grandfather's favorite ice cream store. "He deserves to be honored by us as much as those who admire his work," she said.

"Ice cream?" I asked.

"Your grandpa was such a kid in many ways. He grew up dirt-poor, farming in Monroe. Of course, back then it was just farmhouses and cows." She chuckled. "Anyway, he had never had store-bought ice cream until he and I met in college at the university library. So, naturally, I brought him down here and we shared two scoops of chocolate and strawberry. He was hooked after that."

My grandma hardly ever spoke about my grandpa. I'd assumed it was because they hadn't really been that close, considering the turmoil of their years together, and his having been married. So, I'd never heard this story.

"So, this was your first date?" I asked, and she nodded as she licked the strawberry scoop on her cone.

"Why didn't you ever talk about him?" I asked.

She licked the ice cream several times, thinking before she said, "It hurt. Everything about losing your grandpa hurt."

"And now you've lost his home?"

She patted my knee like she always did when she was comforting me. "No, we preserved it and kept it out of the hands of those horrible Tinkles. You know your grandpa used to complain about the Tinkle who'd worked for him all the time. He was lazy, sometimes didn't come to work at all, but he had connections that made it easier for your grandpa to get his crazy designs approved by the bank he needed to finance the projects."

"Wow, really?"

She chuckled. "They are annoying people, to say the least. I'm so proud we got Rutherford to take this on. To be honest, I'd

have sold to him decades ago if it hadn't been for you and your mom, but thanks to the growth of the real-estate values, holding on as long as we did helped us make out like bandits."

I laughed. "You wouldn't let me share the loot, though."

"I am sharing it, honey," she said as she sobered. "You are my and your grandfather's legacy, in more ways than you can imagine. That house didn't represent him, at least not in the way you do."

I let the emotions take me. My grandma's kind words hit me in the heart. "Thanks for this," I said.

She bumped up against me and stayed like that while finishing her ice cream.

Naturally, I put my arm around her and pulled her to my side. There were few people as special as my sweet grandma. In fact, I could only think of one other, and he was no longer a possibility. I shook off that thought, refusing to let my sadness of missing him interfere with the special moment I was sharing with the incredible woman snuggling into my side.

Forty-Two

Bentley

I HADN'T SEEN MY cousin Melissa Cooper since the big crime syndicate bust and ensuing scandal that shook Seattle over a year ago had played out, when my work had led me to rough up her son Les's boyfriend, Bennett Jackson, as part of the investigation. Even though my actions had ultimately saved Bennett's life, I'd deliberately stayed away after that, not wanting to disrupt the healing I knew they all needed, but now, I needed the favor returned.

I'd called Melissa to let her know I was coming, and to try to prepare Bennett and Les for my arrival. She'd assured me neither of them held any ill will toward me, but I wasn't going to chance it. I wanted them to know I was coming, so they could prepare for any trauma related to seeing me.

When I walked up to the front door, my guards smiled and nodded before opening the door for me to pass through. It was good to see they were still loyal after all that'd gone down with the family and me. Sandra had told me that the guards had really bonded with Les and Bennett, and were now fiercely protective of them.

That made me happy more than anything else. When your employees were good enough to bond with their clients, it showed you'd picked good guys.

Melissa was sitting at a beautiful custom-built kitchen table, and when she looked up, a genuine smile crossed her face. "Bentley, you finally came to visit!"

I chuckled before I acknowledged her slight barb at my absence. "I'm finally here. How's the family?"

"Well, come find out," she said, sliding out of the chair and leading me into the living room, where the finishing touches were being made to the home.

"Melissa, this is amazing. I mean, I've seen your and Vince's work for ages, but I... this is taking another step up."

"I'm so happy you like it," she said, and I could see her pride, although my tough cousin would never admit it.

The family, including Melissa's husband, Vince Cooper, and their adult kids, all came over and welcomed me then. I hadn't seen most of them since they'd moved from Boston out to Seattle. That was strange in and of itself, since I'd made a point of visiting my cousin and her family at least once a month after coming back from the service.

They were the only family I had left, at least real family. I would never forget how Melissa and Vince, as well as my aunt, had put their lives on the line for me all those years ago, but more than that, I just loved them, and truth be known, I thought of the Cooper kids as my own nieces and nephews.

"Where are the little ones?" I asked, perplexed at how quiet the home was, particularly since Melissa and Vince had young grandchildren. The Coopers' home was never quiet, at least not since they'd begun having kids, let alone grandkids.

"Um, school. Duh," Les said as he came over and gave me a hug. "Hi, Bentley. Thanks for coming to visit. We've missed you."

"Really?" I asked, sure he wasn't being honest.

"Really," he said, looking me in the eye.

I nodded, getting the message loud and clear. They were all peeved I'd disappeared. I still needed to see Bennett.

No sooner had the thought entered my mind, than Bennett came into the room. He walked up to me and took the hand I reached out, then he pulled me into a hug. "Thank you," he said. "I haven't had a chance to do that. Thanks for saving me, but more importantly, thanks for saving Les."

I'll admit this wasn't what I'd expected. I assumed he'd be distant, maybe avoid me altogether. I had to force my emotions down to keep from embarrassing myself and ruining my reputation as the iron man, a nickname the kids had given me long before it'd become synonymous with a certain movie superhero.

Bennett pulled back and took Les's hand. "So, to what do we owe the honor?" he asked.

"Well, I need a favor," I said, feeling shy all of a sudden.

"Name it," Bennett said, not even waiting for the rest of the family to reply.

When I mentioned the party to celebrate the completion of their latest home renovation project, they all nodded. "Well, I'd like to bring a date with me."

There were several smiles, but none bigger than Melissa's. "Oh, Bentley, you finally found someone?"

I held my hand up. "Let's not get ahead of ourselves. We've, um... well, we've been having a hard time."

The group didn't press, but all eyes were on me as I turned back to Les and Bennett. "So, this guy, you've met him. He was on the police force when everything went down last year."

Bennett nodded. "Is it Officer Sparks?" he asked.

I looked at him, trying to gauge his emotions, but his face remained neutral. "Yes, Officer Sparks is who I'd like to bring as my date."

Bennett smiled. "I was told he quit the force."

That shocked me. "How did you know?" I asked.

Bennett pointed to an empty chair sitting across from a large sectional, and I sat.

"I went looking for him not long ago. I wanted to clean up the... well, the trauma after all that went down."

"And you were told he'd left?"

Bennett nodded. "I hope it wasn't because of me or my dad," he said, sadness filling him.

"Well, actually, no, this one is on me. Well, it's on Sandra, actually."

Melissa stiffened beside me. Sandra had always been a pill to Melissa. I'd tried to bring my daughter over to spend time with this side of the family while Sandra was growing up, but the girl had automatically hated everything, and anyone related to me.

She had called Melissa various inappropriate things before storming off, never to return. I guessed I wouldn't blame Sandra, but I couldn't really fault Melissa for disliking her either.

Bennett looked confused. "Sandra got him to quit?"

I took a deep breath and admitted what'd gone down. I actually didn't leave much out, which was unusual for me, but I was with family. They should know that the lingering dangers of our Mafia roots were extinguished. Of course, I couldn't tell them who'd killed my father, or where we were when it happened, but I did tell them I'd seen him die.

When I finished, Melissa came over and hugged me. "It's time this was put to rest. I'm sorry it happened like it did, but it's time."

I nodded my agreement. "So, Bennett, Les, you're okay if I bring Cliff?"

They both smiled, and Les said, "He is pretty hot, Bentley, for a cop that is."

I laughed as the family harassed me about my new love interest. Or, at least, who I hoped was still my love interest. Their playfulness signaled to me that something had shifted between us all, too. I mean, we'd been family and we'd spent time together, but they'd never pulled me in, and they'd definitely never teased me before.

I felt like I belonged in a way I hadn't since Sister Clarissa had died.

Before I left, Bennett pulled me aside. "Bentley, Cliff wasn't at fault for anything that happened to me, any more than you were."

I smiled at the kid. He was a brave young man and I'd really messed him up. His dad had killed a man, and was about to kill Les, so I'd had to pretend to try to kill him to get his father to stand down.

Even though I'd done it all for good reason, for Bennett to open himself up to me now, and even to Cliff after all that'd happened, showed just exactly what strength of character Bennett really had.

Forty-Three

Cliff

WHEN A FORMAL INVITATION arrived in my new Post Office box, I was surprised to see it was from Bennett and Les, personally inviting me to the celebration of the completion of their big renovation project on Lake Washington.

I called Jeff and Paul immediately, thanking them for getting me an invite.

"Um, it wasn't us," they both told me.

"Then who? Daniel?"

They both laughed. "Um," I heard Paul say through the speakerphone, "Kaden is working him so hard to finish some of the built-ins for the master suite, he doesn't have time to breathe much less secure party invitations."

I couldn't help but chuckle. The folks in Port Angeles had completely embraced Paul's brother Daniel, and helped set him on the straight and narrow. Kaden, his boyfriend Joseph's dad, had pulled Daniel under his wing, and was teaching him his cabinetry trade.

I thought it was beyond bizarre that our world seemed to work in a circle centered around Bennett and Les. Maybe that was some sort of providence, although I didn't really know if I believed in all that or not.

The mysterious person behind the party invitation became clear the following day, when I was helping Jeff out at the gallery. I was working to repay him and Paul for letting me bunk at their place while I shopped for a new home. I'd fully intended to move into an extended stay hotel, but both of them had insisted I stay with them.

I'm glad they did. I was regretting the sale of my home, and if I had to stay in a small hotel room, I knew I'd be completely depressed about it.

When I walked out of Jeff's office, where I'd been put to work setting up an Excel spreadsheet, I almost literally stumbled into Bentley and Sandra as they came through the front door.

I froze. I'd missed this man in every way possible, and had only just now come to terms with the fact that I'd never set eyes on him again, when here, out of the blue, he showed back up looking just as handsome as ever.

"Hi, Cliff," he said, and shuffled like a kid might do when they were in trouble.

"Um, hi," I responded, just as awkwardly.

We stood there staring at each other for a long time, before Sandra finally cleared her throat and Jeff came around the corner to see who'd come in.

"Mr. Cummings," he said, and I could hear the nerves in his voice. "Is everything okay?"

Bentley turned a warm smile toward Jeff and nodded. "Yes, Mr. Langston, things are good. I actually came, because your husband Paul told me I could find Cliff here today."

I could almost feel the relief coming off Jeff. "Wh... why are you looking for me?" I stammered, before turning to Sandra for the first time since they'd walked in. "Am I in trouble or something?"

"You don't have to assume you're in trouble just because I came to see you," Bentley said.

"Well, probably not, but she doesn't seem to show up unless there is trouble," I said accusingly, gesturing toward Sandra.

She blushed. "Yeah, well, that's why I'm here. I want to apologize for how things went down. I didn't mean for you to be let go from your job."

I'd spent hardly any time with this woman, but as I looked at her more closely, I noticed for the first time a resemblance between her and the man I'd become obsessed with. I knew at that moment she and Bentley had to be related. As I searched my feelings, I realized I didn't feel any animosity toward her. It seemed so long ago now that I'd lost my job, and had she and the FBI agent not spoken to my superior, I would've never known Bentley.

"It wasn't your fault. It was just bad timing. Do you two want to come in for a drink? I'm sure we can swipe some of the fancy bubbly stuff from Jeff's party stash."

Jeff gave me a nasty look, which did more to ease the tension in the room than anything else.

Finally, he turned back to the group, and sighed. "Let me call Paul and have him come meet us here. I would say having a celebratory toast is certainly called for."

The moment Jeff stepped away, Bentley pointed to Sandra, and said, "Cliff, this is my daughter, Sandra. Um... I thought you should know."

I chuckled. "Yeah, I just figured that out."

"Sandra, really, there are no hard feelings."

The rest of that afternoon, we all sat companionably in the gallery's sitting area as Sandra and Bentley explained what they could about what happened after Bentley had left the island. Learning that Agent Ford had been, in essence, a sleeper agent, and that Sandra had been shot and left for dead by him shocked me to my core. The man exuded FBI, it was like his entire persona. I guessed it was impossible to tell the quality of a man by what he presented to the world. *Don't judge a book by its cover.* I had learned that very lesson from Bentley, who, for all of his imposing and steely exterior, was soft, gentle and caring underneath.

Forty-Four

Bentley

W E WERE GETTING READY to leave after the champagne had been drunk and the air cleared, when Cliff pulled me into Jeffrey's office and lifted his hand to my cheek. "I've missed you. More than I thought possible. I need to know if what we had was, um..." I watched the emotions swim across his face before he schooled them. "I need to know if you and I were real."

I nodded, but I didn't try to hide the surge of feelings threatening to engulf me. I pulled Cliff to me like I'd wanted to since the moment I'd walked into the gallery and seen him. Barely able to speak, I whispered, "I've missed you every moment since I left."

Cliff looked up at me with tears in his eyes, tears that matched my own. I pulled him to me and took his mouth with mine, like I'd dreamed of night after night as I lay alone wondering where he was, or how he was doing.

When we pulled apart, I leaned my head against his. "I think I might be falling in love with you. Is that possible this fast?"

Cliff shrugged. "I-I don't know, but I'm feeling the same. I've never felt like this for anyone else."

His admission caused the tears to tumble out of my eyes, but despite how I'd been raised, the years of being told men didn't cry, I couldn't be ashamed of them. These were tears of longing, of desire and loss, but they were also tears of joy for having the man I'd wanted more than anyone back in my arms.

We continued to hold each other there in Jeffrey's office, not speaking, but saying so much more through our shared embrace, for what felt like a glorious hour. "Um, can we spend the evening together?" I asked, breaking the silence, and Cliff nodded into my chest.

"Yeah, I'd like that, but... I sold my house."

I laughed, and when Cliff looked up questioningly, I said, "We're like two lovesick teenagers with no place to go. Sandra and I share an apartment, so that's not an option."

Cliff smiled. "I have an idea." He fished his phone out of his pocket and quickly made a call.

I could hear him talking to someone, and quickly gathered the conversation was about renting a house or something for the evening. "Yeah, I know. No, I'll tell you later. Is the house available or not?" I chuckled at Cliff's frustration. "Cool, we'll come by the bar and pick up the key," he said, and hung up.

"I swear I get the third degree when I just want to find a place to..."

Cliff stopped mid-sentence, and I laughed out loud when he blushed. "When you just wanna find a place to fuck?"

He nodded, but the adorable blush never left his face.

"I wanna do so much more than fuck you, Cliff. I want to make love to you and never stop until you feel how much love I have inside for you. Do you get that?"

Another tear slipped down his handsome face. "Yeah, I get that."

I sent Sandra on her way and followed Cliff as he drove back to Jeffrey and Paul's house to grab clothes and leave his car there. We drove to the dive bar we'd visited once before, and despite desperately wanting the man to warm my bed with me, I couldn't resist at least one pint of the delicious house brew.

Cliff didn't complain when I asked if he minded, and once he'd gotten the key we'd come to pick up, we sat at the same table and held hands while enjoying each other's company. After all the time we'd spent apart, every moment seemed special, and neither one of us seemed to want to let the other out of his sight.

When Cliff went to pay, the old man behind the bar laughed. "Go have your fun. I haven't seen you so gaga over a man, well, ever. I owe you anyway."

Cliff was about to argue, when the man walked out the back, letting the curtain close behind him.

"Guess that's that," Cliff said, laughing as he pulled me out of the bar and to my car.

He gave me the address and pointed down the street.

"What is this? I asked as we pulled up in front of a big and beautiful, if slightly rundown, old Victorian home.

We got out and when I looked around, I could tell why it wasn't that well cared for. We were less than a few blocks from the water, but we were in an industrial part of Seattle. Huge metal buildings surrounded the house, and although it stood on a rather large lot, the grounds were overgrown and few people, if anyone, would want to live in this part of town, no matter how expensive real estate was in Seattle.

"This is my bar partner's mom's former home. His mother used to rent it out as a boarding house to sailors who came in to port not far from here."

I immediately knew I was going to do everything in my power to own this structure, and I hadn't even gone inside yet. It had everything I needed to rebuild here what I'd uprooted in Boston.

I looked over at Cliff, who was trying to get the key into the front door with little success. The fact he'd brought me here, of all places, didn't shock me. Nothing did anymore. I thought of Sister Clarissa and smiled. Maybe she really was looking down on me. When the door finally opened and I followed Cliff into the old mansion, I chuckled and thought to myself, *better not be looking long, 'cause what I'm about to do to this man is in no way saintly!*

Forty-Five

Cliff

Henry, my bar partner, rarely ever rented his mom's old house out any longer. I thought he was afraid of liability, as the old structure was showing some serious need for repair. I knew he didn't have the money for that, but I also knew he didn't really want to part with the building either.

As I pulled Bentley down the hallway to the thankfully clean room—clean only because I'd personally forced Henry to hire a cleaning company to come in behind the guests—I made a mental note to begin the process of talking my friend into letting the old home go.

That night as Bentley and I made love, it was on a level we hadn't experienced before now and had promises interlaced with it. As I lay in his arms, I no longer could resist expressing how I'd felt about him. "Bentley, I love you," I said, then waited for a reaction.

When I looked up, his face was full of emotion. "Yeah... I've been falling in love with you for a while," he admitted. I curled back into his side and fell asleep then, knowing the man I'd fallen in love with had fallen for me as well.

The next morning, Bentley talked me into going for breakfast and we chatted about our lives in general. There were times he dodged my questions, and after the third or fourth time, I finally said, "If it's something you can't tell me, just say, 'I can't tell you that,' okay? Stop trying to dodge my questions."

Bentley laughed. "I used to be better at this, but you've turned me into a mushy mess, so my hard-earned techniques are evading me."

I leaned over the table and kissed him squarely on the lips. "Good, with me you need to be a mushy mess."

A group of young college-age kids clapped behind us, and we both turned to them and smiled. We kissed again just for show.

"So..." Bentley said, after the commotion had calmed down, "...are you gonna accept Bennett and Les's party invitation?"

"You're the one who set up the invite," I said, acknowledging what I'd already figured out.

He smiled at me in his way that caused my insides to melt just a bit. "Yeah, Les is my first cousin's son. I forgot to tell you that earlier."

"Forgot or chose not to?" I asked, but Bentley just kept smiling and didn't reply. "I'm not sure... I mean, Bennett went through a lot."

"He did, and he himself told me he wants you there," Bentley tried to assure me. "Did you know he went to your old precinct looking for you, and was told you were no longer there?"

I looked at Bentley's face, searching for whether this could possibly be true or not. "Why? Why would he want to seek me out?"

"Closure, I imagine," Bentley replied. "He embraced me when I came in, and I assure you, I was a hell of a lot rougher on the kid than you ever could've been."

I had no idea what he was talking about, but I wanted to see Bennett and Les, too. I'd liked the men when I'd met them during my police work, and Bennett seemed to have a good head on his shoulders while all the shit in his life was hitting the fan. It would be good to get to know the couple better.

"So, the party is this Saturday, and I wanted to take you as my date," Bentley continued. "Sandra will be there, too, on security duty."

I chuckled. "Yeah, she and I need to schedule some time to get to know each other better, especially since she isn't trying to send me to prison, or get me fired."

Bentley had the decency to blush, but as things were going now, I was beginning to realize that I'd gained a lot more in Bentley than I'd lost with my job. When I looked at him, his returning smile caused that instant warm feeling to return to my core. *Without a doubt, I've gotten a hell of a lot more out of the deal,* I thought.

Forty-Six

Bentley

C LIFF CALLED HIS GRANDMA to see if she wanted to go with us, but she declined, saying her formal party days were behind her. In a way, I thought she probably made the right choice, because I knew for a fact most of the evening was going to be us milling around meeting people, while Les and Bennett's film crew recorded our every move.

Normally, I'd avoid an event like this out of concern of accidentally being caught on camera, but with my dad's death, I no longer really cared. Still, I'd asked them to try to avoid filming me, if for no other reason than to keep KOPATICAL from having a heart attack.

I picked Cliff up from Jeffrey and Paul's house, despite the fact that they all told me they were going, too. "I wanna arrive with my man on my arm," I told them, causing both Jeffrey and Paul to chuckle and my sweet man to blush.

Cliff was dressed in a tailored suit, and I was rather pleasantly surprised to see him so well dressed, but then I remembered who his grandmother was, and put that thought aside. She might never get him to dress like she'd want in his daily life, but I was assuming she probably put her foot down when it came to formal wear.

I got out of my car and came around to meet him, then when he got close enough, I pulled him into an embrace and kissed him passionately, before squeezing his delicious-looking ass. "You look good enough to eat," I said in his ear.

"Mmm, sounds like a good plan for later."

"I like your planning," I replied, and opened the door for him.

I'd been to more formal affairs during my career than I cared to remember, and to be honest, while I might not hate them, I'd never really seen the point. Tonight, however, was different.

As we were given a tour of the newly renovated house, my cousins showed off their work, and Paul's younger brother Daniel beamed with pride as he showed us all the unique, high-quality cabinetry he'd helped create. I couldn't help but share in the sense of pride they all felt for what they'd accomplished.

I walked over to where Melissa and Vince were sitting, and noticed Les and Bennett were speaking with Cliff. I wandered their way just in time to catch some of the conversation.

"It's not your fault what went down, you were following a lead," Les said.

"I was, that's correct, but it does lead to awkward moments now that I'm dating your cousin."

Bennett smiled, then looked over at me. "We couldn't be happier about that, actually. The two of you are perfect for each other."

I chuckled as I joined the conversation. "We're just starting out, guys, so don't try planning a double wedding or anything."

Les and Bennett looked at each other and grinned. "You should be careful using that word around Melissa or Les's sisters," Bennett said. "They are sorta crazy about weddings."

Les shook his head. "Crazy is the correct word. I swear if it hadn't been for Dad, we would've never gotten this house done."

"'Hadn't been for Dad' what?" Vince asked as he and Melissa wandered up behind us.

"The guys were telling me about juggling between planning a wedding and finishing the house."

Vince just shook his head. "It's been like prying a bottle from a baby to get all the womenfolk to work, instead of staring at those blasted wedding websites."

Melissa grinned and elbowed her husband. "He won't admit it, but he's been just as crazy about it as we have. We can't wait to officially welcome our Bennett into the family."

We chatted, or to be more accurate, they all harassed each other as Cliff and I made eyes at each other. The cameraman called them over to do some final takes, but before Melissa left, she linked arms with me and Cliff and asked us to stick around after the party. She said the family wanted to have a personal celebration without the public and a bunch of cameras following them around.

Just like that, I was back in the family, and apparently, because Cliff was with me, he was, too. I was sure he didn't understand the significance, because Melissa didn't extend that invitation to just anyone, only those she truly saw that way.

I discovered to my surprise once the crowd had dispersed that Sandra had also been invited, which both amused me and gave me a little hope. I had absolutely no doubt it was because of her time helping to keep Bennett and Les safe.

As the light faded with the setting of the sun, the backyard of the mansion glittered with lights the family had strung up in the trees. It was a romantic setting with the warm glow of the light reflecting off Lake Washington, and on the greenery around us.

Champagne was opened, and each of us was handed a fluted plastic glass with the bubbly liquid. I pulled Cliff to me and kissed him as we waited for all the Champagne to be passed out.

"How are you doing?" I asked, wondering if he was overwhelmed by the intensity of my family.

He smiled and snuggled into my side. "I'm good, very good. Almost like I'm in a fairy tale with my handsome prince."

Forty-Seven

Cliff

B ELONGING. THAT WASN'T SOMETHING I felt often, or at least, not since my grandma had gone into independent living. More often, I felt alone or like a third wheel. Jeff and Paul, Daniel and Joseph, and even Bennett and Les, all made me feel like I was an important part of the evening, and of course, there was Bentley, a man who now occupied my life like no other man ever had before.

Being a cop, well, I was usually on the outside looking in, helping to keep things controlled and people safe. Tonight, I was able to be present in a totally different way. I was made to feel like an actual participant, a part of the events as they happened.

When Bennett and Les cornered me, I thought maybe we were about to have *the* conversation. I had prepared to get an earful about how I'd all but accused Bennett of being a part of the... well, a part of his dad's gang.

Instead of being upset, though, they were gracious and un-derstanding... something I was not prepared for.

Bentley stood across from me, looking proud and grand in his tailored suit. I continued to be astounded at how much I cared about this guy. When Melissa linked her arms through mine and Bentley's, and asked us to stay for the family stuff, well, it was like icing on a deliciously inclusive cake.

I snuggled into Bentley as they passed champagne around, and cheered with them in celebrating the end of a very signif-icant accomplishment, then I laughed as they teased each other with stories of things they'd done, or I should say, screwed up, during the renovation.

Most of the teasing was about filming mishaps, but they totally harassed Bennett and Les about all the times they were caught sneaking a kiss in a bathroom, closet, and even the stair-well up to the attic, basically anywhere they thought there were no cameras.

I was feeling just a bit tipsy from all the champagne I'd con-sumed and happy down to my heart when I broke away to use the restroom. I was just coming back out when I heard the crack of a branch to my left.

I turned just as a gun was lifted up to my face. "Don't move," the guy said.

There wasn't much light, and the gunman was standing in the shadow of a shrub that grew next to the house, so I couldn't make him out.

"What do you want?" I asked.

"Your fucking life," he replied, raising a gun. Having had a deadly weapon trained on me twice in a short period of time, I wondered if maybe this time I wouldn't be so lucky.

"Put the gun down!" I heard Sandra yell as she walked around the bush, her gun aimed at his head.

He didn't move, but he shifted just enough that I recognized him as Agent Ford, the FBI agent who'd come with her to Jeff's gallery.

I held my hands up so he could see I wasn't armed, but I knew this standoff could easily lead to my death. Anything could trigger him.

As my eyes adjusted to the dark, I could tell the man was crying.

"What the hell is..." Bentley stepped around the corner, and stopped short when he saw Ford with a gun pointing at my head.

"You son of a bitch, he's dead," Ford said. "He's fucking dead, and I barely knew him!"

"Who's dead, Finn?" Bentley asked, using a name that confused me. Who was Finn?

"Alec. My fucking dad. You goddamned..." He moved quickly like he was about to fire his gun, and I closed my eyes, thinking this was it.

I heard the gunshot, but it didn't hit me. Instead, I heard Ford yell in pain. I opened my eyes and saw blood gushing from Ford's hand that had just been holding his gun.

He looked panicked and began to run, but then Bentley stepped up and busted him in the face, sending him sprawling onto the ground next to Sandra.

I watched as she reached behind her back and pulled out handcuffs, which was strange. Since when did CIA officers carry handcuffs? She rolled Ford onto his stomach and cuffed his bloodied hand behind him.

"You ruined my fucking life, you assholes. You should die. Everything..." he screamed as the rest of the family rushed toward the commotion.

Bentley pulled out his phone, I assumed to call for emergency assistance, as the bleeding man continued ranting on the ground.

"You took everything from me. I had a right to take it all from you!"

Sandra began approaching him when Bentley took the phone from his ear, and said sternly, "Sandra, no, he's down and contained."

She looked at him, then over at the man who they'd told me earlier had attacked her and left her for dead.

"We didn't take a damned thing from you, you scumbag. We come from the same line of people as you. Our lives mirror each other's, but there is a difference." She pointed to Bentley. "My dad chose to fight the corruption and disease that plagued our family, yours chose to embrace it."

She got up then, like she was about to leave, but looked down at him instead, and said, "You had a choice, just like I did. You were a good agent, you could've been even better, but you threw all that away, and for what? Your criminal dad, a man incapable of loving you? God, you disgust me!"

Ford started screaming then, but Sandra walked away toward the lake.

Sirens sounded, and within moments, the Seattle PD descended on us. I recognized several of the guys, my former colleagues, including the one who interviewed me about the night's events.

When I'd finished giving my statement, he closed his notebook and shook his head. "This shit just keeps coming, huh?"

I shrugged like I always did when anyone in law enforcement used that phrase. "It's what we signed up for."

"Maybe what you signed up for," he teased. "I signed up for donuts and hot chicks."

He patted me on the shoulder as he walked toward where Bentley was being interviewed. I chuckled inwardly, because when there was a dude as big and as potentially dangerous as Bentley being questioned. Every officer available would be wanting to stick close in case he went off, but they were barking up the wrong tree. Bentley was an amazing man. Tough, yeah, and physically imposing, but also a good, loving, and caring man deep down to his core.

When they were done interviewing him, I slipped in among them and up to his side. These guys knew me, trusted me, and I felt it was important they knew that Bentley was a good guy, and he was mine and because he was mine, he was theirs as well.

Forty-Eight

Bentley

I WAITED UNTIL THE police interviews were over, then broke away from Cliff, who'd come to sit by me, and walked toward Finn. At first the police wouldn't let me close to him, but when Sandra came around behind me and told them to back off, they did.

Finn's jaw unhinged upon seeing me, ready to spout off defiantly, but fuck him, he was going to hear me out. "I'm going to give you this, and only this, you sack of shit," I said. "Your Aunt Clarissa, she was a saint. She saved me, and helped me in ways that made me the man I am today. She might not have been able to save your father, her brother, from this life, but you could've chosen a different path. You could've told me who you really were, and in her name, I would've turned the world upside down for you. Instead, you chose the wrong family member to admire. You will never get out of prison, not after betraying the FBI, but while you're there, you should pray to Sister Clarissa.

It won't save you from your fate in this life, but perhaps she can still help save your soul."

I walked away as Finn shouted profanities at me. No matter. I'd done my service to her. Sister Clarissa had somehow risen above the horrible fray that was her family, and she'd helped me do the same. I owed it to her to tell her nephew about her, and now that I had, I could leave him to his fate.

I'd wanted and had planned to spend the evening with Cliff, but I could tell Sandra needed me more.

So, after the cops freed us to go, I took Cliff home. "Will you be okay for now?" I asked.

He smiled. "Dude, I'm not a rookie. I also know your daughter needs you right now."

I nodded. "She does, or I'd be here with you."

Cliff leaned over and kissed me. "There will be plenty of time for us. Besides, I have Jeff and Paul. They'll relate to being shot at, and hell, I'm an expert at looking down the barrel of a gun now. I can see my life pass before my eyes in half the time," he said, trying to make light of the situation, which I suspected was all an attempt to put me at ease about leaving right now.

"You're not funny," I said with a groan, and reached over and kissed him long and hard. Being reminded that I'd almost lost him, again, it was almost more than I could bear. I just wanted to pull him into my lap and hold onto him with everything I had in me. I never wanted to let him go.

But Sandra... she wasn't doing well, and remembering how she looked before I left, well, it was important that I get back to her sooner rather than later. A soldier didn't leave a buddy alone, when the darkness was closing in.

Cliff climbed out of the car, but I just couldn't watch him go without holding him first. I climbed out of the car and quickly went to him, pulling him into my embrace. When I finally forced myself to let go, and after watching to make sure he made it inside safely, I got back into my car and called KOPATICAL.

"I wondered when you'd call."

I didn't even bother to respond. "So, I'm headed back to be with Sandra, but I wanted to square things with you first. This is it, the last of Dad's crew, right? We're free of the bullshit?"

KOPATICAL was quiet, I could tell she was thinking. "I can't promise, as you know, we could've missed some errant arm, but no, I don't know anyone who would be willing to follow you to Washington."

I laughed out loud. Of course, KOPATICAL would have figured out I was leaving Boston behind for good. "So, if you know I'm leaving, you know I'm gonna make Cliff Sparks my husband soon, too?"

When she responded, I could hear the smile in her voice. "We assumed that would be the case. I need you to break down what happened tonight, but before I do, we, the agency, want to tell you how happy we are that your guy wasn't hurt. From what we know so far, it was touch and go."

As I thought about that, emotions swirled through me, almost causing me to lose emotional control. Finally, after clear-

ing my throat, I replied in almost a whisper, "Yeah, we were lucky, *again*."

I gave my report as I drove from Jeffrey and Paul's to the apartment I shared with Sandra. I was still answering KOPATICAL's questions, when I walked in and saw Sandra sitting on the edge of the couch. I finished my part of the interrogation and handed the phone to her, so she could answer KOPATICAL's questions as well.

When we were finally done, Sandra handed me back my phone, and KOPATICAL said I had forty-eight hours, then I needed to contact her to *finalize my move*. Whatever that meant. It didn't matter, though. Looking at my daughter, there were more pressing things than trying to figure out KOPATICAL's cryptic messages.

When I sat down next to Sandra, she curled up into me and wept. Only rarely, even counting when she was young, had Sandra snuggled into me and let herself lose control. The only other time I could recall was after she'd gained security clearance to read my file, and realized I wasn't the horrible man she'd grown up believing me to be.

The unexpected reaction caused me to get emotional, too, and silent tears fell from my eyes as grief consumed my daughter while I held her close.

At one point, I knew she'd fallen asleep, so I leaned back and just held her, knowing she'd wake soon and need to talk about it.

When she did, she was able to share with me how tonight had been the culmination of her life's story. The shared similarities between Alec and me, Finn and her. "Dad, I know we were trained to shoot to kill, but killing Finn tonight would've been the same as killing myself. I-I can't explain it. I put you at risk, because..."

"Shh," I admonished. "You did no such thing. You easily took him out, and did so with a simple shot to the hand. You knew you'd hit, and you knew you'd save Cliff, so don't second guess yourself."

She cried more, not releasing her grip on me. Was it bad that it felt good that my daughter had finally turned to me, held onto me, and let me love and care for her when the world had collapsed around her? Probably, a dad should hope his daughter never felt such things, but most dads didn't have a daughter who was a fierce warrior like mine.

Finally, she pulled back, and thanked me. "I needed you tonight, and you've been here for me. That matters," she said, wiping at another tear. "But, I know you must be turned inside out over Cliff, too. Go to him, Dad. I'm fine now."

I smiled. "You are fine. In fact, you're amazing, my daughter. Truly amazing."

She got up, and before I left, I said, "Honey, I can stay. Cliff is fine."

She held her hand up and shook her head. "I'm good. I'm just going to go to bed and cry some more," she said through a watery laugh. "Then, I'm going to finish processing all this and put it aside for good, 'cause neither Finn nor any of the other sons of bitches we are related to are worth our giving them even one more second of our lives. You've got Cliff, and I've got you. So, go. I'll let you know when I need you again."

I knew what she meant, and I knew she would need another crying jag before this was truly over for her, but she was also correct on the processing bit. That was something she'd have to do on her own.

I texted Cliff to see if he was still up, and he texted back right away.

Wanna go on a late-night walk on the beach? I texted, and he immediately texted he would.

After picking him up, we went down to the waterfront, and held hands as we walked along the beach. "I'm not gonna ask if you're okay. None of us are okay, are we?" I asked.

He shook his head. "No, it's gonna take time and maybe a little therapy before I'm okay again." He shook his head again as he looked out over the Sound. "It took a long time to get my mind right after your... well, after your dad and my grandma, but no, this one... well, I feel like something broke in me this time."

I nodded. "Yeah, me too. I think I might need to pull back a little on my work for the government. I can't see ever putting you in harm's way again and, well, in the past, that would've been inevitable."

Cliff leaned into me as we walked. "Let's not think about it right now. It's too fresh to make a decision about that. Just hold me, okay?" he asked.

I did just that. We found a pier that poked up out of the water, blocked from the wind, and lay up against it while watching the tide go out. When the sun started to come up behind us, the light began to touch and chase off all the dark shadows. It almost seemed like it was clearing out the ugly spots of our souls.

I looked down and almost chuckled when I noticed Cliff had fallen asleep in my arms, not unlike my daughter had earlier. Life could be odd. The past few months had been one hell of a roller coaster ride. Since I'd lost Sister Clarissa, whether by circumstance or by choice, I'd been alone. Now I had two incredible people in my life, an amazing daughter who had finally opened up and let me be her dad, and an incredible man who I'd fallen in love with and who loved me back.

Cliff felt like he could be my soulmate, someone I felt was specially designed for me. When the sun rose enough that the sparkles on the water began to dance, I could've sworn I saw an image of Sister Clarissa smiling back at me.

I blinked twice, and when I looked again, she was gone, but in her place was a feeling of serenity. She'd said she was going to watch out for me. Apparently, she'd meant it.

Forty-Nine

Epilogue: Cliff

As we were coming up on our one-year anniversary, I decided to propose to the man I loved more than life itself.

Grandma had to have procedures done to help prevent her from having another stroke, which reminded me once again that my time with her was limited. It prompted me to push the timeline a bit, since because, for the life of me, I couldn't even imagine marrying my love and not having her there as a witness.

So, with Jeff and Melissa's help, I planned a huge get-together at Bennett and Les's newly finished loft and commercial building. Luckily, the property was big enough to accommodate all our friends and family, and it was also a perfect excuse to keep Bentley from being able to figure out my plans.

Sandra had gone with me to pick out her dad's engagement ring, which had been a sweet bonding experience for us. Of course, we both spotted the perfect ring at the same time.

The jeweler came over and in a distinct Irish lilt, said, "Oh, this is a beautiful ring." She pointed to the center where a pinwheel swirled out away from the Celtic knots that surrounded it. "This is the symbol of truth..." she continued, and almost as a secondary thought, said, "...and justice."

Both Sandra and I became emotional, as if by some providential means, we'd found the absolute perfect ring for the man we both loved.

The night of the party, I stayed close to Bentley as Melissa and her daughters gathered everyone together in the huge main room of Bennett and Les's flat. Once everyone was gathered, Melissa stood on the fireplace hearth and got everyone's attention.

"We are here to celebrate another accomplishment of the relationship between the Cooper/Jackson merger. However, we were a bit sneaky, as that's not the main reason we are here tonight."

Melissa looked over at me, and winked. "Show's yours, kid," she said, loud enough for everyone to hear.

I drew in a deep breath and let it out, before turning to Bentley. "Bentley, you've changed my life..." I began, then cleared my throat dramatically, before adding under my breath, "...in mostly good ways." Then, I winked at Sandra, causing her to blush.

"I love you, Bentley Cummings. I love you so fiercely it sometimes overwhelms me."

Bentley stood unmoving with the mask he put on when emotions were overwhelming him. A year ago, I'd have interpreted that mask as arrogant or intimidating. Today, I knew it for what it really was.

I knelt down on one knee, and asked as loud as I could for the crowd, despite becoming choked up by my own emotions, "My love, will you marry me?"

Within seconds, the giant man I loved more than I had words to say lifted me up into his arms. My legs completely left the ground while he repeatedly kissed me, and said, "*Yes, yes, yes,*" over and over again.

When he finally put me down, the first person I saw was my grandma, and the smile that lit up her face contrasted with the tears that fell from her eyes.

She was the first to congratulate us, and the rest of the evening was filled with our family and friends congratulating us as well.

That night, as we made love, Bentley kept telling me how much he loved me. "I can't believe you're mine," he repeated, as much to himself as to me.

When we finally snuggled into our favorite position, with his huge body curled around mine as we were both about to fall asleep, I whispered, "You are my light, Bentley. You're the love I never dreamed I'd have. Thank you."

Fifty

Bentley

"**S**ANDRA, IF YOU POOF my hair one more time, I'm going to blow my top." My daughter ignored me, other than to chuckle a bit. She stood behind me while we both looked into the mirror as she once again tried to force my cowlick into place.

Finally giving up, she leaned down and kissed my cheek. "I'm so proud of you, Dad. Cliff is an amazing man."

Fuck, if that didn't make me misty-eyed. *Again!*

I leaned my head into her as she hugged me. "Thanks, honey," I said, and she wiped a tear and turned around as Melissa walked in with her daughters.

"Okay, one more glance over, and it's time to send you down the aisle." Melissa leaned down to whisper in my ear. "Bennett and I have the plans printed and wrapped. Sandra stuffed them in your bedroom for the big reveal when it's just the two of you."

Melissa had gone with me to look at the Victorian dump owned by Cliff's bar-owner friend Henry. Of course, I'd had to all but beg Henry to let me have a look.

Cliff had talked to him already about selling and that had helped. I also thought when I told him I wanted to turn it into something nice for Cliff, that had been the thing that helped convince him the most.

Melissa turned her nose up at the old manufacturing places that surrounded the building, and when she walked into the old house, she just laughed at me, but no matter what she thought, the home was perfect for Cliff and me.

My Boston home had been in an industrial area as well. I'd learned very early on in my career that, especially in the evenings, if someone was lurking around, it was easy to spot them. Residential or commercial areas weren't as easy to keep surveillance of your surroundings. In my line of business, that was a problem.

I'd decided to present Melissa and Bennett's renovation plans to Cliff as my wedding present to him. He'd still not found a new home, and although I knew the old house was in many ways an opposite of where he'd lived before, I knew with a lot of TLC and some creative design to the exceptionally large lot, we could make it a nice home for the two of us.

I smiled at her and stood up as the women in my family led me out the door, and into the arms of my sweet, soon-to-be husband.

A brisk summer breeze blew Sandra's hard work into chaos as we walked out onto the large deck of Phil and John's island home. When I'd asked them to let us have our wedding there, they'd readily agreed. Of course, they had no idea that one of the main reasons I wanted the wedding to happen here was because I now saw their home as the place marking my ultimate liberation, the place where, with my father's death, I had earned my freedom to love the man I was marrying today.

Cliff had a strange effect on me. He seemed to crush the hard exterior I'd kept in place my entire life, simply by loving me. As a result, I pretty much wept through our wedding.

We'd both predicted we'd be this way, so we just let the preacher recite the traditional vows, and we didn't try to read our own.

The reception was held at the Guemes Island Resort, which we'd booked for the entire weekend. The islanders were invited to celebrate with us since it was a Friday, and we all knew there would be animosity that lasted for generations if we blocked them from a Friday night fish fry at the resort.

The island was certainly an option for us to live on, but ultimately, it was just a bit too secluded for the security company I ran and had managed to convince Cliff to help me operate.

I'd intended on backing off, or maybe quitting the business altogether, but Cliff had talked me out of it. "You and I, we… we aren't people who will ever live a normal life, Bentley. Whether or not you pull back, I'm not going to stop doing what I do. I'm just made that way, and you are, too. It's in our blood, but maybe we can plan together. It's doubtful I'll ever go back into law enforcement. I'm tainted. Even some of my buddies who've left Seattle without the issues I faced are struggling with getting hired outside of town, but well, I've been thinking. I like detective work. I like looking for clues and helping to bring bad guys to justice, so why not work for..." He hesitated a moment, then smiled slyly. "...I mean, *with* you."

I chuckled. "With me, huh? So, you want a cut of the business?"

"Well, of course. I am gonna be your better half, after all."

Cliff hated to be tickled, and I rarely did, but I ended up holding him down and tickling him, before letting our wrestling turn into something more passionate.

We returned from our wedding reception to an empty cabin. Phil was staying on Peter's sailboat, and John and Cliff's grandmother were bunked at their friend Patricia's house. I pulled the plans out to show Cliff what Melissa and Bennett had designed, and he looked them over silently before looking up at me. "You want to buy Henry's rundown boarding house?"

When I nodded, suddenly feeling nervous that he'd hate it, he laughed out loud. "I was actually going to suggest it. It's perfect for your business, especially when you have to keep someone safe and hidden away."

My mouth dropped open. "You were, really? Wait, did Henry tell you?"

He shook his head. "No, really, I had the same thought myself."

I grinned. "So, this is a go?"

He nodded. "But, on one condition."

I felt my left eyebrow go up. "What condition?"

"Patricia Gomez approached me tonight at the reception saying that she had decided to move next door to Grandma to keep her company in the independent living facility. I guess her sons are threatening to force her anyway. She wants us to buy her place."

"Have you seen it?" I asked.

He shook his head and laughed. "No, but John says it's a beautiful place tucked back and secluded from the rest of the village, and that it has its own beach access as well. I'm sure she'd show it to us tomorrow before we fly to Greece for our honeymoon."

It was my turn to laugh. "Husband, I'll do whatever you want. I'm the happiest man alive right now, and you're the reason for that happiness."

The intensity of our shared emotions engulfed us both as we gave ourselves over to our happiest passions. We were perfect lovers, compatible in every way—we had been from the first time we'd touched—but the thing I loved most about my new husband was that our love was so much deeper than I'd known was possible.

My life up until now had always been dark, but Cliff Sparks was indeed like the sparks his name indicated. He was a light that lit up my world. I knew as long as I had him and his love, total darkness would never find its way back in.

Aiden's art is his passion, but he's lost inspiration. When he meets the gruff but sexy rancher Devin, his life is changed forever.
Aiden Inspired

Available at your favorite bookseller

Join Blake's email list to get advance notice of new books and receive his occasional newsletter:

www.blakeallwood.com

MM Romance By Blake Allwood	**Romantic Fantasy By Adam J. Ridley**
Transitions Series Aiden Inspired Suzie Empowered (MF Romance) Bobby Transformed	**Big Bend Series** Love's Legacy (1) Love's Heirloom (2) Love's Bequest (3)
Chance Series Love By Chance Another Chance With Love Taking A Chance For Love	**The Witch Brothers Series** Emerald Earth (1) Diamond Air (2) Ruby Fire (3) Sapphire Water (4)
Romantic Series Romantic Renovations (1) Romantic Rescue (2) Romantic Recon (3)	
Melody Series Melody of the Heart Melody of the Snow	
Road to Rocktoberfest Anthology Changing His Tune - 2022	
Coming Home Series (2023) A Long Way Home Family Home Discovering Home Finding Home Bound For Home …and many more	
Novellas Tenacious Moon's Place	

Blake Allwood was born in west Tennessee, then moved to Kansas City MO after earning a degree in Early Childhood Education from Graceland College in Lamoni, Iowa. He met his husband Shaun in 1995 and they officially married in 2015, once gay marriage was legalized; although they still consider Valentines Day 1995 as their true "anniversary date". Twenty-two years later (2017), after fostering 12 children together, he and his husband sold their home, purchased an RV and began traveling the country with their two dogs.

Typically, Blake can be found relaxing in the RV or by the fire with his laptop and their Jack Russell Terrier, Buddy, curled up between his legs demanding attention. Denver, their Siberian Husky mix is often asleep at his feet or playing tug of war with Blake's husband.

Most of Blake's stories are inspired by the places they have visited in their ongoing travels. His first book, ***Aiden Inspired***, was released in 2019 and he has now written over 20 books. In 2023 he is releasing the ***Coming Home*** series which is comprised of ten-plus sweet contemporary romance novels that are based on a fictional town in his home state of Tennessee.

Blake also writes under the pen name of Adam J. Ridley for his urban fantasy fans looking for stories revolving around gay characters. His first series is The Witch Brothers Saga, starting with ***Emerald Earth***.

biblipride.com

Books by LGBTQ+
authors